# miss Match

### The Truth About Destiny

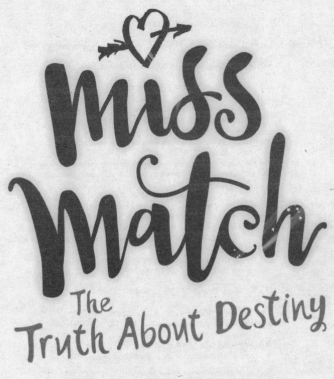

# miss Match

## The Truth About Destiny

### CRYSTAL CESTARI

Quercus

QUERCUS CHILDREN'S BOOKS

First published in the United States by Hyperion, an imprint of Disney Book Group

First published in Great Britain in 2018 by Hodder and Stoughton

1 3 5 7 9 10 8 6 4 2

A CIP catalogue record for this book
is available from the British Library.

ISBN 978 1 784 29914 9

Typeset by Hewer Text UK Ltd, Edinburgh
Printed and bound in Great Britain by Clays, Ltd, St Ives plc

The paper and board used in this book are from well-
managed forests and other responsible sources.

Quercus Children's Books
An imprint of
Hachette Children's Group
Part of Hodder & Stoughton
Carmelite House
50 Victoria Embankment
London EC4Y 0DZ

An Hachette UK Company
www.hachette.co.uk

www.hachettechildrens.co.uk

To Molly, who is fated for greatness

# One

MOUNTING EVIDENCE SUGGESTS I MAY BE A MASOCHIST. I wouldn't have thought this until recently, with my previous top character descriptions being 'sunny,' 'winning,' and 'eager to please' (jk, they'd be 'misanthropic,' 'sarcastic,' and 'cantankerous'). I guess part of the human experience is to grow and change, though I didn't think it could happen all at once.

Why else, other than a deep-rooted desire to see myself suffer, would I be in my kitchen, elbow-deep in powdered sugar, making peach tarts for a girl who is predestined to ruin my life? If I'd been asked a few months ago what kind of social activity I'd be least interested in, pretty much all situations involving other people would have made the list, but a front-runner would definitely have been inviting over an alleged rival to sample my latest culinary endeavor. Yet here I am, carefully plating a masterpiece for someone who may someday cause me severe emotional pain. Am I deranged? Insane?

Don't answer that.

'Oh my goodness, these fruit-pie thingies are amazing,' says Kim Li, licking the final crumbs of my legendary baking skills off her lips. An adorable pixie-size girl (though not of pixie descent), Kim has the poreless complexion face-wash commercials promise and a worldly style cultivated after living on several continents. She currently has an entire rainbow of barrettes clipped in her jet-black hair yet still manages to look sophisticated and not like a five-year-old gave her a makeover at Claire's.

She was invited by my best friend, Amani Sharma, who is also finishing up her dessert. Never to be outdone, Amani makes being a girl look easy, with a pink dress I wouldn't even know where to buy. Per usual, I am the least done up in the room, wearing jeans I picked up off the floor this morning, and my only accessories being peach flesh and flour. 'Really, Amber, nicely done,' Amani confirms.

They're both lounging on my couch like it's the most natural thing in the world and not some freak occurrence where I suddenly have more than one friend and we get together for girl time. Maybe, in addition to my being insane, a shape-shifter has stolen my body and taken over my social calendar?

'You both are too kind, and also correct,' I say. 'These tarts came out perfectly.'

'What's next on the menu . . . humble pie?' Amani asks, with an exaggerated wink, wink.

'Ugh, humble pie takes way too long to bake; I don't bother with it.'

'Clearly.'

Kim laughs sweetly beside us. Even though we've been hanging out for a few months now, I think we're all trying to decide how she fits in. Especially me, since I'm the one with the potential roadblock. Kim is, after all, my alleged competition, based on nothing except the visions of her and my boyfriend, Charlie Blitzman, living happily ever after in my head. In fact, I knew her before I knew her, getting more and more peeks into her personality every time Charlie was near. So when she showed up at school two months ago, I handled it with my usual finesse and grace (i.e., I lost it). It would be easier to hate her. To prick a voodoo doll and put a curse on her children's children's children. But as the Fates would have it, Kim is actually a delightful, interesting person, making it nearly impossible to churn up negative feelings around her. And since she and Amani seem to have almost identical class schedules, they've been getting to know each other at a rapid pace, whether I like it or not. In an effort to be a Bigger Person™, I've kept a running mental list of Kim's positive attributes to pull out whenever I feel myself having irrational feelings. For example, reason number three: Kim is always ready with a compliment. I've never had to work so hard at maintaining a friendship, but then again, that may be why I don't have many friends.

The entrance buzzer goes off, though we aren't expecting any other guests to this already-out-of-the-ordinary gathering. I'm very comfortable buried under a pile of blankets and a plate of tarts, so I don't feel like moving if it's a solicitor or drunken neighbor punching the wrong button.

'Amani, should I bother to answer?' I ask my friend, who is slowly rejoining the fortune-telling fold. For way too long, she kept her unique brand of magic under lock and key, but now she's welcoming it back in. Most of the time her visions come to her fast and furious without her control, but other times, for very mundane happenings, she can conjure up a visual or two. Her precog abilities are the extra cherry on the awesomesauce that is Amani, and I'm so happy she's opened up this part of herself again (not just because it works to my advantage from time to time).

She taps her chin thoughtfully, fluttering her ridiculously long lashes. 'Hmm, let me see.' The buzzer sounds again. 'Yes, I'd say this visitor is worth your while.'

'Scale of one to ten?'

'A solid nine. Maybe a nine point five, due to provisions.'

'That sounds promising!'

*Bzzzzzzzzz!*

'All right! I'm coming!' I yell, although the mystery guest is two floors below. I almost drop a pastry in prying myself from the couch, but Kim manages to catch it (reason number twelve: has good priorities, and number thirteen: excellent reflexes). I pound the button to open the front door, and before long, there's a tap at our apartment entry. Our visitor is dressed in an orange gingham tie coordinated to his glasses, and holds an extra-large vanilla cupcake with a disproportionately large cake-to-frosting ratio that looks like something from a My Little Pony coloring book. It's Charlie.

'Well, there's a masculine treat,' I say.

'Why, thank you,' he says, putting his free hand over his heart and performing a small bow.

'I was referring to your pastry.'

'Oh, this?' He turns it around, showing off the density of pink sprinkles. 'Yeah, it's pretty freaking delicious.'

'It's also pink.'

'So? It could be a rainbow swirl topped with unicorn wings, and I'd love it just the same.'

'Unicorns don't have wings. You're thinking of a Pegasus,' I correct.

'You know what I mean.'

'I've never seen a guy so devoted to buttercream,' I say.

He leans in close, his lips hovering by my right ear. 'Well, I got it for you, so what does that say about my devotion?' A plague of goose bumps covers my skin, and I have to playfully push him away before I grab his face and lay one on him.

'Can you guys, like, turn the cuteness down a notch?' Amani calls from behind us. 'Some of us are trying to keep down our peach tarts.'

'Yeah, all this adorable affection is making me nauseous,' Kim chimes in.

Charlie grins at me, all white-toothed and proud, and I take a deep breath in preparation for his match reel. Looking into his dark green eyes, my matchmaking abilities activate, giving me an unfiltered view of his romantic future. This would be fine, of course, if I were his destined leading lady, but instead, I'm treated to scenes of him and Kim drinking piña coladas on a white-sand beach, and sipping coffee on a lazy Sunday. I work through them quickly, not eager to linger, and refocus on the actual boy in front of me.

'Hey, Amani. Hey, Kim.' He waves. I try not to cringe when her name passes his lips.

'Hi, Charlie,' they respond in a unified monotone, though I know their mocking disdain comes from a place of affection.

'What are you doing here?' I ask him.

'Oh, you know, I was in the neighborhood.' He smirks. This is definitely not true, since Charlie and I are at completely different pinpoints on the Chicago map. Maybe, just maybe, he could spot my tiny Wicker Park apartment from the top of his Gold Coast penthouse if he had a set of quality binoculars. This is not the first time he's found himself so far from home; I expect it won't be the last. 'I forgot you were having the girls over.'

'Yeah, well . . .' In all honesty, I've about had my fill of female friendship for the night, as Amani and Kim are much better at finding acceptable conversation topics not involving witchcraft tangents and supernatural subplots. They can riff on deep conditioner treatments for longer than I thought possible. And yet, being a hostess with the mostest means suffering for the benefit of your guests. (I guess. I'm still not very familiar with this role.) 'Can I call you later?'

'You better,' he says, planting a small kiss on my forehead before calling out, 'Bye, ladies!' I watch him disappear down to the first floor, and then I retreat to my living room, where Amani and Kim are hanging themselves on fake nooses of sweetness.

'All right, I get it,' I concede, biting into the offensively pink cupcake. 'Our undeniable chemistry makes you queasy.'

'You guys are just perfect.' Kim sighs. I tense at her praise, trying to focus instead on the swirling sugar on my tongue. 'You make me simultaneously happy and jealous.'

Amani, knowing my pulse will race at Kim's envy, quickly interjects, 'Yeah, but mostly grossed out.'

'Sorry, not sorry,' I singsong just as there's another knock at the door. I thought Charlie had left by now, but maybe he's being oversentimental in his need to see me. 'Geez, back for more already?' I call out, turning the knob.

Yet instead of being greeted by my delectable boyfriend, I'm met with something truly stomach turning: Ivy Chamberlain.

# Two

'IVY? WHAT IN THE GODS' GOOD NAMES ARE YOU DOING HERE?'
I ask, making a mental note to check on where Mom keeps
her protection potions. Wherever they are, they need to be
relocated to the front entry closet ASAP.

Ivy Chamberlain, resident teenage dream/nightmare
(depending on how you look at it), crosses her arms across
her ample chest and lets out the world record for longest,
most exasperated sigh. You'd think I'd dragged her away
from her usual Friday night football-player make-out session
to be here, not that she came here of her own mysterious free
will. Seeing most Manchester Prep students outside of school
is an unpleasant experience, but interacting with Ivy when
not absolutely forced to is the highest level of torture.

'Don't for one second think I didn't explore literally every other option in this world and beyond before coming to you,' she sneers, her spun-from-gold locks falling over her shoulder. 'I'm desperate.'

I try to hold it in, but I can't. 'Oh, Ivy, acknowledging the problem is the first step. Bravo.' I do a slow clap.

'I knew this was a bad idea,' she mutters as she starts walking down the apartment building stairs. I look back at Amani, completely flabbergasted, and use sign language to ask, *Do I stop her? What is happening?* Silent communication definitely comes in handy at times like this.

Amani shrugs, looking just as confused as I am. I definitely have zero desire to have my mortal enemy in my sacred space, though I am puzzled (and admittedly intrigued) by what could've brought her here.

'Ivy!' I call out. Damn curiosity! I hear her stop somewhere on the first floor. 'C'mon, now. Tell Auntie Amber what's wrong.'

She hesitates, then huffs dramatically as she makes her way back up, glaring at me as she enters.

'Please, come in.' I gesture sarcastically.

She barely surveys our quaint apartment, not even peeping into my mom's office, which is right off the living room and filled to the brim with every supply needed to start a Wiccan apocalypse. Yup, just a totally normal home.

'So this is where you live,' Ivy says, keeping her limbs

close, like she doesn't want to accidentally brush up against something.

'Obviously.'

'And you have friends?'

'Yes. Shocking, I know.' I wave at Amani and Kim, who are in stunned silence over the sudden vibe change to our gathering. 'Say hi, friends.'

They both wave robotically. The whole thing is going really great.

'So, um, what can we do you for, Ivy?' I ask, my thirst for knowledge waning. 'I can whip up some poisoned brownies if you're hungry.'

She gives me the evil eye, which, in her case, is just her eyes. It must be hard, I guess, to be a siren and not have people fall all over you like normal. Since Amani and I are mystilogically inclined, Ivy can't pull her usual mental manipulation on us, and Kim's doing her best to blend into the background. We've mapped out a Manchester survival guide for Kim, with Ivy starring as Public Enemy Number One (we even drew her as an Ursula-esque sea urchin). Kim has transferred to many schools, so she's pretty street savvy on her own, but even having lived on different continents never alerted her to the presence of earthbound supernaturals. When she learned of our particular strains of magic, Kim opted to stay out of any future forecasting or matchmaking, declaring she desired a life 'full of surprises.' This proved to be incredibly fortunate for me, seeing as how revealing her match would bring me a life 'full of devastation.'

'I'm here because of my sister,' Ivy finally admits, though it's clear how much it physically pains her to do so.

'Iris?' I ask, memories bubbling in my brain. Iris was a senior when we were freshmen. While she didn't abuse her siren abilities during high school the way Ivy does, Iris was still adored, successful, and drop-dead gorgeous. She was student body president and gave many rousing speeches during her last year at Manchester, her words managing to reach even the most cynical of souls (mine). Iris had a stage presence that couldn't be taught; when she spoke, you listened, but not in an against-your-will, bow-before-the-queen way. Every time she spoke, it was clearly from the heart; even if she was using her siren charms to boost her appeal, there's no magic that can duplicate authenticity. I remember listening to her speak about school pride and how every person can make a difference, and as a result, I almost signed up for the environmental club. That's how good she was: I nearly participated in a school organization.

But that's not why I remember her.

It may be hard to believe, but I wasn't always the self-assured, amazing matchmaker I am now. During freshman year, I was still very much struggling with getting my powers in line, learning when I should spread the love and when to keep my mouth shut. Since everyone around me was dating and I could see how every blossoming relationship was doomed to fail, I wanted to save people the heartbreak by ending things before they began. But as it turns out, ninth-grade girls aren't into hearing a total stranger reveal that their crushes are douche bags.

In my effort to help, I got bullied. A lot.

On one particularly wonderful afternoon, a group of girls cornered me behind the auditorium. Things had evolved beyond the typical girl-on-girl violence of backstabbing and spreading rumors, to actual physical violence. Four floozies with razor-sharp nails were about to beat the crap out of me, when Iris walked by. She stepped in mid-punch and spoke about sisterhood and how ladies need to stick together. Miraculously, they listened and didn't bother me anymore. I never saw Iris again – her graduation came quickly after – but I never forgot her selfless act of kindness.

'Yes,' Ivy confirms. 'She's getting married.'

'Well, mazel tov,' I offer. 'I know a great caterer.'

'NO!' she responds with unnecessary volume. Amani, Kim, and I brace ourselves. 'This wedding CANNOT happen.'

'And why is that?'

'Because! Her girlfriend is not good for her, OK? You have to understand; she's making a huge mistake.'

Oh great. Here we go again. Am I somehow putting out off-brand messaging? Do I need to switch from matchmaking to match*breaking*?

'What makes you think that?' Amani asks. 'I mean, you're not just jealous that your sister is stealing the spotlight with her wedding planning?'

An excellent question, and definitely something I wouldn't put past Ivy. I'm not about to jump into some big family drama just because she has to play a supporting character for once.

'What?' Ivy snaps. I swear the room temperature drops ten degrees. 'Are you for real? What kind of person do you think I am?'

'Well . . .' I start.

'Don't answer that. This isn't about me. Iris is too young and too beautiful to throw her life away for Brooke. My whole family is just standing by, and I've gone to every shaman and warlock I can think of. No one will help me. You are, for better or worse, my only hope.'

I pause, letting the last few words hang sweetly while Ivy stews. When I don't answer, she adds an impatient, 'So??'

'Hold on, I'm trying to savor this moment.' I take one giant breath, exhaling slowly. 'Ah, yes. I feel good about this.'

'What does that mean? You'll help? Or you're just relishing my pain?'

'Both, actually.'

'Ugh, you are sick. This makes me sick.'

'It will cost you, you know.'

'Oh, trust me, I know. I can already feel a knife slicing my pride.'

I smile. 'I meant dollars. But that's an acceptable payment source as well.' Ivy rolls her eyes. 'Just bring Iris by Windy City Magic; I'll do a reading there.'

'Fine.' Ivy bolts for the door, not saying good-bye or anything more. We sit in silence for a minute, letting the weirdness dissipate.

'Good Gods, are you really going to help her?' Amani eventually asks.

'Yeah, although I'm looking at it less like I'm helping Ivy, and more like I'm helping her sister. And if it turns out Iris is already with her match, it will piss Ivy off, which is a win-win if I ever saw one.'

Kim laughs, releasing angelic tones that could summon woodland creatures. Sometimes I wonder if her insides are actually made of sugar. 'That's going to be some session. I feel like Ivy will lose it if this doesn't go her way.'

'Oh, they'll both question it, for sure,' Amani adds. 'A matchmaker telling a siren how to live her life? No way.'

'Ivy will have to accept it. I mean, have you ever been wrong before, Amber?' Kim asks. Now there's the million-dollar question. A few months ago, I would have been offended, defending my abilities with my final breath. Matchmaking had always been an absolute, a function so central to my being that to question it would mean questioning my existence. But now I debate it daily, constantly rolling certain events and scenes in my head before I fall asleep. Have I ever led lovers astray? The possibility haunts me. I long for my past certainty, where I could brush off doubt like flour off a rolling pin. These days, the only thing I know for sure is that every time I'm with Charlie, my feelings for him shake me to the core. His companionship and affection are things I not only crave, but that make me a stronger, better version of myself. But that doesn't change what I see in his eyes. The Fates, those bastards, are taunting me with this push and pull, leaving me with riddles and forcing me to live a puzzle. Have I ever been wrong before?

Good Gods, I hope so.

# Three

THERE'S SOMETHING IN THE AIR AT WINDY CITY MAGIC. I don't know if it's Mom's two-for-one permanent perfume potions or the free corn dogs in the Navy Pier food court, but the shop is jam-packed. I've already done twelve matchmaking sessions at my so-pink-I-could-puke table o' love, and poor Bob, our part-time employee and recovering magic addict, was needed for eight sketch-artist additions. Even though he's surprisingly good with a pencil, he doesn't always thrive under pressure. Earlier today, I was describing a man's match as someone having 'dainty, birdlike features,' and Bob started freaking out about this giant peacock that once attacked him while he was trying to steal an egg from its nest. Luckily, he managed not to divulge the horrible details surrounding the type of hex one does with a peacock's egg, but still, Bob's ranting was so incessant, it scared the customer off. Mom put Bob back on the register after that, and I put away my matchmaking sign, trying to tidy up the messes left by meddlesome tourists.

'I swear, everyone just has to rub their fingers all over the crystal balls,' I say to no one in particular as I Windex away prints. 'Everybody wants to play fortune-teller, but no one wants to pony up the cash. Why do we even stock these?'

'You can't have a magic shop without crystal balls,' Bob says, refilling the magical mints we leave at the counter. (They are magic in that they freshen your current breath and keep it fresh through your next meal, even if your last meal was garlic coffee.) 'Everyone knows that.'

'Oh really? Everyone?'

He nods, quietly rubbing his 'lucky' rabbit's foot with his meaty right hand. Bob's not the most riveting conversationalist, but we've had a few magic-related debates in our day. Most of his former life is still a mystery to me, but there's a lot of passion rumbling through that boulderlike body, and I always wonder if one day he'll just completely explode.

'Excuse me, do you know where I can find Madame Sand?' a woman asks from behind me. I can tell right away she's not a 'typical' customer. A lot of our clientele, especially on the weekends, are suburbanites spending a big day in downtown Chicago, with Navy Pier serving as their main attraction. I personally would throw myself into the frigid waters of Lake Michigan before choosing to spend a day here for fun, and most locals would say the same. These weekend warriors usually wander in here by mistake, confused as to why we don't sell T-shirts or shot glasses with 'I ♥ Chicago' emblazoned on them, but our selection of magical goodies is so enticing, they rarely leave empty-handed. Who could resist, after all, a potion promising to block out any human voices for one solid hour? Not me.

Money is money, and we certainly don't judge (OK, maybe *I* do), but Windy City's real patrons are those looking for a magical solution. A fairy in need of a delicate wing patch, or a wizard who needs authentic ground wormswort. This woman here could be a vampire or maybe one-sixteenth centaur, but either way, the fact that she knows my mom's name proves she's on a different level.

'Sure. Is she expecting you?' I ask.

'No, but I need some help with a custom spell I started working on at Dawning Day the other night.'

'Oh, um, sure. Right this way.' I guide the witch to the back of the store to Mom's private quarters. I pull back the red velvet curtain and peek inside. Mom's mixing something sour smelling in her stone pestle. 'Mom? You have a Dawning Day peep here to see you. I don't recognize her, but—'

'It's OK. Send her in,' she says without looking up.

'Oooookay.' I turn back to the unknown witch. 'She'll see you now.'

The woman thanks me politely and disappears behind the curtain. I hang out for a second to try to overhear what's going on but then decide against it. Even though it was a hard adjustment at first, I haven't been to a coven meeting since the blowout over whether someone so low on the magical food chain (i.e., *moi*) should be allowed to enter the sacred union that is Dawning Day. A newer member, a despicable wretch named Victoria, declared that I was somehow discrediting the group by proximity – me not being a full-fledged witch. It was insane, of course, and Mom ultimately put Victoria in her place (quite literally, since she rendered her motionless with a severely scary choking spell). We haven't seen Victoria since, but I've still kept my distance from the coven. Victoria, for all her surgically modified ways, did have one thing right: witches, Gods bless 'em, are not my people. I can't aspire to anything they work with, and they have no idea about the things I tackle. I always hung around coven meetings because I was looking for a place to belong, but now I know that's not it. I can't force myself into a box that doesn't fit, and no spell can do that for me either.

Still, it's good the group is accepting new members, though after Victoria, I hope Mom is being a little more cautious in the screening process.

I get back to helping customers and perform a demonstration on how our teeth-whitening tar works (rub on chompers, let sit for ten minutes, and – voilà! – good-bye stains!). It's five minutes to closing when I realize Ivy never came by. Huh. For all the spectacle she made showing up at my place, I thought for sure she'd drag Iris in here today. Whatever. Makes no difference to me. Rather than getting into it with a couple of sea witches, I may actually have a shot at leaving on time and toying with that cinnamon dolce crepe recipe I've been dying to try. I've got a new friend who I'm sure would love to sample it.

# Four

'ORDER UP!'

I pass off a plate of chilled cow's heart in a honey pear sauce to a tuxedoed server. Hopefully that will satisfy the diner's request for something 'sweet, yet hearty.' My next order is for a warm intestine compote, and I'm not sure where to start on that one.

Being that it's my last year of high school (praise the Gods!) and the Future looms near, Mom loosened her death grip on my Windy City schedule and started letting me rotate two shifts elsewhere. And since it's my dream to feed the masses large quantities of sweet, hyperglycemia-inducing desserts, I split my time between two of the most unique eateries on complete opposite sides of the spectrum:

first is MarshmElla's, the 100 percent mortal-owned-and-operated bakery that is an actual slice of heaven on earth, and then the Black Phoenix, proudly serving the hidden supernatural community, whose particular palates keep me on my toes. With my buddy Ella, we've brainstormed treats that will keep dentists living plush for years to come, but working in the Black Phoenix kitchen has really been a challenge. I thought having a best friend with a spice affinity forced me to think outside the box, but Amani's preferences are nothing like what I've seen at the supernatural hot spot.

'Customers are really liking those candied bat wings you invented,' says Marcus, a line cook I'm usually stationed next to. 'Something about the chewiness of the wing combined with the sugared coating; they really go after 'em.'

'Yeah, I'm glad. Though it's weird, because I usually taste-test my recipes as I go, but with this one, I just had to *wing* it,' I say with an over-the-top wink.

He smiles at my stupid pun while peeling a pile of gross-looking eyeballs. Marcus is a poet, but more important, a freshman at the Chicago Culinary Institute, aka my dream school. He works here a couple days a week to help pay for tuition. He's a nice guy, a little on the reserved side, definitely embracing the 'contemplative poet' vibe. He plates like a pro, though, making super-weird menu items look almost appetizing. Also, he's a werewolf.

'Have you applied to the Culinary Institute yet?' he asks, dropping the eyeballs in a deep fryer. 'The deadline is probably coming up, right?'

'Thanks for the reminder.' I sigh. My application has been ready for a week, but I haven't had the guts to stick it in the mail. 'I'm working on it.'

'You know, I could help you with it, if you want,' he offers. 'I've been through it already.'

'I just may take you up on that.' A second pair of experienced eyes couldn't hurt.

He nods. 'It's good that you're staying in the city,' he says so quietly I almost don't hear him over the clangs of pots and pans.

'Why's that?' I ask as I add a cherry to my last blood orange cake of the night.

Marcus looks down at the floor as if he'll find an answer down there, but our boss, Vincent, glides in before any words come. 'Amber, your arm candy is here,' he delivers in his cool baritone. As always, he's dressed like he's going to a black-tie gala, rather than managing a secret supernatural restaurant. He's so obsessed with keeping up appearances, he makes the kitchen staff wear full makeup even though hardly any of the customers see us, and we're typically sweating like pigs over open flames and ovens.

'Thank you, sir.' I untie my apron and check my reflection in a sauté pan hanging on the wall. I quickly run my fingers through my black, blue, and green hair, giving it my trademark 'carelessly tousled' look. 'See you next week, Marcus!' He responds with an almost sad, lopsided smile and halfhearted wave. Poets, man.

Vincent escorts me to the front, acting as a pseudo-bodyguard. Candles dance off the golden tabletops as a lonely saxophone player croons in the corner. It's not like I'm in danger from the night crawlers and blood suckers who dine here, but ever since the regulars learned a matchmaker is on staff, my attention is in demand. I often get pulled aside for some quick and dirty relationship advice at the end of the day, which is not preferable since I'm usually pretty tired and not really up to sitting through love reels. I am weirdly popular here – a feeling I'm not accustomed to – and have even had customers order my desserts just in the hope I'll deliver them with a side of happily-ever-after.

'Are you meeting up with Amani tonight?' Vincent asks, trying (and failing) to casually bring up the object of his affection. Ever since I introduced him to my best friend, he's been completely smitten: the correct response, seeing as how they are each other's match. Amani had to be stubborn, though, and jumped on the repulsion train instead, describing Vincent as 'slimy.' She's right in that there are times he does get involved with unidentified goos (just a side effect of catering to this particular clientele), but personality-wise, I still think she's wrong. Vincent's a vampire, so he came of age in a different time – the 1920s – and has a different idea of what impresses a lady. He's old-school, using lots of flash and cheesy lines, when he should just drop the wannabe-gangster act and be himself: a nice guy with a lot of patience and heart. Now that I work with him, I want them to fall in love even more. I'd coach him, but I've been ordered to STAY OUT OF IT, so I do.

'Nope. No Amani tonight. Just me and the boy,' I say.

'Well, that should be fun,' he says, clearly disappointed. 'Great job tonight.'

'Thanks . . .' I start, but I'm already checked out because I see Charlie at the door, and he looks so cute in his navy peacoat and knit beanie I just want to scrunch his face. I throw my arms around him and pull him in close, breathing in his scent. Heaven. Too bad for him my current aroma is a lovely combination of hog bowels and skunk spleen. Still, he kisses my forehead and lays a cheek on the top of my head, completing the hug and ignoring my stench.

'Hey,' I say, muffled in his coat.

'Hey, you. Ready to go?'

'Yes, please.'

We walk out into the cold Chicago night; small flurries twirl around us in the evening air. There's a light dusting of snow on tree branches and rooftops, but the sidewalks are blessedly clear. Charlie's building is only a few blocks away, so we walk clutching each other's mittened hands.

'How was work?' he asks.

'Good. You know . . . weird. I keep hearing my desserts are a hit, but they look so disgusting.'

'Yeah, I hope you aren't mad that I haven't asked to try them.'

'Dude. I haven't even tried them. So you're good.'

Out of nowhere, he steps in front of me, taking my face in his woolen palms. Tiny snowflakes catch on my eyelashes as he leans in for a kiss. The warmth of his lips quickly spreads through me, till I almost forget we're standing outside in January. The heat builds, and I pull the ends of his scarf to bring him as close to me as possible. It's exactly what I want after a long shift, and I know I won't be the first one to pull away.

'I missed you,' he whispers when we do come up for air.

'You just saw me at school.' I laugh.

'But that was, like, hours ago.' He strokes my cheek with his thumb. 'And school is overwhelmingly filled with people who get in the way.'

'Agreed. People are the worst.'

'So I like it when I can focus on only you.' I see my spellbound expression reflected in his glasses. Sometimes I don't know what to do when he says things like this. It's not like I don't believe him, or that I'm unworthy of his affection; I sometimes still can't believe our relationship is even happening, against the odds, the Fates: everything. Blessed, beautiful Charlie: I wish I had such sweet sentiments always queuing on my tongue to respond.

I grab the collar of his coat. 'Why are you so—'

'Charming? Amazing? Irresistible?'

'—good to me?'

His smile softens from cheesy game-show host to something more genuine. 'Oh, that's easy. You make me happy, so I want to make you happy too.'

'Well, you're crushing it, Blitzman.'

We walk a little farther, hand in hand, when I find myself asking, 'Charlie?'

'Yes?'

'What do you want to be when you grow up?'

He strokes an imaginary beard. 'Hmm. A rock star?'

'Really?'

'Not really. I have no musical talent.'

'Right. OK, then what?'

He shrugs, like I'm asking him about what he'd like for dinner and not what he'd like to do with his life. 'I'm not sure, to be honest.'

I try not to make a face. 'Well, I know you've kicked all your volunteer work up ten notches, and you've been busting out your college applications . . . How are you bundling together all your hopes and dreams for your essays?'

'I'm not, I guess,' he says. 'I'm keeping things open-ended, talking about how the future is bright with possibility, and I can't wait to seize the day!' He pumps a triumphant fist in the air.

As adorable as that is, I shake my head. 'I can't function like that.'

'Like what?'

'Like . . . whatever happens will happen. "It will all work out somehow."'

'But won't it?'

'Not without a plan.'

Now he's shaking his head. 'It's the classic rivalry: head versus heart. You're lucky; you hit the jackpot early by figuring out what you want to do. You've mapped out the future with your love of baking. But this ol' slot machine' – he taps at his temple – 'has yet to land on a winner.'

'Doesn't that stress you out, though? Not knowing?'

'Nah. I just go with my gut, wherever it leads me.'

I scrunch up my nose. 'I don't know, sounds risky. What if you have irritable bowel?'

'Oh, baby, I love it when you talk dirty.'

'Gross, Charlie!' We both laugh and land in a kiss, which turns into several kisses, which turns into an impromptu make-out session right in front of his building. Charlie starts to pull back, but I lean in for more, leaving us breathless before his doorman.

'Hey, um,' Charlie whispers in my ear, 'do you want to come up for a bit?'

Usually I'm supposed to be home by eleven, and staying out late will definitely incur the Wrath of Mom, but even with that dilemma hanging over my head, I can't fathom leaving his side right now.

'Well, I mean, the restaurant *did* need me to stay longer for extra help tonight,' I say with a wink.

As the elevator doors glide shut, Charlie's hands slide up my back, and I know I've made the right choice.

# Five

Senior year is truly an academic conundrum. On the one hand, our entire educational lives have led to this point: every quiz, every paper, has been completed with the intent of positioning ourselves appropriately for this moment in time. Colleges want to see your history and progress to ensure they're investing in a good egg. And yet, the actual work of this final semester will likely go unnoticed, since transcripts won't be updated until we're packing our bags to say goodbye. There's that usual drive to succeed, infused with a creeping malaise; my Culinary Institute application is in the envelope, ready to go, so what does it matter how I do on this test? I don't really see how calculus will apply to my actual life; the only math I need is kitchen measurement conversions, which I mastered before I lost my first tooth. Or so I tell myself, as I try to solve for $x$ in the most absurd problem of all time.

I look around the classroom, seeing if any of my Manchester comrades are experiencing a similar existential crisis, but it's hard to tell, since everyone's quietly working away in their plaid skirts and button-downs. I don't have any friends in this class, so it's not like anyone would shoot me a sympathetic look anyway. I scribble down something resembling an answer and then focus on the clock in the front of the room. Three more minutes until lunch. Bless.

When the bell rings, I'm free for forty-five blissful minutes. I usually brown-bag it; I don't trust the cafeteria offerings, mostly because the head cafeteria lady, Ms Dench, is half orc, and orcs are wildly mischievous. Who knows what she could be slipping into the vats of corn dogs? Mystery meat, indeed.

'What's up, friend?' I take a seat with Amani, who is fearlessly chowing down on a tray of sriracha-soaked chicken fingers.

'Nothing really, just your standard day,' she says with the tone of a sad trombone.

'Why so glum, chum?'

She shrugs, but before she can answer, Kim comes bouncing up, with the pep of a human rabbit. I can almost feel sunshine radiating from her smile, and unfortunately I left my shades at home.

'Hi, guys!'

I offer a tight-lipped smile, while Amani is more taken with her charms, scooting down on the bench to give Kim a seat. I guess she's having lunch with us now?

'What are we talking about?' Kim asks.

'Actually, Amani is not really having the best day,' I start.

Kim whips her head in concern, touching Amani's arm. 'Oh no! What's wrong?' I try not to feel territorial, even though *I* was the one talking to my best friend about her problems. I wasn't really looking for an assist, but Amani doesn't seem to mind the backup.

'Ben Shelldon tried to ask me out again,' Amani reveals while licking hot sauce off her thumb.

'Wow! That's exciting,' Kim exclaims, putting down her sandwich in hopes of a gabfest. 'Are you gonna say yes?'

Amani and I eye each other, psychically connecting in that special way only best friends can. Ben has been chasing her for months, but she's wisely kept him at bay, mostly because she knew her real match was right around the corner, and also because Ben is a disgusting example of the human race. But after meeting her 'true love' turned out to be the biggest letdown of all time (her words, not mine), she's definitely chilled out on all things *amore*. No longer is she the girl drawing hearts on the edges of her notebook or planning out the perfect wedding place setting. My dear sweet bestie has let a level of cynicism into her heart that I thought was only reserved for crusty, old matchmakers.

'I don't know,' she answers. There's a vacancy in her eyes that reads straight-up defeated. 'Maybe.'

'Excuse me . . . maybe? Is that your final answer?' I ask. Ben's not supernatural, but somehow I associate his limbs with slime. I don't know how anyone could consider going anywhere with him voluntarily, least of all someone in my social circle.

'I mean, I don't have anything to lose.'

'Except maybe your pride, your standards, and, oh yeah, your lunch.'

Amani pops a flaming-hot Cheeto in her mouth. 'Yeah, well, at least he doesn't drink blood.'

Sheesh. 'That you know of! Who knows what that dude is into! I once saw him eat pizza out of the trash.'

Kim giggles softly, then wipes her face clean of expression, definitely unsure of the conversation's context. 'Amani, you're awesome and can have any guy you want,' she offers. 'There's no reason for you to settle.'

This would be my cue to say something as to how she could do a lot worse than Vincent (ahem, BEN) and that a perk of dating the undead is that his love would be eternal, but I don't have a chance because Amani just says, 'Thank you. And I have no intention of settling. I—' She breaks off, as her whole face suddenly morphs from dead-fish blaze to consternation. Whatever future sneak peek just interrupted her train of thought is not good. Her eyes twitch, and her whole head jerks side to side two times. 'Something annoying is about to happen,' she warns.

We sit on high alert, waiting for a fire alarm to ring or a food fight to break out among the meatheads sitting next to us, but even in our heightened state, we all jump back in surprise when Ivy drops her tray in the middle of our table.

'Good Gods, Ivy!' Amani yelps. 'What the hell?'

'Oh, did I interrupt something important?' She practically pushes Kim over to make room for herself, clearly having no issue invading personal space. Kim, almost an actual doormat, scoots over to suit her, eyes so wide it's amazing they haven't popped out of their sockets. 'I need to talk to you,' Ivy says.

'I'm sorry, but this is a designated siren-free zone,' I say, waving my hand around the table perimeter. 'You have not been cleared to enter.'

Ivy crosses her arms. 'I thought you agreed to help me.'

'Yeah, and I thought you agreed to bring Iris by the shop. That's where I conduct business.'

The siren looks off into the lunchroom, pouting her perfectly pink lips as she surveys the scene. There's something off about her appearance that I can't put my finger on . . . It's not just that she's sitting here (which is weird in and of itself), but that her physical presence is different somehow. Her skin is still blemish-free, and her nails in precise ovals; it gags me to confess she's still the most beautiful living creature I've ever seen. But then it hits me: she's usually flanked by a set of interchangeable lackeys who follow their leader without question. Ivy's used her siren powers to rule the school for so long, I can't even remember a time when she's been alone. Maybe she's instructed her groupies to get her a beverage or cry quietly in a corner until she's returned. Either is plausible.

'She won't come,' Ivy finally admits, still turned away.

'And you can't just, like, make her?' I ask.

She snaps back, shooting daggers in my direction. 'A siren can't force another siren to do something. Duh.'

I turn to Amani. 'Do people still say "duh"?'

'Apparently.'

Ivy scowls, twisting up her exquisite features.

'Ivy, of course your sister isn't gonna want to see me. If she's secure in her relationship, she has no reason to visit a matchmaker. Especially if you've tried dragging her to me under the pretense of breaking them up.'

She impatiently taps red fingernails against her green cardigan. 'Well, then I need you to go to her.'

I burst out laughing, until I realize she's serious. 'Are you for real?'

She reaches into her backpack and hands me a thick envelope. I peek inside, and there's too many hundred-dollar bills to count. 'What the what?'

'That is how serious I am,' Ivy says. 'It's clear from your dollar-store beauty products that this is more than you typically make matchmaking. So this better get your ass in gear.'

36

'Joke's on you – I don't wear makeup. This is just my face.' Ivy makes a grunting sound like a constipated grizzly bear. As much as I'd love to swindle money from someone I despise, this is a lot of coin for a result I cannot guarantee. 'Ivy, this is too much—'

'Are you listening to me? Money is not important; my sister's future is at stake.' She's standing now, leaning over to hover in my face. 'My address is in that envelope. Meet me there after school.'

'Uh, I have to work.'

She pounds her fist on the table, making us all jump again. How infuriating it must be for her to not get her way. 'I'm pretty sure I just covered a year's worth of shifts. Meet me there, or I'll make Ben Shelldon follow you everywhere you go for the rest of the year.' Ivy grabs her tray and storms off. I can almost feel the waves of frustration left in her wake.

'Ha! See? Even Ivy thinks Ben is the worst,' I say once she's gone.

Amani fights back a smile. 'How much money is in there?' she asks, nodding toward the envelope.

'I don't know, but definitely enough for us to get a round of cafeteria cupcakes! Excuse me, garçon?' I snap my fingers at no one in particular. 'Little help, please?'

# Six

TRY TO IMAGINE THE RESIDENCE OF YOUR MORTAL ENEMY. Depending on the depth of your hatred, you'd probably envision a home covered in thorns, with menacing gargoyles and maybe a moat of molten lava. While logically I know Chicago's neighborhoods are not zoned for large pools of volcanic liquid, I am disappointed to find Ivy lives in a typical Lincoln Park brownstone. No sinister fog or rusty gate: not even a foreboding vulture circling the property. Kind of a bummer, to be honest.

The doorbell is a regular chime (not a human scream), and I'm greeted by an ordinary butler, not one missing a head or made of bones. Neither of Ivy's parents is home: her mom, also a siren, is a cancer researcher (an instance of using siren powers for good and not wasting them on pep rallies), and her dad, just a regular joe, has some sort of fancy-pants finance job, hence the butler.

'Would you care for something to drink?' asks the non-ghoulish butler. 'We have Perrier, tea, espresso.'

'Ooh, yes, I'll take an espresso,' I say. Might as well. I mean, it'd be rude not to, right?

'Excellent,' he says with a nod. 'I'll alert Miss Chamberlain of your arrival.'

I wait in a sitting room that's probably larger than Windy City Magic. I can't even imagine having this much living space. I should be at MarshmElla's right now, whipping bowls of frosting, and yet I'm here, covered in frost. When I called to say I'd be late to work, Ella was decidedly displeased, even though she did admit curiosity about the whole siren employment of a matchmaker. Luckily, I have a recent influx of cash to buy that set of candy molds I know she's had her eye on. Hopefully, that will make it up to her.

Ivy eventually emerges, cascading down a fairy-tale staircase as I sip my notably delicious coffee. Mmm, money buys good beans.

'Well, I see you couldn't wait to get your mitts on some free drinks,' Ivy says, flopping down on a chaise.

'Thanks for the hospitality!' I say, raising my cup in her direction. 'Where's the bride-to-be?'

'She should be home any minute now.' We sit in horrible silence, staring at each other. I can actually hear the passage of time, thanks to the grandfather clock in the corner of the room. Ivy looks just about as uncomfortable as I feel, fidgeting like the chaise is made of spiders. 'So you're still with Charlie?' she asks, grasping for something to break the awkwardness.

'Yup,' I say, unable to hold back a smile. 'Wait, that's not why you asked me here, is it? You're not still hung up on that whole thing?'

'Please, I couldn't care less.' She swats the question away.

'Well, you must care a little.' I bat my eyelashes while I take another sip.

She glares at me with such intensity, I wonder if it's a natural talent or if she practices in the mirror like a deranged pageant queen.

'As I'm sure you've noticed, I have half the school falling over me, so I don't have time to focus on one at a time.'

'Hey, you brought it up,' I say, and Ivy rolls her eyes. 'Do you want to give me any more insight into your sister's relationship peril? Why is it so necessary to stop this wedding?'

She tilts her head in suspicion. 'Will what I tell you influence your . . . "magic"?'

'No, and there's no need for air quotes, thanks.'

She thinks it over, but before she can spill any details, a Disney heroine walks through the door. Equally as beautiful as Ivy, only less severe, Iris is like the softer, sweeter siren sister. She looks just like she did in school, and I wonder how she's been using her powers since then: Saving puppies? Helping the homeless? Either way, an imaginary halo sparkles over her golden hair. The fact that Ivy emerged from the same family tree seems like a joke.

'Iris, finally!' Ivy sighs in relief.

'I'm sorry, were you waiting for me?' Iris hands her coat to the butler, offering him a heartfelt thanks.

'Yes! Obviously!'

'Sorry, Sis, what's wrong?' Her flawless forehead wrinkles in concern.

I sit to the side like a nature photographer, observing the scene in silence. I thought Ivy would thaw in the presence of the sister she's so desperate to help, but somehow she's still the same abrasive wench. Lovely.

'Nothing's wrong, I just wanted you to meet my . . . friend.' She winces like she's bitten into a lemon upon saying 'friend,' and I make a similar sour face.

'Oh! Well, that's nice.' Iris looks my way, radiating sunshine. 'I'm Iris.'

I take her hand, using the opportunity to lock eyes before she realizes my identity. It's the most thematic matchmaking montage I've ever seen; usually I get a glimpse into a variety of lovey scenes and situations, but these sneak peeks are all the same. Everything is aquatically angled: at the beach, swimming, ocean on the horizon. Lots of flowing hair. And her match: somehow I'm only seeing her face, which is odd, but it is stunning. Sun-kissed skin, aqua eyes, strawberry-blond hair. They're a very attractive couple, almost disgustingly so, if this is the girl Ivy's worried about.

'I'm Amber,' I finally reveal once I've seen my share.

'Amber, lovely to . . .' Iris gets a knowing look, reminiscent of most of Ivy's evil-expression collection. 'Wait a minute! You're that matchmaker Ivy's been wanting me to see!'

'Yes, um, that's me.'

Iris spins around to her sis. 'Ivy! When will you let this go?'

True to form, Ivy stands her ground, never backing down from a fight. 'I'll let it go when you dump Brooke.'

Iris's jaw drops. 'Why can't you just be happy for me?'

'What is there to be happy about? She's taking you away from us!'

'That is *my* choice, and none of your business.' With every comment, the siblings inch closer together, refusing to let either have the upper hand. Holidays must be fun in this house.

'It *is* my business!' Ivy yells. 'You're *my* sister!'

Iris sighs, fingers at her temples like she's warding off a migraine. 'For heaven's sake, Ivy, not everything is about you.'

It'd be really cool, from a spectator's standpoint, if sirens could shoot sparks or something when they're angry, but even without, the energy in the room is downright electric. My aura is all shook up, and I kind of wish I'd videoed the whole thing. *Dueling Sirens*: the next big YouTube sensation!

Suddenly, they seem to remember I'm in the room, and turn to me in sync. Both of them have a hunger in their eyes suggesting they'd easily claw information out of me.

'You know already, don't you?' Iris says coolly. In a matter of minutes, she's gone from sunshine and rainbows to a creature ready to attack. I'm wondering if sirens can somehow control the sun, because I swear the room has dimmed and the temperature has dropped. It's like all the happiness has left the world. Lesson learned: never, EVER be lulled into submission by a siren.

'She better, if she knows what's good for her,' Ivy snarls, her usual bloodthirsty self.

I'm literally being backed into a corner as the siren sisters slowly edge up on me. I wish I had one of Mom's instant fog potions so I could make a magical escape, but all I have on me is a half-eaten bag of M&Ms. Typical Amber: always choosing chocolate over safety.

'So what's the verdict? Have I found my match?' Iris insists. With my back against the wall, there's no winning scenario here. I honestly don't know who my answer will piss off more, and both Chamberlains look like they could torture me in very specific, painful ways. What a great day.

'OK, guys, I did see Iris's match, but do you think we could ease up on the dramatics a bit? I feel like I'll have to go into the magical witness protection program after this.'

Ivy, unsurprisingly, does nothing to alter her energy or stance, but Iris pulls herself back from the veil of evil.

'I'm sorry, Amber,' she concedes, blinking furiously like she's coming out of a trance. 'This has become a very sensitive issue between Ivy and me. I'm sure you see this a lot in your profession.'

'Heightened emotions are the name of the game, sure,' I say, downplaying my rattled nerves. Somehow being cornered by a pair of sirens is right up there with nearly becoming a vampire's chew toy.

'Let's give her some space.' Iris leads me away from her venomous sister, and I take a seat across from the two of them. Suddenly, I feel like a daytime talk-show host ready to reveal paternity. One of them is about to get super angry, and I don't know which.

'OK, so, I saw Iris's match,' I start slowly. They're both breathless, hanging on my every word. 'And she has long strawberry-blond hair, blue eyes . . .'

Iris's face lights up. 'That sounds like Brooke.'

'Hold on,' Ivy interjects. 'Anyone can have strawberry-blond hair and blue eyes.' She turns to me, nostrils flared. 'Didn't you get a name or something? Social security number?'

'That's not really how it works . . .'

'Are you serious? What good are you?' Ivy stomps around the room like a toddler mid-meltdown.

Sigh. 'If you have a picture of Brooke, I can confirm whether that's who I saw.'

Iris pulls out her phone, where the girl in my vision lives as her wallpaper.

'Yup, that's your match. Congratulations.'

Iris squeals and gives me a squeeze. I guess since I validated her love, we're best friends again. 'Thank you so much! You know, you look vaguely familiar to me. Have we met before?'

Not wanting to get sentimental in front of Ivy, I say, 'Maybe. I was a freshman when you were a senior.'

'Of course. I'm sure we crossed paths. And I'm so glad we did today!' She skips off into the other room, presumably to tell her girlfriend they've been officially sanctioned by a bona fide matchmaker, leaving me with Ivy, who's digging her claws into her sides in a murderous rage.

'Well, I guess I'll be going, then.' I stand to leave, but Ivy grabs my wrist.

'Do you have any idea what you've done?' Her voice has dropped an octave, effectively dropping my stomach.

'Yeah, I confirmed a couple in love. Clearly, I deserve to be punished.'

Ivy shoves her gorgeously scary face in mine. 'You saw her, then? Brooke? Notice anything peculiar, or is everything you see covered in candy hearts?'

'Well, it was one of my more narrowly focused visions . . .'

She shakes her head in disgust. 'Brooke's a mermaid!'

Whoa. That explains all the $H_2O$. 'OK . . . Neat?'

'No! God! How do you think the two of them will spend their life together, huh?'

'I don't know. Buy a house with a pool?'

She pinches my wrist tighter. 'Dammit, Amber, stop joking around. Because of our siren heritage, Iris has the option to live in the sea. But she'd have to renounce her family and surrender her magic to do so. We would never see her again, and she'd be giving up everything.'

The pieces start to fall into place. 'You mean . . . she'd be pulling a reverse *Little Mermaid*?'

Ivy groans. 'Essentially, yes.'

'Wow, that's . . . intense.' I'd hate to admit I ever see anything eye to eye with Ivy, but that is definitely a huge sacrifice. To give up a central part of your being for another person (or, in this case, *mer*person) is no small gesture. There's no turning back once you've sprouted scales.

'Wait a minute,' I say. 'How is she going to pull this off? She can't just manipulate herself to grow a tail, can she?'

'Do you hear yourself?' Ivy yells. 'Of course she can't. She needs the help of a witch.'

I try to keep up, even though this whole thing is crazy. 'Has she seen my mom?'

'She has, actually, but your mom turned her down. Said she wouldn't do it . . . something about mystical limitations.'

That sounds like her. 'Well, you should be fine, then. I don't know any other witch who'd be powerful enough to pull off a transformation like that. That is some straight-up "wielding the magic of the ancients" if I ever heard of it.'

'Yeah, well, Iris said she found someone who doesn't give a crap about the Fates and will do it for the right price.'

Now, that is not something any witch worth her salt would say. Witches aren't − or shouldn't − be swayed by money like mortals. They're generally guided by a higher power. So any Wiccan willing to perform a spell unsanctioned by the Fates is not someone you want to mess with. 'Who is this witch?'

Ivy slumps back on the chaise, defeated. 'I don't know. She said her name is Victoria.'

# Seven

GREAT. GREAT. I'VE SOMEHOW FOUND MYSELF TANGLED UP WITH a siren, a mermaid, and a homicidal wicked witch who has made it clear on more than one occasion that she is definitely NOT Team Sand. Way to go, Amber! Why don't I just arm-wrestle a dragon and piss off a necromancer while I'm at it?

'Can you believe all this?' I say to Ella as we prep her bakery's kitchen for a fresh round of pies. She ties her apron in place, though I don't know why she bothers, since half the ingredients will end up on her person regardless. Ella's not supernatural, but we've known each other so long, I can trust her with weird stories that border on insane.

'You know what I wonder,' she starts, rolling out dough for the crust. Her hands (and somehow, her back) are already covered in flour. 'How did Iris and Brooke even meet? It's not like you can pick up a mermaid at Starbucks.'

'I know! Is there a dating site for the aquatically bent?'

'Maybe Iris was scuba diving and their eyes met across a school of fish.' We both laugh as I stir the lemon custard filling.

Ella pops three crusts in the oven, setting the timer. I love being here. The anticipation of pulling out something scrumptious in less than an hour fills me with childlike glee. You'd think I'd be used to it at this point, but I still bounce like a five-year-old on Christmas morning when a treat is ready to go. Being in this kitchen, digging through Ella's endless supplies, working with professional-grade tools: Heaven. Pure heaven. She's taught me her secrets for making macaroons and why it's best to use room-temperature ingredients. I've learned how to weigh (not measure!) flour, flambé fruits, and whip sugar into something lighter than air. Everything I need is here, everything I want. This is the real magic.

'You have to admit,' Ella continues, 'it's really romantic.'

'Living underwater does not sound romantic. It sounds . . . cold.' I wipe the prep table clean, getting ready to start on a large batch of chocolate oatmeal raisin cookies.

'No, I mean, the gesture. Risking it all for love.' She washes her hands, then tousles her blond waves for any stowaway ingredients. 'Imagine if Charlie did something like that for you.'

'I prefer him to be landlocked, thanks.'

Ella twists her hair in a high bun, shaking her head. 'Joke all you want, but I know he'd melt your heart down to butter if he made a life-altering surrender to be with you.'

'Yeah . . .' I trail off, knowing full well he already does a pretty great job of turning me to mush whenever he's around. I grow more attached to his goofy comebacks and never-ending collection of tie clips every day. And unbeknownst to him, he may already be sacrificing something to be with me: love with his true match, Kim.

But this is my happy place, so I push the thought away, squeezing cookie dough with more force than needed. After this, I'll be responsible for prepping the next day's early morning treats. Recently, Ella introduced a full line of breakfast pastries, including chocolate hazelnut croissants, raspberry cream Danishes, and homemade Pop-Tarts. My personal favorite is the cinnamon sugar churro donuts that are so light and fluffy, they're like a cloud dissolving in your mouth. Pair that with her side of mocha dipping sauce, and I'm a goner. DEAD. Now that MarshmElla's offers breakfast, there's really no reason to eat anywhere else.

I slip into a happy trance of sucrose and sauces, and get home smelling like butter and cream, which is quite possibly the best scent on earth. (Other than bacon. Obviously.) I always bring something sweet home for Mom so she's continually reminded of how beneficial it is to have her daughter take a break from magic and dabble in desserts.

'Hey, Mom.' I peek into her office, where she's sitting on a floor pillow, poring over a grimoire. 'Want a midnight snack?'

At the sound of 'snack,' she perks up, snapping out of her trance. 'What did you bring me?'

'A caramel pretzel puff,' I say, presenting the salty-sweet mound on a napkin.

Mom brews a desire potion that puts people into temporary states of hypnosis, but I'd say this treat accomplishes a similar effect. Her eyes widen, and while no actual drool emerges, the way her lips are moving, it's clear saliva production is up. Sugar: nature's ultimate magic weapon. 'Thanks, hon.'

I place the puff by her knee, taking a quick peek at the grimoire. This isn't one of her personal tomes; the handwriting is too loose and swoopy. Mom's script is so precise, you'd think she's still going after that elusive A in Penmanship. This writing looks more like Grandma Edith's. Witches are all about sharing their secrets . . . Well, as long they are magical secrets. Meticulous grimoires are kept to track the mythological journey of a Wicca. Spell successes and failures are documented so that the next era of witches can build upon those of the past. We have several generations of Sands' grimoires on our shelves, and even though I'm not technically a witch, someday they'll be passed to me. If I happen to birth magically inclined offspring, these books will give them incredible insight into the supernatural world, whereas my biggest gain will be creating a cool-looking library.

'What are you reading about?' I ask, pulling up a pillow. 'More on Grandma Edith's time living with the nudists?'

Mom chuckles, mouth full of caramel. 'Actually, I was looking for her spell for hair-growing tonic. I've had several requests at the shop, and I seem to remember her befriending a werewolf with alopecia.'

I try to picture a bald werewolf and envision a hairless cat. 'She really knew some interesting characters, didn't she?' I say. The events of the day gurgle inside me, and I know there's no point in trying to keep them down. 'Speaking of which, guess what I got myself into today?' I quickly recount the early details of Chicago's newest hit soap opera, *The Siren and the Mermaid*.

Mom leans back. She looks uncomfortable, and she shifts around on her pillow. 'Yes. Iris did come to me. But that was a while ago.'

'And you didn't jump at the chance to send a siren back to the sea?'

She hesitates, chewing her treat much longer than necessary. 'It would take exhaustive resources, and ultimately, the fallout with the Fates would be tremendous. They're not fond of witches acting like Gods.'

Ah, the Fates. Unwilling to help yet pissed when others step up. Such a delightful bunch.

'But . . . you *could* do it, right? If the Fates weren't such controlling jerks?'

She tilts her head, looking upward for an answer. 'Theoretically, yes. I could perform such a spell. But I still wouldn't. Think of all the princes transformed into frogs over the years. Do you know what happened to those witches and sorcerers?'

'OK, so you don't want to be smote from on high. But if *you* could do it, could another powerful yet mentally deranged witch pull it off too?' I cross my fingers, hoping the answer is no.

Mom raises a brow. 'I suppose . . . ? But only someone with no regard for mystilogical boundaries.'

Dammit. 'Yeah, well, apparently Iris has hooked up with just such a person.'

'Who?' Yet as soon as the question leaves her lips, she narrows down the field to one horrible option. 'Victoria.'

'Ding, ding! I'd give you a prize, but you already ate the caramel puff.'

'It was delicious, by the way.'

'Thank you! I made it myself.'

'But Victoria – this is a problem.' Her eyes grow cloudy with concern.

'I was kind of surprised to hear she's still around after you showed her what's up a couple months ago.' The image of

Mom going Dark Willow and turning a spell meant to attack me back around on that hag remains firmly in my top-five favorite visuals, just behind Charlie's first attempt at making crème brûlée and almost setting his sleeve on fire with the torch. Adorable.

'Unfortunately not. Victoria is a plague not easily erased.'

Sensing an opportunity, I ask, 'Well, how did you get rid of her before?'

'Before?'

'You know, when you knew her earlier in life, during a mysterious time that you've inexplicably chosen to keep secret from me? Back then.'

Mom rubs her hands over her face, letting her fingers rest at her temples. 'It's too late to be getting into this, Amber.'

Evaded again! 'OK. I mean, I know you have some alleged skeletons in your closet or whatever, but revealing this admittedly scintillating information is actually pertinent to the scenario at hand.'

'You know,' she says, squinting with suspicion, 'I find your involvement here confusing. Isn't Iris's sister the girl you punched in the face? Why help her?'

Number one all-time favorite visual. With a bullet. No regrets. 'Yeah, so?'

Her eyes bore into me, practically forcing me to spill.

'OK, fine!' I throw my hands up, guilty. 'Maybe Ivy paid me an obscene amount of money to help Iris. And Iris is actually a decent person, who may or may not have been nice to me in the past. This mermaid is her match, and the two of them look insanely happy; I want them to be together. But using Victoria as a stop on the path to true love? I can't just stand idly by.'

'Well, that is noble. Sort of.' She thinks for a minute, flipping a page in the grimoire back and forth. 'I know that any warnings I give regarding dealing with dangerous witches will be disregarded, so let me cut to the chase by offering my help.'

'Aww, thanks, Mom.'

'It seems like Iris is determined to make this happen, regardless of the consequences. So we'll need to find out when exactly she's making this commitment.'

Something catches her attention, a memory perhaps, and her expression fades to somber. Her forehead is heavy, creased with anguish, her focus lost in subconscious. 'Iris is taking a big chance, letting herself be overtaken by love. I don't know if she realizes what she's getting herself into.'

# Eight

'HOW'S THIS?' AMANI ASKS, STRAIGHT-BACKED, PINKIE OUT, sipping daintily from a teacup. She's discovered a coffee shop in our neighborhood that serves high tea on Sundays, and while I personally think tea tastes like liquid dirt, tea parties usually come with an assortment of sweets, so I opted in.

'Wonderful, darling,' I say, copying her posture. I pretend to sip, then quickly abandon my cup for a pink-frosted petit four instead. Amani grabs a yellow one but adds a chili-powder jelly bean to the top before popping it in her mouth.

'I feel so fancy,' she announces, fluffing out the skirt of her dress. In addition to a taffeta petticoat, she's also wearing a white satin headband in her shiny brown waves, along with lace fingerless gloves.

'You definitely look the part.' In my effort to be fancy, I wore jeans without holes.

'Thanks. It's fun to dress up sometimes.' As if she isn't always walking around like a dress pattern from the 1950s. Out of nowhere, she cocks her head to the side, brows furrowed, distracted by a vision. 'Someone's about to make a mess.'

Sure enough, seconds later we hear a crash in the back of the room.

'Rest in peace, fragile porcelain,' I say. We both raise our non-broken cups in solemn salute. 'That was pretty seamless, by the way. Your vision came in and out without much disruption.'

She blushes and smiles down at the table. 'Yeah, I still can't always control what I see and when, but I'm definitely trying to limit the whole poltergeist face whenever I can. Not sure that will leave the best impression around campus next year.'

At this, I occupy my mouth with a cranberry-orange scone. Nothing is official yet, but since Amani is still unsure of her future path, she decided to apply to state schools, where she can explore her academic options without spending a ton of money. Her parents have six kids to put through college, and she's very conscious of this burden. I always support her 100 percent, but most state schools are located far from Chicago in the cornfields of Illinois, and I'm already (selfishly) missing her.

'You're probably right,' I finally add. 'Though it would be an interesting way for you to make a name for yourself.'

'Ha, true. I can haunt the dorms or something.' She takes a bite of a cucumber sandwich. 'I applied to U of I and Illinois State.'

I nod, trying not to mentally calculate the distance of these schools. 'Good, good. Classic choices.'

'How's your application going?'

'Oh, you know, patiently waiting to be released from the confines of my drawer.'

'They'll accept you. Obviously.'

'Is that an official premonition?'

'You know what I mean.'

Our pact, while frayed around the edges, is always annoyingly upheld at the most inconvenient times.

'Has Charlie applied?' she asks.

'Yeah. He's already been accepted at Notre Dame, his dad's alma mater. But he's hoping to hear back from Northwestern.'

'That'd be good. Then he'd be close to the city.'

'It's definitely the preferable scenario.' And I can't stop myself from smiling, because having Charlie be only a short 'L' train ride away means we wouldn't have to become one of those doomed high school couples that tries to hold on to the past even through they're screaming into the future. We won't be in the same zip code, but we won't require airfare to see each other. I could jump on the Purple Line after pulling out a fresh batch of cookies and be sharing them with him once they've cooled. It would be perfect, if only the Fates would allow it.

'Well, I think I'm done with tea,' Amani decides, tossing her napkin on the table. 'This was fun, though. It's nice that your mom has been easing up on your shop schedule.'

'Yeah, I think she's trying to prepare herself for when I'm at school. I mean, I'll obviously still work there, but my hours will be more sporadic. Bob's gonna have to fill in the gaps.'

'How is Bob these days? Still curbing the urge for world domination through wizardry?'

'Aren't we all?' I snort. 'Sometimes I catch him muttering an incantation under his breath, and then a super-annoying customer will suddenly be silenced, so . . . he's still got some work to do.'

'Classic Bob.'

We bundle up for a walk down snowy sidewalks, but when we hit the pavement, I'm instantly paralyzed by the sight of Kim and Charlie walking toward us. Together. Not like holding hands together, but laughing and talking and so totally entranced by each other's company, they don't even notice Amani and me until they're almost on top of us. Even wrapped in winter gear, I still see smiles hidden by scarves. They look so good together it's painful: both so classy and stylish with individual flair. Both funny and smart in a way that never makes you feel less so. Seeing them like this is straight from my visions of them as a couple, and I have to rub my eyes to make sure it's real.

It is.

Amani curls her arm around mine, steadying me with her grip. Because she is wonderful and correctly assumes my insides are dying, she takes charge of the situation. 'Hey, guys,' she calls out, startling the pair. 'What are you two doing here? Together.'

Charlie's face, already pleasant, brightens further upon seeing me. 'Hey, you,' he says, stepping close for a quick kiss. 'You girls done being fancy? I thought I'd surprise you and join.'

'For tea?' I ask.

'Excuse you, yes. I am a very sophisticated man.'

I want to smile, but I refuse.

'Of course you are, Charlie,' Amani says. 'And you brought Kim?'

'Oh,' Kim pipes in. 'We just got done with an MA meeting.' MA (short for Manchester Ambassadors) is a community service club at school. I didn't even know such a thing existed until I started dating Charlie, who's been a member all four years. 'Member' is kind of a loose term, because (per his words) he's probably been to 1.5 meetings during the course of his school career. Even though he likes the idea of helping people, he doesn't particularly care to be around *Manchester* people, which is quite the conundrum. Still, he's been trying to be more involved lately to both help with college applications, and make his dad – Chicago's 'community comes first' mayor – proud. I didn't realize Kim had taken up the call of service, though.

'You're meeting on a Sunday?' I ask.

'Yeah, well, I blame our whip-cracking *presidente*, Alison, who got the bright idea of doing a winter carnival fund-raiser, and since it's winter *now*, we have to hustle to actually pull it off,' Charlie says. 'Something about that girl freaks me out.'

Seeing as how Alison Bleeker is one-quarter banshee, yeah, you can't help but jump into gear when she shrieks, er, talks.

'Well that's . . . fun,' I say.

'I think so,' Kim says. 'I haven't really joined a club like this before, but my parents promised we'd stay here until graduation, so I figured, why not. Might as well do something. And carnivals are cool, right?'

'Carnivals are the epitome of cool,' Charlie says, and the two of them laugh, at what I can only assume is an inside reference, since carnivals don't exactly rank.

I try not to let the sound of their mixed laughter melt my eardrums. I have no real reason to distrust either of them. Kim seems so pure, her words may actually be candy coated; she's been nothing but a sweet and supportive friend since we've met. And Charlie – he's his own brand of magic. I don't want to be this girl; I refuse to transform into someone who double-checks intentions and digs way deeper than face value. The path of jealousy is lined with thorns, and I'd rather steer clear. If only my head weren't clogged with these visions, if only I could see straight. I want to stomp on their seeds of burgeoning romance and wipe away the happy ending. All I want is the security of Charlie's feelings and to ignore the circling sharks. But I don't know how.

'Well, I look forward to dragging around a cheap stuffed animal after winning at the ring toss,' Amani adds.

Kim smiles, and we all stand there awkwardly for a minute.

'So, Kim, do you want to hit Sephora with me?' Amani asks, cleverly pulling her away from Charlie. 'Amber's not really into mascara shopping.'

'Definitely not,' I confirm. 'I like my lashes to be pale and lacking flirtation.'

Kim lets out her twinkly little laugh. 'I'd love to. I'm in the market for some new nail polish, myself.'

'Great!' Amani gives my arm one last pinch, then latches on to Kim instead. I don't want Amani to go; I want to unload all my insanity and have her tell me it's OK. But because she's wise and less certifiable than myself, I have to assume she's doing this for a reason.

'Bye, all!' Kim waves.

As they walk away, Charlie wraps me in a tight hug, picking me up an inch off the sidewalk.

'What are you doing?' I squeal.

'Squeezing the weirdness out of you.'

'What?'

'You have a weird vibe. What's up?'

'I am a vision of normalcy.'

'False,' he says, glasses sliding down his nose. 'I know you, Sand, and I know when you're wigged out.' He sets me back down. 'Spill.'

Damn. I'm caught. And I thought I was such a good actress. What do I do now? Pull the paranoia rip cord, or let it lie?

'Turns out tea doesn't agree with me.'

'Tea doesn't agree with anyone. It's like dirt water.' Oh, this boy. 'But that's not it.' He still has his arms locked around me, so it looks like I'm stuck until I talk (although, truthfully, there are worse places to be).

Deep breath. 'Seems like you and Kim were having fun,' I slowly venture.

'Sure, I guess,' he says. 'I've never really had an MA buddy, so it's nice to have someone to talk to.' I search his face for any deeper appreciation, any beyond-friendship feelings growing inside, but I guess my detective mask is not very sneaky. 'Wait a minute – why?' he asks.

'No reason,' I lie.

Wheels click behind his lenses, trying to pinpoint my problem. 'Do you have some sort of weird thing with Kim?'

he asks. I shake my head. 'You act different when she's around.'

'What, I have to be exactly the same all the time?'

'No, but there's a distinctly different vibe.'

'Like what?'

'Like . . . it wouldn't surprise you if she suddenly sprouted fangs.'

'To be fair, I think that of most people,' I say.

He pinches his lips, keeping himself from laughing. 'Is this one of those weird girl-world things where you say you're friends but you secretly hate her? Because, honestly, that's the worst.'

'That is the worst. And no, I don't hate her. She's my friend.' But I say 'friend' with so little enthusiasm, even a deaf troll would detect the fault in my voice.

Now Charlie's the one hunting for clues, his dark green eyes going to town. 'Are you . . . jealous, or something?' he correctly guesses.

I release an offended huff. 'Jealous? Me? Matchmakers don't feel jealousy. Only satisfaction at witnessing fledgling love.'

He frowns. 'I know you're trying to be funny, but I already know you're tough, so drop it. Just talk to me.'

But I don't want to talk; I don't even want these feelings. I want to take this cute boy and smother him with kisses and not have a care in the world. The problem is, I do care – a lot

– more than I thought possible. It's the caring that consumes me, and morphs from a positive sensation to negative obsession. If I tell him – if I release this poison swimming in my system – will it make things better, or worse? Will I look like a fool, or will it confirm my fears?

'Well . . . you do look cute together,' I eventually say.

'Cuter than this?' He pinches my cheek.

'Stop. And no, obviously not.' My cheeks are burning, and not from his touch. I can't even look him in the eye. 'But you two mesh well.'

He considers this, and my heart actually stops. Good Gods, did I just give him an idea? Open his heart to a new possibility?

'I don't think of her that way,' he answers, and I want to vomit from relief. 'She's your friend, and I figured part of the boyfriendly duty was to be nice to your lady's pals. If you'd prefer, I can go all "raging jerk" when she's around. You're the boss.'

I find his response so overwhelmingly comforting, and I'm so embarrassed by the whole exchange, I bury my face in his coat. 'No, don't do that.'

Charlie rests his chin on the top of my head and strokes my hair. 'You have nothing to worry about, OK? You're the only girl for me.'

If only that were true.

# Nine

THE FINAL BELL RINGS, AND I'VE SUCCESSFULLY MADE IT through another stretch of school. The hallways fill with chattering groups buzzing about their days, but I'm not one to linger; the sooner I can step off campus, the better. What's there to talk about, anyway? OMG, can you believe what so-and-so said? Yes, I'm sure so-and-so is a total idiot, and anything verbalized is an accurate portrayal of sub-intelligence.

I'm at my locker, packing up my stuff, when an icy shard digs into my shoulder. I whip around to see who'd dare assault me and am annoyed (but not surprised) to see Ivy, in full siren power pose (i.e., hands on hips, chest out). Sometimes I think she forgets her magic is lost on me, but it's fun to see her try.

'Was that . . . your finger that tapped me just now?' I ask. 'If so, you should be checked for hypothermia—'

'Don't even try making a cute reference about me being cold because sirens lived in the ocean, blah, blah. There's no time. We gotta go,' she commands.

'I'm sorry, where are we going?'

'I hacked my sister's phone; she's meeting with that witch tonight. We have to spy on them.'

I'm impressed by her initiative, even if the results mean mortal peril. 'You know that's completely unsafe, right? Victoria's a straight-up lunatic, and she would have no problem murdering you on the spot.' I try to hold back a smile but fail. 'Although I'm sure that's a common reaction after meeting you.'

'Like you've never received a death threat,' she throws back. Touché. 'So what do you suggest, then?'

'Well, where are they meeting?'

'Someplace called the Black Phoenix. Although I couldn't even pull it up on Yelp, so it must be a dive.'

Ah! For once, the Fates make my life easy. 'Perfect. I was actually heading there myself.'

'What? Why?' she asks, horrified.

'I work there, one night a week. Don't worry,' I say, patting her reassuringly on the shoulder. 'You'll fit right in.'

She tosses her hair in my face, taking off two steps ahead of me. I consider jumping ship until I realize we've just passed a group of football players who didn't even turn when Ivy walked by. No catcalls, no displays of desire. For my entirety of knowing her, there's always been at least one hopeless, slobbering pile of boy-shaped Jell-O. Even if she weren't actively twisting the knobs of her siren charms, sheer beauty alone has been enough to turn the masses to pudding. It's been such a constant occurrence, you start to take the nonstop adoration for granted, until it's suddenly gone. But why? Where did her admirers go? She's still painfully beautiful as far as I can tell.

Ivy too seems oddly indifferent to cultivating their attention. She's usually shoving her boobs and butt toward anyone who will look. But right now she's steady, focused, ignoring all flanking man meat. Maybe she's already sampled all the Manchester offerings and isn't interested in seconds?

When we get outside, I start walking toward the bus stop, but Ivy snaps her fingers at me (rude) and points to her red Mercedes-Benz in the parking lot. Leave it to a siren to snag a spot in the faculty-only lot. Even though getting in a car with my enemy behind the wheel isn't exactly my idea of a good time, I'm not one to turn down a free ride.

'So where is this dump?' Ivy asks, turning the key.

'Oh, we have to make a stop at my apartment first so I can change.' Before her eyes can roll, she looks down at her own plaid skirt and seems to decide this is a good idea. When I'm at work, I'll be covered in an apron, so it doesn't really matter what I wear; I just prefer my daily uniform doesn't come out smelling like boiled bat wing. Plus, Vincent does prefer we make some sort of effort to be presentable, and even though my hair is too short and choppy to tie into a full updo, I've invented a little twisty, bobby-pin solution that appeases him. It's better to show up ready to go, because I've definitely received more than one side-eye from the boss man when my hair is hanging in my face.

At home, after I've changed into some leggings and a white button-down, I see Ivy brought a spare outfit too, though hers is certainly more asset-baring than mine: skintight jeans and a low-cut top. I guess those are a siren's tricks of the trade, but I'll need something other than jaw-dropping curves to provide backup for this evil-witch surveillance. The Black Phoenix may give me a slight home-court advantage, but if I've learned anything about dealing with my supernatural kinfolk, it's that it's better to be safe than strangled.

I peruse Mom's office for anything easily accessible and deployable in case of emergency. Most of her completed one-stop spells in a jar are at the shop, while she keeps the separate ingredients at home. There's a lot of power packed in these shelves, but without an official witch to mix them all together, they're pretty worthless to me.

'Ugh, what are you doing in there?' Ivy moans from the living room. I made her stay away from the goods on the off chance her aura would make everything wilt.

'You never learned patience, did you?' I call back.

'What good is patience when you can get whatever you want, whenever you want?'

'Right, right.' I finally spot what I've been looking for in Mom's charm drawer: a pair of sound-amplification amulets that act like magical walkie-talkies. The stones vibrate at the same frequency and are tethered together via some sort of wavelength I don't fully understand. All my simpleton, non-witch self knows is that using these will allow us to listen in on Victoria and Iris without being seen.

We go through the Black Phoenix back entrance just before 5:00 P.M. Ivy, completely appalled at having to enter through an alley, huffs the whole time. The smell of the kitchen is what really puts her over the edge, though, and I can tell she's questioning her devotion to her sister when a seared liver passes by her nose.

'People . . . eat here?' she asks, positively green.

'Well, I wouldn't say people, but yes, edibles are consumed in this establishment.' I tie on my apron and add a dab of colorless lip gloss for good measure.

'Is this some sort of freaks club?' Her eyes widen as Alessandra, the sphinx hostess, glides by, wings draping down her backless dress. I remember having a similar reaction the first time I saw her, but now that chilling with a sphinx ain't no thang, Ivy's bewilderment makes me feel worldly and superior.

'Yup, and as a siren, you're an automatic member here. Welcome!' I congratulate her. I stick out my hand, but she's keeping herself drawn inward, not wanting to physically interact with anything around her. 'Let's go find Vincent,' I suggest.

'And what is he, a goblin?'

'No. Just a vampire.'

'Great.'

Vincent's wiping down the bar, doing his last-minute checks before the doors open for dinner. He waves when he sees me but doesn't stop racing around.

'Hey,' I call out, trying to catch him. 'Can I ask you a favor?'

'You're late. Why aren't you in the kitchen doing prep?' He's always cranky before the sun goes down.

'Sorry. Something came up, and I need your help real quick.'

He stops adjusting an arrangement of black silk flowers at the coat-check desk. 'What?'

'I need you to place one of these' – I hand him an amulet – 'at a particular table tonight.' I give him the backstory while Ivy shifts uncomfortably.

'Victoria's coming here?' he groans, exposing a razor-sharp canine. Looks like he's been another casualty on the Victoria pain train.

'You know her?'

'Let's just say . . . our paths have crossed.'

Ugh! Why are people so reluctant to share information about this witch?!

'C'mon, Vincent, you gotta give me something.'

He shoots me a look that reads 'no, I really don't' but then relents. 'She used to date a regular of mine, another vamp. Not a good guy but a good customer: always ordered appetizers and drinks. They came in here pretty frequently for a while. But when things ended, they really ended.'

'What does that mean?'

'Rumor has it she dragged his mattress outside in the middle of the day while he was sleeping. Then, poof.' He snaps his fingers. 'He was gone.'

'Holy crap!' I look over at Ivy, whose face is frozen in a silent scream.

Vincent nods, his pale, sun-never-touched self shuddering at the thought.

'Sheesh, what's up with your shady clientele?' I tease, trying to lighten the suddenly grim vibe.

'You have no idea.' The clock strikes five, and he runs his fingers through his slicked-back hair, giving a final pull on his bow tie. He shakes his shoulders like he's shedding a skin, and the poised, charismatic restaurateur I've come to know and love starts to emerge. Vincent may be dead, but he's really alive when it's time to be on. He replaces his fangs with a charming smile and settles into his showman role. 'I'll pass this on to their waitress when the time comes; I don't want to be anywhere near that witch.'

'Fair enough.'

'You better hope she doesn't see it, though,' he adds. 'I will disavow any knowledge of its existence if discovered. I can't have you causing another scuffle in my place, Miss Sand.' He winks and heads off to greet the first diners of the evening. I grab Ivy's hand and drag her back to the kitchen, where I start setting up my station. Marcus, who's already chopping ghost peppers, gives me a little wave.

'What's new?' I ask him. I pin the other amulet back behind my ear with several bobby pins. It looks like a hearing aid, and essentially, it is. 'Did I miss anything over the last week?' Marcus keeps to himself, but I can usually pry some gossip out of him.

'Well,' he starts, removing the scalding seeds from the peppers, 'Thursday was open-mic night, and a banshee went on for over an hour. It was awful, but no one was brave enough to get him offstage.'

'That's amazing. I'm sorry I missed it.'

'It really wasn't—' He stops, interrupted by Ivy sighing louder than the sous-chef sharpening knives behind us. We both turn her way.

'Yes, princess?' I ask.

'What am I supposed to do while we wait?' she whines.

'You could peel onions.'

'No.'

'Or peel eyeballs.'

'GROSS.'

Perhaps out of boredom, but more likely because she just noticed Marcus is the only line member not sporting some sort of face fungus or pointy horn and is actually decent-looking, Ivy suddenly lights up, shaking her fingers through her hair so it perfectly cascades down the sides of her face. She shimmies between Marcus and me, leaning on the counter to best reveal her décolletage, leaving me with a view of her butt. Now it's my turn to sigh.

'Hey, there,' she purrs in Marcus's direction. He gives me a 'what is happening?' look over her shoulder.

'Uh . . . hey,' he replies.

'You're pretty cute, you know that?'

'Um, thank you?'

'And you're really talented with those knives. Good hands. I wonder what else you could do with them.'

Good Gods. Flirting? Now? I should have realized bringing her here meant I'd need to protect more than myself. 'Yes, Ivy, that's called a skill,' I interject. 'Some people actually work to achieve goals, instead of performing brain melts like you're trying to do to poor Marcus here.'

She looks back at me with doe eyes. 'I'm just talking. He doesn't have to answer.' Of course we both know that's not how sirening works. If she's looking to converse with this innocent werewolf, he'll participate, whether he wants to or not.

But in a delightful twist, Marcus goes right back to chopping, completely bypassing Ivy's feminine wiles. It's an excellent choice, but the fact there was a choice at all is . . . odd.

'Amber?' says a whisper in my ear. It's Alessandra, chatting through the amulet. 'Your party is here. I'm going to slip the amulet in the table's centerpiece, OK? Hope it helps.'

'OK, it's showtime,' I say to Ivy. 'Marcus, I'll be back in a minute; can you cover my station for me, please?'

'Sure,' he says, blushing. He's probably relieved at my removing such a foul creature from his workspace. I lead Ivy to the supply closet, where it's quieter, and we crouch down in a corner, pressing our ears to the amulet. We hear some shuffling and silverware clinking on the other side.

'This is quite the place,' we hear Iris say sweetly through the stone. Ivy tenses at her sister's voice, unconsciously gripping on to me. I let it slide and make a mental note to properly disinfect the area later. 'I've never been here before.'

Skipping pleasantries, Victoria cuts to the chase. 'So are you ready for the transformation or not?' The deep tone of her voice instantly sends a shiver down my spine. I can just picture her cartoonishly 'beautiful' face, forehead frozen and lips permanently pursed.

'It's not that I'm not ready; I'm dying to be with Brooke,' Iris says, losing confidence. 'I'm just worried about the possible side effects from the spell.'

'Side effects? Darling, I'm a professional. I don't make mistakes.'

'But magic always has consequences, doesn't it?'

'And who told you that?'

'Lucille Sand.'

Victoria lets out a horrible laugh that crackles through the stone, making both Ivy and me squirm back and hit our heads against the vegetable crates. 'You poor thing. You talked to Lucille? No wonder you came to me.'

'HOW DARE SHE!' I say in an intense whisper. Ivy slaps her hand over my mouth, not wanting to miss a word on the other side.

'What I don't understand is: Why are you willing to perform the spell, but she isn't?' An excellent question, and I'm glad to hear Iris isn't completely lost to the pulls of love. She still has a good head on her shoulders.

There's a pause, and I can't wait to see what angle this liar will spin. 'Well, Lucille likes to think she operates by a higher mystical code, but that excuse allows her to pass judgment on everyone around her. She hides behind the Fates, when really, she just doesn't have the skills.'

It's a good thing I'm holed up in a closet, away from the knives, because I want to stab a witch right now.

'Oh.' They're both quiet, Iris letting Victoria's claims sink in. The waitress comes by and delivers the night's specials, and I look at Ivy, who is curled up and perched like a gargoyle, eyes wild but frozen, poised to attack. This exchange is putting both of us on edge, but Ivy seems extremely disturbed at being forced to stand impotently by. 'Lucille warned me about taking such a big risk,' Iris continues. 'She said I may regret it one day.'

'Just because she made foolish life choices doesn't mean you are. She's projecting. I, on the other hand, don't judge my clients. You're an adult; you can make your own choices. If you have the cash, I'll get you that tail.'

Charming. Their drink orders arrive, and after a few sips, Victoria follows up with, 'So?'

Ivy's biting her lip; her sister's life is on the line. I've never seen her so small; she's always a mountain among men. To see her here, nearly drawing blood from both her mouth and my arm, it's almost . . . humanizing. We hold our breath as we wait for the verdict.

'OK,' Iris declares, quiet but assured. 'I'm ready. Let's do it.'

# Ten

'IVY, WAIT!'

The siren is on her feet, running through the kitchen, with no regard for the flames and forks around her. She's a wild animal, tearing through a culinary jungle, but luckily, she's headed for the alley and not the dining room. I can only imagine what she'd do if she were face-to-face with her sister right now: Drag her by the hair to an underground lair and throw away the key?

As I follow her out back, the amulet begins to make a crackling sound, like land lines losing connection, then falls silent. I'm too far away to pick up the signal from the dining room (#oldworldproblems). I don't really want to miss the rest of Victoria and Iris's conversation, but loose-cannon Ivy is my most immediate concern. I find her pacing like a caged lion. I can't tell if she's going to scream or cry, so I decide to keep a safe distance.

'Are you OK?' I call out in the darkness. There's a real tornado of special smells happening back here, as Ivy's chosen to melt down in direct proximity to our Dumpster. I don't even want to think about how many unidentifiable body parts are rotting in those bins.

I hear her sniffle, her face turned away. I'm guessing she doesn't want to cry in front of me, and I don't blame her; I'm not sure if I'm the right person to comfort her right now. Wait, no, I'm sure I'm not.

'Don't you want to hear the rest of their conversation?' I ask. If I know anything about evil types, it's that they like to finalize contracts: not always in blood, but definitely making their victims sign on the dotted line. There's no way Victoria's leaving tonight without a clear plan of attack.

'What does it matter?' Ivy whines.

'What do you mean? You wanted to come here—'

'Yeah, to stop her! But she's hell-bent on becoming a fish, no matter the cost! Nothing I do matters!' she yells. I can see her better now; she's wiped away her smeared mascara, but she's not up to her siren standards.

'Speaking of hell-bent, I don't get what your problem is here. Your sister found her match. Isn't that a good thing? I mean, I know you'll miss her, but—'

'This isn't about me!' Ivy says indignantly. Her wide eyes glow through the darkness. 'You don't understand.'

While I'm not really interested in the inner workings of Ivy's brain, I feel like I don't have all the pieces of the puzzle. 'OK, so make me.'

She huffs at first, almost as unwilling to share as I am to listen. But we've somehow found ourselves in this unholy alliance, and if we're going to make any progress, we need to bridge the gap.

'What the hell is she going to do all day, huh? What kind of life can she have at the bottom of the ocean?' Even though her rage is building, her voice softens, turning sad. 'Her dream was to be a senator, to use her siren powers to make real, impactful change. But what kind of impact can she make underwater? Foster peace agreements between a dolphin and a shark? She's throwing her life away, and for what? Love?' Ivy shakes her head. 'Ridiculous.'

I can honestly say I've never thought about a mermaid's day-in-the-life. It seems relaxing, at first glance, to lie among seashells all day. But Ivy does have a point: What do they do down there? What will Iris's life become?

Back when she was in school, no matter the topic, Iris could command any room. I have no doubt she could dominate the Senate floor with her ideas, using her influence for good, but she can't conference in from the coral reef. She'd have to leave that dream behind. Has she thought this through? Is she ready to sacrifice not only her body but her ambitions as well?

'Hey, um, Amber?' I hear Marcus call from behind me. He's peeked his head out in the alley, like an expectant puppy. 'Your station is getting pretty backed up. You may want to get in here soon.'

'Thanks, Marcus,' I say, giving him a wave. When I turn around, Ivy is gone, disappeared into the night. It's just as well. I honestly have no idea how to process Iris's situation. I can't reassure any of the Chamberlains that love conquers all, and if a matchmaker can't, who can?

Once I'm inside, the amulet crackles back to life, allowing me to catch the tail-end details of Operation Sea Bound, which are: Iris must pay Victoria in full in advance so she can acquire the proper supplies. The actual spell must take place on a full moon, the soonest being in three weeks. They'll rendezvous by Lake Michigan at midnight. Then good-bye, legs.

I pull the amulet out of my hair and tuck it in my back pocket. Now that I know the particulars, I don't need to listen to further small talk. I trudge over to my station, the weight of Iris's decision weighing heavily. I barely even know her, but I can't help agreeing with Mom that this could be a huge mistake.

'Let me ask you something,' I say to Marcus, sliding my hands into a bowl of dough. 'Would you ever sacrifice a part of yourself for someone you loved?'

He flinches a little at my return, a smile tucked in the corner of his mouth. 'Um, that's random, but OK. I don't know . . . Which part?'

'Any part. A body part, I guess.'

Long curls of carrots cover his area, as he glides the peeler up and down; he takes several contemplative seconds before responding. 'I surrender my body once a month for the whole wolf thing,' he says, voice soft with sorrow. His gaze is distant, mind elsewhere while his hands work. 'It's not easy. Nor fun. I can't imagine voluntarily going through something like that.' More carrots coil below him. 'But if there was no other answer, then yeah, I guess I would. In the name of love.'

'In the name of love,' I repeat, nodding. I'm pretty attached to my appendages, so switching them up for someone I love would be extreme. But then again, what if Charlie's arm got ripped off by some freak dragon accident, and giving him one of mine would be the only way for him to survive? Granted, I can't foresee us being in any situation where dragons are present, but the whole thing is hypothetical, so whatever. The point is, would I give him my admittedly less-cool, non-tattooed arm in the name of love? Would I? Or would I keep myself whole while he struggled? I don't think I'd really *be* whole if the person I loved was suffering.

Furthermore, could I give up one dream in exchange for another? If I had to live underwater to be with Charlie, that would mean never being able to bake again. No cookies, no pies: I'd never feel the warmth of an open oven for the rest of my life. Is that something I could really sacrifice?

It's too heavy to think about, especially when my first dessert order is in: sugared calf's brain à la mode. I quickly switch the subject. 'How is the whole werewolf scene, anyway?'

'What do you mean?'

'Like, I've always been curious . . . Does your skin or hair color influence your fur color?'

Marcus laughs, and I can't help but turn to watch him. He's not an unhappy person in the least, but seeing him laugh openly is rare. Watching his face shine with humor brings a smile to my own, and I have to look back down at my bowl of dough to regain focus.

'I've never really thought about it,' he admits, still chuckling, 'but yeah, my fur is black.'

'Awesome. Do you think mine would be blue and green striped?'

He shakes his head, smile hanging on. 'You're crazy, Amber,' he says. 'But I like it.' We lock eyes for a minute, and I'm treated to a glimpse of his future love life: him squeezing the shoulders of a short leading lady, with two puppies playing at their feet. I have to wonder if they are their kids or actual dogs. But before I can decide, we look away, getting back to actual work. Marcus is a sweet guy; I know he'll make a great pack leader someday.

I get lost in the dinner rush, and before I know it, it's past the time Charlie usually picks me up. He always swings by before closing, forever protective after that vamp tried to make me his main course. I check my phone and find his missed text:

> Dad dragged me to a charity dinner last minute to be his +1. I'd much rather be with you, sorry. If the desserts look up to your standards, I'll snag you some. XO.

Ugh, great. Guess I'm bussing it home.

As I pull on my winter gear, I think about Ivy and wonder if she got home OK. She was pretty upset, but I don't see her Benz parked outside, so she must've managed to find a different place to rage. Actively worrying about my enemy has me spooked for a second, but the chilly night wind forces me to focus on the journey ahead.

These are the moments – all bundled up, heading for the bus stop – I wish my magic went beyond matchmaking. I'm not really a fan of being the cute single girlie walking alone at night, because the world is full of weirdos, and I don't mean the supernaturals. I hear footsteps crunching in the snow behind me, so I quicken my pace, but the footsteps do too. I swing my bag to the front to whip out my pepper spray just as the stranger reaches for my shoulder. My finger's on the nozzle when he calls out, 'Hey! It's me!'

I recognize him seconds before blinding him. 'Marcus! Good Gods! You scared me half to death!'

'Sorry,' he says, head hanging low. 'I didn't realize you'd be going home alone. Doesn't your . . . boyfriend usually pick you up?'

'Yeah, well, he had to go be Mr Fancy-Pants tonight,' I gripe, with more bitterness than I mean.

As my heart rate returns to its normal, non-fight-or-flight pace, we start walking together. 'It must be weird, going out with the mayor's son,' Marcus says.

I shrug. 'Not really, I don't know. There's definitely less conventional issues.'

'Such as?'

'His dad holds him to really high standards, so there's a burden for him to do well, carry on the family legacy, blah, blah. But you've seen Charlie: it's not like he's gonna win a Super Bowl. So he's pressured to be great in other ways.' I pause, realizing I'm revealing a lot of personal information that's not mine. 'I mean, Charlie *is* great. But I mean, professionally great. With a capital G.'

Marcus nods, pulling his scarf tighter. 'You don't feel that kind of pressure? I feel like most kids get that from their parents on some level.'

'I have, in the past. Being a matchmaker in a family of witches is not exactly ideal.'

'I know what you mean. Now that my wolf gene emerged, I'm not in med school like my dad planned.'

The image of a wolf with a stethoscope pops in my head. 'You were going to be a doctor?'

'That was the plan. Until my sixteenth birthday turned into a scene from *Teen Wolf*.' He seems like he's trying to make a joke out of it, but his staring contest with the sidewalk indicates there's some real pain there.

'You definitely have the bedside manner for it. You're so chill and patient,' I say, trying to be helpful.

We're stopped at a crosswalk, the red light casting a glow on Marcus's cheeks. 'Thanks. But it doesn't matter now. It's not like I can go all monster in the middle of an ER.'

'It might be the best place to wolf out, though. You'd get instant medical attention.'

He looks off. 'Sure. Right after I've scarred a patient for life.'

I've unintentionally hit a nerve. It's easier for me to have one foot each in both the 'normal' and supernatural worlds, since for all intents and purposes, I'm just a regular ol' human. But for those who carry physical proof of their lineage, it's much harder to keep it on the down low. It would be beyond awful knowing I couldn't bake or work in a kitchen because of an anatomical trait getting in the way.

'But I guess in the end, it's OK,' he adds, 'because once the doctor thing was no longer a possibility, I turned to other things. Writing. Cooking. Things that can make people happy, without me being around.'

'Where do you go, during a full moon?' I ask gently.

He kicks a dirty clump of snow. 'My parents' basement. It's pretty destroyed by this point.' Another clump goes sailing. 'They're less than psyched. They were hoping the gene would skip over me.'

Well, I definitely know a thing or two about being on the wrong heredity branch of a supernatural tree.

We wait in silence at the bus stop, warm puffs of breath illuminated under a streetlight. It's late and cold, but this city is always in motion. I sense a few supernaturals passing by, probably heading home after a night of gross-out cuisine. One couple, both vampires, dance down the snowy sidewalk, with moves rivaling Fred and Ginger's, and I realize they could have learned the steps from the famous dancing duo themselves. Immortality is so weird. I don't think I could deal with people for the rest of time. In seventeen years, I've only managed to gain a few acquaintances, and I don't see that changing exponentially anytime soon. I've never really mastered the recipe on how to make friends.

While I was watching the impromptu ballroom show, Marcus inched his way closer to me. He must be cold, and I decide it's too bad he can't sprout fur whenever necessary. I'm about to comment on this very point when he says, 'Hey, Amber?'

Away from the harsh kitchen lights and in the moonlight, he looks different. His features are so soft, so unassuming, I can't picture them transforming into a snarling, predatory creature. In fact, if I had to choose someone most fitting to wear a wolf's clothing, it would never be sweet, poetic Marcus. He can barely chop through dead meat without flinching; how would he hunt down breathing prey?

'What's up?'

'I'm glad we work together.' He meets my eyes for only a second before burying his face back in his scarf.

Well. Maybe I'm learning that friendship recipe after all.

# Eleven

I WALK OUT OF CHEM LAB TO A HORRIBLE SIGHT: AMANI chatting (and flirting!) with Ben, that no-good bottom-feeder of a boy. Backed against his locker, his meaty hands positioned on either side of her head, she's just inches from being smothered. But she's not trying to get away. She's actively flashing her pearly whites at whatever idiotic story he's telling. And Ben, while wearing a tie, is no gentleman; there's a hunger in his eyes that makes me want to immediately shower. What in the holy hell is she thinking?

'Hey, guys,' I butt in, wedging my body between them before anything gross happens. 'What's going on?'

Amani, caught, looks away and starts picking at her cardigan. Ben gives me a slow body scan, then smiles hungrily.

'Amber Sand, you're looking hot today,' he oozes. Ugh, even hearing my name on his lips makes me shudder.

'If by "hot" you mean "angry," then yes, that is my general state.'

'I meant like delicious, just like Amani here.' EW, EW, EW. 'She and I were just making plans to hook up, but there's no reason we can't expand the guest list.'

Amani cringes, and it takes everything I have not to vomit on his khakis. 'First of all, I doubt that. Second, BYE.' I grab Amani's hand and yank her away, not stopping until we're halfway across campus. I practically shove her in the corner by the vending machines.

Before I can start, she stops me with, 'I know, OK?'

I'm pacing like an overprotective parent five minutes past curfew. 'Do you? I mean, how'd that little exchange even start?'

She sighs, shoulders slumped. 'I don't know. I'm lonely, OK? Not all of us can have adorable billionaire boyfriends following us around like golden retrievers. And Ben is the only guy who's shown me any attention this year.'

I clear my throat. 'Well, not the *only* guy.'

My comment is not well received. 'I'm sorry, let me clarify: the only LIVING guy.' Amani buries her face in her hands, shaking her head back and forth. 'This can't be it for me. I can't have only freak shows look my way. I mean, I'm smart, pretty, funny, and I can see the freaking future, for

Gods' sakes! You're telling me that still leaves me with chum?'

My heart clenches tight, struggling to function at hearing my best friend talk this way. 'No one is telling you that, certainly not me. You deserve a prince on a white horse with a shining sword and a pure heart and a big castle and a basket of puppies with a double rainbow sunset surprise,' I say, hoping to make her laugh.

But she doesn't. 'Then why don't you see that for me?' Glistening with doubt, her eyes search for the answer. And for the millionth time, I see Vincent, feeding her chocolate-covered strawberries and stroking her hair while she sleeps. Loving her, adoring her. If only I could play her this footage so she'd understand.

'I see only happiness for you, BFF,' I say gently. 'I would never lead you astray.' I take her hand, and she squeezes back. 'But I will one hundred percent always lead you away from disgusting douche bags like Ben.'

She smiles weakly. 'Yeah. I'm sorry you had to see that.'

'Um, so am I. I almost barfed. Like actual vomit.' Amani laughs, wiping away a stray tear. 'Don't settle,' I demand. 'Don't be that girl.'

We walk to English, arm in arm, where we're promptly split up by Ms Dell, who has some sort of personal vendetta against Amani and me ever being partners for a project. Instead, I slide up next to Kim, with whom I'm partnered to discuss William Faulkner's touching tale of mental instability and incest. Surprisingly, I wasn't exactly thrilled with the pairing, but at least Kim actually read the book, unlike most, who probably would've left me to suffer on my own. There's no point in making matters worse, I guess, so I try to be friendly.

'I think . . . this may be the worst book of all time,' Kim decides, flipping through her copy of *The Sound and the Fury*.

'No, no, you're mistaken. It's a classic,' I reassure her.

'But who writes like this? There are literally pages without punctuation! That's not genius – that's bad editing.'

I look around the room to see how others are faring. I guess it could be worse; in doing a quick survey of partnerships, it looks like Ivy ended up alone, the victim of the odd-numbered class size. She sits staring out the window, not even pretending to work on the book, which honestly is a move I support.

'Yeah, screw it,' I say. 'Let's talk about something else.'

'OK!' Kim shuts her book and wiggles happily in her seat, shining those cheery eyes my way. I can't avoid it, so I take a deep breath and let her match reel play: a moonlit scene of her and Charlie taking a horse-drawn carriage ride through downtown Chicago. Blech. Make it stop.

'So!' Kim exclaims, blessedly breaking my trance. Now that we're no longer talking about fictional sociopaths, she's all perked up. 'What are you and Charlie wearing to the winter formal?'

'Oh, uh . . .'

'I mean, I know you're not into that stuff, and I love that about you, but you've probably at least picked out your dress? Right?' She's gripping the edge of her desk like she might float away otherwise, like the idea of a school dance is filling her soul with helium. This is one of those situations where I feel like I have to fake girlhood because I have no idea what the 'proper' reaction to the formal-wear question should be. Also, Kim is not exactly my number one pick to chat about my boyfriend with.

'I'm not really sure if I'm going,' I admit. Charlie hasn't mentioned it, and since I've never had a boyfriend when one of these things has rolled up before, I pretty much scrubbed all future events from my mental calendar. I guess, though, I'm supposed to set my watch by them. Although who wears watches anymore, really?

'What? Of course you're going!'

I have to laugh at her adamant confirmation; she looks positively appalled I'd think otherwise. 'Charlie said so!' she adds.

Now I'm gripping my desk. 'He did? When?'

'During Chem lab last week. We were supposed to be changing liquids different colors on the pH indicator, but it was taking forever, so the conversation migrated elsewhere.'

'I didn't know you two were partners,' I say, trying to keep my eyes from spinning.

She brushes it off. 'We're not, usually. But both our partners were out that day, so Mr Longhorn matched us up.'

DAMN YOU, MR LONGHORN. You have no business matching people! My evil brain whips up a visual of Charlie and Kim, sitting close together over warm, bubbling beakers of chemicals, all cute and nerd-chic in their goggles and lab coats, and it's all so adorable I want to SCREAM.

'You know, it's really sweet, the way Charlie talks about you,' Kim continues, oblivious to my inner meltdown. 'I've never heard a boy be so romantic and loving, and I've lived in Paris.'

Yes! I leap at the chance for a subject change. 'What are boys like in France?'

'Oh, you know, everything is so heightened; everyone's a poet.' She frowns. 'But it's hard to tell what's real and what's just playing into a part.'

I nod, though I don't fully understand. The most exotic locale I've ever visited is Des Moines. 'But Charlie . . . ?' I press.

'He's so genuine. You know he's not saying things for show. He'll say things like "Amber just lights me up," and he literally brightens, as if simply saying your name is some sort of internal light switch. On anyone else, it'd be corny. But for Charlie, it's endearing.'

It takes all my mental strength to focus on the overall idea she's selling, rather than my romantic rival describing my boyfriend as endearing. It's nice – more than nice – to hear he talks about me with such affection, even if he's sharing these feelings with someone he may share his life with someday. I keep a lot of that emotional goo to myself, but I guess it's sweet to have someone shout it from the rooftops. Oh, Charlie, if I could kiss you right now.

I'm smiling, and find myself saying, 'He is pretty great,' before I can hold it in. Ms Dell, zeroing in on my grin like an anti-happiness hawk, circles around us, knowing full well there's nothing in this assigned reading that could make anyone joyful. Kim and I flip through the book, and I ramble out some nonsense about symbolism and imagery until our disapproving teacher wanders away.

Once she's gone, Kim sighs dreamily. 'Anyway, I hope I can find someone who loves me like that someday.' *Don't react, don't react, don't react.*

'Well, maybe you will, at the dance,' I offer.

'What? No. I'm not going to the dance.'

'Why not? You're telling me I have to get all gussied up while you lounge at home in sweatpants? Nuh-uh, not fair.'

She shrugs. 'I don't have a date.'

'So what! You're an independent woman; you don't need a man,' I say, waving a finger for emphasis.

'But I want a man.'

'Right. But you don't *need* one.'

Her twinkly laugh surfaces. 'Point taken.' She leans back in her chair. 'OK, maybe I'll go. But only if a certain matchmaker agrees to set me up on a date.'

A lightning bolt pierces my nervous system. 'Uhh . . .'

'I mean, I'm assuming my actual match is not lurking the Manchester halls' – *breathe, Amber, breathe* – 'but maybe you can help point out someone decent for one night of fun?'

'Well, I don't usually do it that way . . .'

'Please?' She clasps her hands together like an angel-faced child begging for candy. How can you say no to that?

'I guess I can try,' I relent.

'Yay!' Her cheerful cry breaks the somber vibe of the room, which, given the book we're supposed to be discussing, is not a shock. Everyone looks over at us, including Amani, who signs a quick *What's going on?*

*I'm trying not to be that girl,* I sign back. Amani looks confused but nods in acknowledgement.

Once everyone turns their attention back to the trials of Yoknapatawpha County, Kim whispers to me, 'In return, I'll help you find the perfect dress.'

I'm guessing this is a gesture of friendship, so I fake a happy face.

Yay?

Later, in my bedroom, I light a sage stick in an attempt to clear my physical and mental space of stupid energy. I cannot turn into an envious loon every time Kim and Charlie are somehow linked. 'Jealous she-devil' is a female trope I'd like to avoid. Feelings? I don't succumb to feelings! I am Amber Sand, matchmaker and molder of feelings, ha-ha! Only I am in control of my destiny (well, me, and the Fates, of course).

Yet after stinking up my room for several minutes, I feel less enlightened and more ready for a treat. The best answers are usually found at the bottom of an ice-cream pint, right? I head to the kitchen to be sure, where I find Mom furiously scribbling something in her grimoire. She doesn't even look up as I pop the top off a fresh Ben & Jerry's.

'Did you finally crack that pesky water-into-wine spell?' I ask, taking a seat next to her.

'Hmm?' She looks up, blinking furiously like she just touched down from a different planet. That's some deep concentration right there. 'What's that smell?'

'Sage. Also, Cherry Garcia.'

'Something wrong?'

'Nah, just dumb stuff.' I take a massive bite, letting the dark chocolate chips fill the holes in my soul. 'Whatcha writing? New spell?'

She closes the soft leather cover. 'Oh, no, just a few personal musings.'

'Really? I thought you witchy types only recorded the nuts and bolts of magic.'

Mom reaches for my spoon. 'Emotions play a big part in magic; temperament can either make or break a spell. It's just as important to document one's state of mind to accurately measure the journey.'

'Interesting. So how are you feeling?' I stroke my chin, giving my best therapist face.

'I'm more interested in what's going on with you. School stuff? Boy stuff?' After Mom takes a bite, she passes the spoon back to me, and I scoop another heaping mouthful. 'Ah, boy stuff,' she deduces.

'There's no *actual* stuff,' I confess. 'I'm creating all my own drama.'

'Meaning . . . ?'

Sigh. 'Do you have any anti-jealousy spells?'

The corners of her eyes crinkle. 'I tried to brew one once. Thought it'd be cute to call it Green Monster Be Gone or something. But I never quite got the right combination. The closest I came was a liquid that made me cry for five hours straight; I think the concoction was literally trying to dry out all my feelings.' She chuckles to herself. 'Anyway, some emotions refuse to be tamed.'

I don't really want to talk about this anymore, and this is the perfect segue. 'On that note, Iris is definitely going through with her journey to mermaid land.'

Mom splays her fingers on the table, taking a deep breath. 'Please don't tell me you went to see Victoria.'

'No! Well, not really. She came to the Black Phoenix, on her own, and I was there. I overheard the whole plan.' I give her the details before she can get too mad.

'I need to talk to someone,' she says after digesting the information. 'Someone Iris is close to. At this point, only a loved one will be able to talk any sense into her.'

'Like who? Brooke?'

'Perhaps.'

That seems like a difficult undertaking. 'I don't know, Mom. Don't you think Iris and Brooke will be pretty united on that front? I mean, Brooke is probably super-psyched that this is happening. Why would she do a one-eighty and say, "Hey, girlfriend whom I miss and love, please do not join me in the ocean blue"?'

'If she knew Iris was in danger because of who she's working with, she might change her tune,' Mom says sternly.

'I guess, but how are we supposed to find a mermaid anyway? With a snorkel?'

'I'll do some research.'

'Supernatural research? Like watching *The Little Mermaid*?'

She stands, kissing the top of my head. 'Something like that.'

# Twelve

'No, there's no way,' Charlie says, staring out at the murky water of Lake Michigan. 'You think she's out there?'

'I mean, I hope not. How would Brooke befriend a crab with a Caribbean accent living in a Midwestern lake?' We're snuggled up on a Navy Pier bench, sipping hot chocolate and watching flurries disappear into the waves below. I've been poring over an illustrated copy of *Mythological Creatures and Beasts* all through my Windy City shift, but the section on mermaids was not particularly insightful. The author skewed romantic while penning about Ariel and friends, dubbing them the 'pearls of the sea.' This is not helpful because, one, there are already pearls of the sea (they're called pearls), and two, it does nothing to help me pin down their general aquatic whereabouts. Also, I've been very preoccupied picturing what mermaid life could possibly be like, but these pages offered no insight either. I'm going to suggest Mom stop selling this book, because it is way dumb. 'For Brooke's sake, I hope she lives somewhere warm and colorful. I feel like the bottom of Lake Michigan would be fifty shades of gray.'

Charlie gives me a side-eye.

'As in color scheme!' I add.

He laughs, pulling me closer to him. 'Agreed.' After one last sip from his drink, he sets down his cup, and I rest my head on his shoulder. He lays his cheek on my beanie, and I breathe in his delicious boy smell.

'We've been so busy lately,' he says, voice low. 'I feel like we hardly see each other anymore.'

I kiss his shoulder, nuzzling into him deeper. 'I know.'

I wouldn't say things are strained between us, but there's definitely been less snuggle time than I would like. Between working at MarshmElla's, the Black Phoenix, and Windy City, I've been all over the place, and that's not even counting my involvement in this siren love affair. And it's not like Charlie's just been sitting around waiting for me; he's been hustling himself, really throwing himself into this winter carnival business, not to mention working on college applications and squeezing in more community service time to satisfy both his dad and the university admission Gods. I think about him all the time but only get a few minutes with him in the flesh. It's not fair. Stupid life getting in the way of my Charlie time. In fact, I'd instigate a full-on make-out session with him right now if I didn't have to be back in the shop in two minutes.

'Hey, um, question for you, sir.'

'Answer for you, m'lady.'

'Um, are we – and not that I care either way – but are we making an appearance at the winter formal?'

He sits up, mouth and eyes open wide in excitement. 'Oh, darling, I thought you'd never ask!'

I give him a playful punch on the shoulder, to which he fakes injury. But after he rebounds, he adds, 'Yes. I already planned my outfit.'

'Of course you did,' I say with an adoring eye roll. 'What am I supposed to wear?'

'Anything you want. You always look good.'

'Thanks, but aren't we supposed to coordinate? Isn't that a thing?'

'I mean, I'm going to wear a shirt that has little bow ties printed all over it, with a navy suede blazer.'

'Sounds cute.'

'It is cute.' He leans in, kissing me lightly. 'Though not as cute as you.' I kiss back, lacing my hands behind his neck. I should probably care that we're in public, but I don't, and I climb onto his lap, just as his pocket starts buzzing.

'Well, hello, sailor.'

'Sorry,' he groans. He pulls his phone from his pants and smiles at the screen.

'What?' I ask. 'Who texted you?'

'Kim,' he replies, all nonchalant, unaware of how her name alone paralyzes me.

'Excuse me?' I spit, unable to filter.

He recoils in surprise. 'Is that a problem?'

I move back to the bench, putting distance between us. 'I mean, it seems kinda weird for her to be texting you.'

'Not really. We're both at the mercy of this carnival craziness, and now we're partners in Chem,' he says, tone sharpening. 'We have a project to finish by Friday.'

'How convenient.' I slump back, arms crossed.

'Yes, solvents are nothing if not convenient.' He unlocks his screen, shining it toward me. 'Here. See for yourself.'

Kim's text reads,

What in the freaking freak are nonpolar solvents?

Fine. So it's not a sexy note. Still I offer no reaction.

'You know, Amber, green is not a flattering shade for you,' Charlie says, staring at the lake.

'And you don't think I have any reason to be upset?' I scoff.

'No, actually, I don't.'

'Charlie, we were literally lip-to-lip, and another girl was blowing up your phone.'

'Yeah . . . about chemistry,' he says.

'Yeah. CHEMISTRY!' I let the word hang, but he's not connecting the dots. 'Hello?!'

'OK.' He stands up. 'I'm leaving.'

'No you're not!' I demand. 'We are still talking about this.'

'No, you are overreacting about something I already told you is not a problem. Kim is my partner: not in life, not in love, but in school. I would hope my actual partner could understand that and trust me. But clearly, you don't, and honestly, it feels like garbage.' He storms off, quickly disappearing into the Navy Pier crowd.

'Charlie!' I call out, but he doesn't turn around, and I can't even chase after him because I have to return to my stupid shift. I stomp back inside, ripping off my beanie and coat before throwing them in the back room in frustration. Bob gives me a wary look as I return to my matchmaking table, annoyed at the world, but I meet his gaze with extra intensity until he's forced to rub his rabbit's foot and turn away.

'Amber.' Mom glides over, nose in a book and thankfully not noticing my embittered state. 'I'm waiting for the Chamberlains to arrive. Please let me know when they get here.'

'OK – wait. Which Chamberlains? Ivy and Iris?'

'No, their parents.'

'Oh. Sure.' I'm about to ask why, but Mom has already retreated back to her office. The shop is quiet, except for the vaguely mystical Pandora station we have playing in the background. A lot of chimes and gongs. Desperate for something to do, I walk over to the feather section and make sure the individual plumes are divided by their respective birds. They're all mixed up, so I start organizing, noticing we have an excess of owl and a drought of crow. I'd think the owl would be more popular, but what do I know?

Just as everything looks neat and tidy, a real-life Barbie and Ken enter the shop, and I instantly recognize them as Ivy's parents. Who else could produce such perfect-looking children, other than perfect specimens themselves? They look lost, clutching their designer coats and handbags. I slip into customer-service mode.

'Welcome to Windy City Magic,' I say in the sweetest tone I can muster. 'Can I help you?'

'Yes, we're looking for Lucille Sand. We have an appointment. We're the Chamberlains,' says Ivy's mom. I stare at her for a moment longer than I mean to, only because she has the most precise hairstyling I've ever seen; absolutely flawless pin curls frame her face. I must look like a wildebeest in her eyes.

'Any relation to Ivy Chamberlain?' I ask innocently.

'She's our daughter.' They both smile proudly. 'You know her?'

'Oh yes, we go to school together.'

'Wonderful!' The mom beams. 'It's so nice to meet more of Ivy's friends. She's had so few come by the house lately.'

Interesting. 'My mom is expecting you; please, right this way.' I guide them toward the back of the shop, deciding it best to end the Ivy exchange before my true feelings wiggle out. Mom seats them around her star-print tablecloth, instantly lighting some serenity incense. She must be nervous about how to approach the very sensitive topic of one's daughter switching species. But for the first time in the history of ever, she doesn't pull the velvet curtain closed tight, leaving a small gap through which I can hear every word. I soak up the opportunity.

'Thank you for coming,' Mom begins.

'Yes, you said this had something to do with Iris and Brooke? Is something wrong?' Ivy's mom asks.

'Not wrong, per se. But as a mother to a mother, I have a concern.' Everyone shuffles uncomfortably in their seats, waiting for the reveal. 'As you know, Iris is considering renouncing her siren heritage to become a mermaid. She came to me about performing the spell and I turned her away, expressing my opinions.'

'Why did you refuse her?' asks Ivy's dad.

'Because of the complexity of the spell, the possible ramifications. It takes a tremendous amount of energy for something like this to be successful.' Mom pauses. Her voice lacks the confidence it usually has when talking magic, like she isn't quite sure how to phrase her thoughts. I picture her face creased in worry. 'And, quite frankly, I was concerned. She's young, only twenty. This isn't something she could reverse if she decides later it was a mistake.'

The Pandora playlist fills the empty space, soft pan flute warbling while Barbie and Ken must be gathering their thoughts. It's not like Mom is friends with these people. Who knows how they'll react to what is essentially her judgment of their parenting? Hopefully they don't fly off the handle like when Ivy and Iris went all primal in their sitting room.

'We appreciate your looking out for her,' Barbie begins, 'but Iris is not the first in my bloodline to have done this. Sirens and mermaids have a long and tangled history; we are one and the same.' This surprises me. Sirens become mermaids on the regular? Somehow I pictured Iris as a revolutionary, paving the way for aquatically challenged love affairs everywhere. Mom made it seem like the Fates would lose their shit if this happened, but maybe that's not the case?

'Yes, but—' Mom tries to interject.

Barbie continues. 'Brooke is a lovely girl, and we've never seen Iris so happy. Ever since they met, it's like she's found herself.'

'I'm not trying to undermine their relationship—'

'Iris is an adult, and we support her decision,' Ken adds. 'We trust her to know what she needs.'

Mom takes a deep breath, trying to maintain her Zen. 'You are her parents, and you know her best. But what I know best is magic, and the witch Iris has chosen to complete this spell is not to be trusted. She will not take your daughter's well-being or safety into consideration; she only cares about her own personal gain. Performing a spell like this . . . it will give her access to power she will not handle with care.' Mom's voice wavers, making her argument all the less convincing. She's not one to cower in the presence of other supernaturals, but she's definitely not leading the charge here.

'With all due respect, Ms Sand, it sounds like you regret passing up the opportunity to wield such a magnificent spell, and are now trying to discredit a colleague.'

I almost gag upon hearing 'colleague,' since putting Mom and Victoria on the same level is like comparing buttercream frosting to tar.

'That is not—'

'We've heard what you have to say, but we both have very early mornings, so we'll need to cut this short. Good night,' says Barbie.

The Chamberlains exit, looking only slightly ruffled, with Mom emerging after they're gone, rubbing the corners of her eyes, shaking her head slightly. She's defeated, but for a brief second, I have to wonder: Did Barbie and Ken have a point? Was it out of concern or regret that Mom brought them in?

I know Mom is worried about Victoria's involvement, but is there a small part of her wishing she were doing the spell? Is there a witchcraft 'transformation' merit badge she's missing out on now? I know she's not one to throw herself into a power struggle, but her involvement in this whole thing has been murky. I feel like there's another reason why she rejected Iris in the first place that has yet to be revealed.

'Well, that could've gone a lot worse,' I say, trying to comfort her.

Mom's looking toward the shop door, but her gaze is much farther out. 'They are only very loosely tied to the supernatural community, so they don't understand. And I can't make them.' She disappears back behind the curtain, this time pulling it completely shut.

Later, from the comfort of my bed, I send a simple *sorry* text Charlie's way. I should not have attacked him like that; he has every right to be upset because he hasn't done anything wrong. I'm the one projecting the details of a yet-to-be-lived romance onto his actions, and without knowing the truth about his match, he has no way to understand my actions. Maybe I should just tell him, follow through with my matchmaking duties and get it over with, only I'm so scared that information will lead him straight into Kim's arms, I can't bring myself to do it.

A few minutes later, he responds with an *it's OK*, but I know it's not. I'm so afraid of getting burned, and yet I can't stop sticking my fingers in the flames.

# Thirteen

I DECIDE IT'S TIME TO STOP BEING A BABY AND JUST MAIL MY Culinary Institute application already. What's the worst that can happen? They reject me and my life plan flushes down the toilet? Ha-ha-ha, see if I care. (I care immensely. Please don't let that happen.)

I stand before the corner mailbox, my hopes and dreams compacted in an eight-by-ten envelope, and drop it below, wondering how something so important can lie in wait next to the humdrum of cable bills and get-well-soon cards. I instantly wish I had coated the package with one of Mom's tracking serums so I could at least know when my application was being reviewed. I contemplate bashing into the box to get my envelope back, but I'm not in the mood to be arrested for mail fraud.

In a weird twist of fate, I have the afternoon off to do as I please. Ah, if only I had someone to share it with! I was supposed to be catering a bridal shower with Ella, but I guess the bride got cold feet, and now Ella's left with four dozen champagne cupcakes (there are worse problems, to be sure). Charlie is tagging along with his dad to some Chicago Bears event (ugh, sports), and when I called Amani, she and Kim were shopping for formal dresses, which is not exactly 'my jam.' I didn't realize the two of them were spending separate friendship time together, but I try not to let it consume my thoughts. I go for a long walk, wandering around aimlessly, until I find myself in Ivy's neighborhood. Knowing full well the Ice Queen will be at cheerleading practice, I figure there's no harm in trying to chat up her sister to gain any more insight into what's going on in her head.

Just as I'm walking up the front steps, Iris emerges from the front door, wrapped in a long white coat, giving her an angelic silhouette. I've never understood how people can wear such bold blocks of white; if I slipped my arms in that coat, I'd somehow instantly stain it with chocolate or mud, even if I wasn't in close proximity to either. Her wardrobe choice alone makes Iris intimidating, but she's also giving me a perplexing scowl, despite the fact I confirmed her true love status.

'Oh, hello, Amber,' she says coolly, locking the door behind her. 'Are you looking for Ivy?'

I stifle a laugh. 'No, actually, I wanted to talk to you.'

'About?'

'Well, I was just curious, I guess, about how everything's going. With your girlfriend.' My mind races, trying to find a probable reason for me being here. 'I like to follow up on my matches, from time to time.'

Iris looks at her watch, distracted. 'Um, that's very kind of you, but I'm on my way to an appointment.'

'I can walk with you, if that's OK. I won't take much of your time.'

Her mouth bends in a slight grimace, but unlike her sister, she's not inclined to instantly banish those she doesn't need. 'Well . . . sure.' She brightens, consciously changing her disposition. 'It's always nice to have company.'

We head off, down the prim and proper sidewalks of Lincoln Park. Row after row of distinguished brownstones look down at us, as ice-covered tree branches sparkle in the sun.

'It's very sweet of you to ask about Brooke,' Iris begins, smiling as her lady's name graces her lips. 'It's been a difficult couple of weeks.'

'How so?'

'Well, as you know, Ivy's really having a hard time with it all. The transformation, I mean.'

'She must love you a lot.'

Iris nods. 'And I love her too. I'm not doing this to hurt her. It's not like I will disappear from her life. I think that's what she's worried about.'

I don't really know if this is my place, but I seize the moment anyway. 'Honestly, it seems like she's more worried about what will happen to you.'

Iris's brows crinkle. 'What do you mean?'

'Well, Ivy will obviously miss you. But I think she's scared about what you'll be missing out on. Like, it will be kinda hard to come home and open presents Christmas morning unless there's a kiddie pool under the tree. And living in international waters will make it pretty impossible to run for Congress.'

Her face hardens. 'She told you about that?'

'Even if she hadn't told me, I can totally picture it. I remember when you used to give speeches for student council; you are the only person who's ever made me feel even a glimmer of school spirit. You have a real gift; you could change the world.' And in that moment, for the first time, I'm truly worried Iris is making a mistake. It's not that I didn't hear both Ivy's and Mom's concerns before, but somehow, talking out these points makes it clear how Iris's plan is miscalculated. What if it doesn't work out? As a matchmaker, I want to take solace in knowing Brooke is her match, but who even knows if that's enough? It goes against everything I believe in, but right now, I feel strongly that love won't even the scales. I want them to be happy, yes. But there are so many factors that play into a relationship's success. Brooke isn't giving up anything, while Iris is changing her entire world. What if Iris hates being a mermaid and regrets giving up her dreams? What if this life change is too much? What if the love in her heart cannot overpower her sacrifice? Just because you love someone doesn't always mean it's meant to be, a reality I struggle with every day.

'But how can I change the world when my world feels incomplete?' Iris continues. 'I can't turn my back on Brooke. Being separated from her is like missing a part of myself.'

I grit my teeth, not loving her answer. 'Aren't you scared, though? I mean, it's not just like you're moving. Your entire world is about to go underwater. Literally!' I swing my arms out for dramatic effect. 'Becoming a mermaid: that's not a small change.'

'It will be a transition, I'm sure.' Her head tilts to the sky, sunlight kissing her cheeks. She looks happy, confident, secure in her decision. If I were about to switch species, I would be a complete mess. Hell, I *am* a mess, and this isn't even happening to me. 'Not doing it would be the bigger risk. And besides, I've always loved to swim,' she says with a wink.

I'd like to smile in affirmation, but I can't. While Iris has no qualms about going full-on Ariel, I worry about her future. I think about that day she saved me from bullies; she didn't even know me, yet she cared enough to help. How can I repay the favor? She stopped a fist from hitting my face, and I need to stop a witch from ruining her life. But how?

'You know, I'm glad you stopped by, actually,' Iris says, suddenly scooping her arm around mine. 'Would you mind going to this appointment with me? I'm a little nervous, so it'd be nice to have some support.'

'Uh, sure.' I don't have anything else to do, and maybe if we spend more time together, I can convince her to change her mind. 'Where are we going?'

'Well, I have to meet the witch who's helping me with my transition. She's been gathering all the elements for her spell, and I guess she needs one last thing from me.'

Alarm bells ring in my skull, causing me to temporarily seize by her side. Luckily, I happen to spaz out right in front of a coffee shop, giving me a logical cover. 'OK,' I say, trying to smooth any visible shaking. 'Mind if I grab a latte real quick?'

'Of course, I'll wait out here.'

I run inside and instantly start blowing up Mom's cell. She doesn't answer, so I call the shop, but Bob answers, reciting our shop spiel at the speed of sloth.

'Thank . . . you, for calling . . . Windy City Magic, where . . . magic is . . .'

'Bob!' I yell, trying to break his auto response. 'Is Mom there?'

'Amber? Is that you?'

'YES.' Gods. 'Put Mom on the phone.'

'She's not here right now.' He pauses for an unnecessary dramatic effect. 'She went to get change.'

ARGH! 'OK, can you have her call me back? It's an emergency.'

'Yup.' I hang up before he can draw out anything further. I try calling everyone in my phone (which is not a lot of people, to be fair), and when no one picks up, I text Mom:

VICTORIA 911

and head outside, surely covered in an unattractive sweat.

'Where's your latte?' Iris asks.

'Oh, um, I realized I already had two today,' I lie. 'I should probably cut back.'

She shrugs, and we march off to what will definitely be a dangerous exchange. Victoria knows Iris previously reached out to Mom about performing this spell, but doesn't know about her client's present Sand entanglement. If she sees me, she'll have to assume something is up and could pull something sneaky on either Iris or myself. I can almost feel my throat tightening, reminiscent of our last encounter. Yet I don't want to leave Iris alone; who knows what Victoria 'needs' to complete this spell? I pray to the Gods Mom gets my cry for help and ends the appointment before it begins.

We reach an empty dry cleaner's storefront, and Iris looks at the address she has scribbled down, confused. The sign says closed, but the door swings open to a cleared-out space free of hanging garments or detergent smells.

'I guess this is the place?' Iris says, unsure. 'Victoria?'

This could easily be a murder den or meth lab, and honestly, I'd feel more comfortable in either if I knew Victoria would not be around. Why she'd have a client meet her here is inconceivable, though if she's going for 'building terror,' then she definitely nailed it.

Finally, she emerges, like a lizard slithering out of the grass, covered in animal print and ready for prey. With hair a few shades beyond platinum, and skin a confusing color of tangerine, Victoria stands like a real-life plastic-surgery fail. Every part of her being has been tightened or tinted beyond human limits, her efforts resulting in a disorienting display. It doesn't help to know that underneath all that work lies the beating heart of a lunatic.

'Iris, how lovely to—' She comes to a halt, her big reveal ruined by my presence. Though she recovers quickly, pointing her chin high and casting her gaze down the tip of her rhinoplasty, it's clear she's been rattled. It's not the first (and certainly will not be the last) time I've made someone stop dead in her tracks. I soak in the momentary satisfaction.

'Why, Amber,' she resumes in her dissonant baritone, 'I didn't know you'd be joining us today.'

'You know her?' Iris whispers to me.

'Uh, sort of,' I say, leaving out the part about Victoria nearly ending my life. 'We've met.'

'Iris, I wasn't expecting you to bring a guest,' Victoria says between clenched teeth. She keeps inching closer, filling my nostrils with her horribly musky perfume. 'Is there a reason why you felt you needed backup?'

'Oh, no, of course not,' she says, clearly lying. Even through her coat, I can tell she's covered in goose bumps. I mean, I know I am. 'I just happened to bump into Amber on the way here.'

'How convenient,' Victoria hisses. She takes a lap around us both, trying to detect any concealed spells, I'm sure. Her stilettos click on the linoleum, in time with her acrylic nails tapping at her side. Once she's decided we're free of magical ammunition, she stands before us, hands on hips, towering above us both.

'Luckily, Amber is very ineffectual magically, so she won't be able to interfere with what I need.' Her carnivorous smile will haunt my dreams for weeks, guaranteed.

'And what do you need, anyway?' I ask, my knowledge of how Victoria operates being my only advantage here.

'I'm sure it's too hard to wrap your non-magical head around this' – UGH, wench! – 'but a spell of this magnitude requires a considerable amount of resources. Brave Iris is giving herself over to love, and I need something of hers to help see that through.'

'Such as . . . ?'

Victoria shrugs, pulling on the gaudy string of pearls around her neck. 'Nothing she'll miss. Just a part of her essence.'

'Her essence?!'

'Relax. My Gods, you Sands are so overdramatic.' She cackles, as if losing an undetermined personal element is nothing to react over. Ha-ha, no big; good-bye, part of myself!

'No, she's right; what do you mean, part of my essence?' Iris's sweet face is turning sour, losing certainty in the situation.

Victoria, ever the snake oil salesman, swoops in to reassure her wavering client. 'Darling, don't worry. You know this spell is no joke; we talked about it. You will be going through a major transformation. Just to be sure nothing gets lost in the balance, I'll take a small, unnoticeable slice of your soul and keep it safe until we're done. That way, in the unlikely occurrence that something goes wrong, we'll still have a part of you to help restore your true character. Make sense?' She flutters her lashes, making me sick. This sounds like the most insane bull I've ever heard, but Iris seems to be buying it.

She nods slowly, trying to determine if this logic is sound. I want to shake her, to throw her over my shoulder and hightail it out of here, but I know an easy escape is not in the cards.

'What do you think, Amber?' Iris asks, her voice small and

fragile, like a child asking for permission. I don't want to crush her dreams, but this does not feel right.

'I don't like it. I've never heard of my mom taking a part of someone in order to complete a spell. A real witch would figure out a less invasive way.'

Victoria is laughing to herself. 'A real witch? You mean, someone who sells fairy figurines and pentagon pendants in a tourist attraction? That's who you'd trust your life to?'

'Hey!' I spit back. 'You know full well my mom has the skills, and we sell a lot of actual magic in our shop!'

'The Lucille Sand I knew was capable of real power, and had she continued studying with me, maybe she'd be the one standing here now, with the ability to change a life. But she made a poor choice, and now Iris has only one hope if she ever wants to be with her true love.'

I'm not going to win this; Victoria is too persuasive, playing too hard on Iris's emotions. How can I stop her when love is on the line? I can't do this alone. *C'mon, Mom,* I think. *Burst in right now, please.*

But she doesn't.

'It's OK, Amber,' Iris reassures me, giving my shoulder a pat. 'This is what I want, remember? And I'm sure Victoria wouldn't do anything to hurt me.'

'Ha!' I burst. I'm actually shaking with fear, knowing there's no way this turns out well. 'Don't trust her, Iris. We can find you a different way!'

'That's enough from the peanut gallery,' Victoria grumbles, snapping her wrist and instantly flinging me against the wall. Iris screams. The wind is knocked out of me, yet I try to run back, only to find I'm stuck to the wall, like a bug on flypaper, forced to watch against my will.

'Damn you!' I screech, straining against intangible glue.

'Is that really necessary?' Iris asks, lip trembling as she takes a step back from the wicked witch.

'Quiet,' she bellows, wrapping a bony orange hand around Iris's neck. 'I need to focus.'

It happens quick: for a moment, Iris tenses, making a faint, choking yelp as Victoria perches a claw just outside her mouth, which is slowly turning blue. Iris is convulsing like she's going to vomit, her whole system shaking and fighting this mystical lobotomy. With one final gurgle, Iris projectiles something, like a translucent hairball, which Victoria catches and pockets inside a small leather pouch. Iris falls to the floor, just as I'm released from my concealed web; I rush to her side, while her breathing slowly returns to normal.

'What did you take?' I ask, peering over my shoulder. Victoria pretends not to hear me, freshening her bloodred lipstick instead. 'What did you take?' I repeat.

'Just like I said, a part of her essence.' A brow raises in amusement. 'The free part.'

Now I feel like I can't breathe. 'You took her free will?! Are you deranged?'

'Not in the slightest. Now I know she won't back out of our arrangement, and I'll become infamous in my success.'

'You're sick,' I hurl at her, but she's unfazed. She crouches down, pinching Iris's cheeks with one hand, forcing her victim to look her way.

'Now listen to me,' Victoria says, enunciating every syllable. 'You will go straight home, without making any stops, without any alarm. You will stay in your house until the full moon, upon which we will meet for the spell. You are not to leave for any other reason, and you are not to tell anyone what has happened here. You will not listen to any instructions from anyone else but me.'

Iris doesn't nod or make any acknowledgement but pops up, immediately heading to the door. She says nothing, looking neither at me nor at Victoria, making a beeline in the direction of her house. Without free will, she's incapable of doing anything other than what Victoria instructed.

I start to chase after her just as Victoria adds, 'Give my regards to your mother,' before disappearing back into the dark.

# Fourteen

THE WHOLE WAY HOME, I TRY TO TALK SENSE INTO IRIS. I plead, I yell, I slap her in the face. I pull her, yank her, even get a running start to try and push her off course, but nothing works. She's like a robot wearing an Iris costume, capable only of completing her programmed task. When she finally unlocks her front door, she sits down in the foyer, successful in her mission. Then I swear I hear her make a whirring sound, after which she closes her eyes and falls asleep.

It's awkward, standing in a stranger's house with an almost-comatose body at my feet, but I know I have to tell someone. The Chamberlains' butler has not come to greet us, so I call out a tentative 'Ivy?'

My phone starts to ring, just as Ivy walks in from the kitchen, balancing a plate of cucumber slices. She drops it upon seeing her sister, porcelain shattering as she runs to her side. Mom's face flashes on my screen, but it's too late now.

'What happened to her?' Ivy cries, pushing Iris's hair back off her face. 'What did you do?'

'I . . . I did what I could to stop this,' I say, realizing Victoria has much more power than I thought. 'Iris was on her way to meet Victoria, and we happened to run into each other. I tried to call for backup, but . . .' Clearly, my efforts failed.

'Why does she look like human pudding? What did that witch do?'

'She . . . She said she needed something else for her spell. A part of Iris. She took . . . her free will.'

I may as well have knocked Ivy across the jaw. I expect her to launch herself at me, make me a punching bag for her pain. But she doesn't. Instead, she looks up, on the verge of tears, and asks, 'What do we do?'

As Victoria so preciously noted, I have no magic; I have no idea what comes next. So I call back my mom and recount the events, putting her on speaker to hear her reply.

'Ivy, I'm so sorry this happened,' she says, her voice echoing throughout the room. 'The only thing we can do now is wait for the full moon and thwart the spell.'

'What?' Ivy yells. 'That cannot be the only option.'

'Victoria holds Iris's free will, which we'll obviously need to obtain. Though your sister is powerless right now, at least she's safe at home for the time being. I will work on gathering resources to ensure Victoria does not complete her spell as planned, and we'll successfully restore Iris.'

'And I will too,' I add, trying to be comforting but feeling pretty useless. 'I know weird people who can help us out.'

Ivy stares blankly, like someone has scooped out her soul and there's nothing left to guide her. She looks haggard, beaten: completely un-siren-like. Even during times of anger or frustration, she's always maintained her perfect gloss, careful not to expose her inner core. With dark circles under her eyes and hair clumped in a messy tangle, she looks like a regular teenage girl.

'Can you help me get her upstairs?' she asks, so softly I almost miss it. 'My parents will freak if they see her like this.'

'Yeah, sure,' I say, though it's entirely disarming to hear Ivy ask permission, rather than demand assistance.

We manage to drag Iris's lifeless body upstairs; she's like a Costco-size bag of potatoes. We practically drop her into bed. She makes no notice of our efforts; we could have plopped her into a bathtub, and I still think she'd be sleeping soundly. Ivy stands in the doorway, watching her sister sleep, her own eyelids heavy. Her grief is palpable; usually when I'm around her, I feel her icy chill, but now all there is is sadness.

'After everything I did, it didn't even matter,' Ivy says, her voice hollow but words weighted. 'I couldn't protect her.'

'What do you mean?'

A memory presses, causing an emotional implosion. She seems to shrink before my eyes. 'I used it all up. My siren powers. I tried to change her mind and stop her from doing this.' Her head hangs lower. 'But it didn't work.'

The Fates were insightful enough to place some mystical checks and balances on sirens: so that they don't have the ability to rule the world forever, they each are granted a finite level of power. Once they've used up their storage of magical manipulation, then they're done, and have to live as run-of-the-mill humans. I always thought it was wasteful of Ivy to exert influence over high schoolers, but putting that energy toward her sister is a sacrifice I didn't expect.

'I thought a siren couldn't manipulate another siren,' I say.

'We're not supposed to; it's like a moral code. But I tried anyway.' She turns to me, face painted with regret. 'And now it's gone.'

It all makes sense now: her solo ventures through school, her inability to snake-charm Marcus or any other warm-blooded male. Ivy's no longer a siren, and she can't force the masses to flock to her side. She relied so heavily on that persuasive well of magic she never took the time to cultivate any real, lasting relationships. And now she's alone.

'That was very brave of you,' I confess. The words taste funny, but it's the appropriate flavor.

'You think I'm an idiot.'

'Usually, yes, but right now, no.' I conjure up a sad smile. She reciprocates, and there's a moment of understanding between us that I don't think even Amani could have predicted, and I do my best not to freak out over having a heart-to-heart with my nemesis.

'Can I, um, do anything for you?' I offer. I don't know what the etiquette is after dumping someone's lifeless sibling at one's door.

'No, I just want to be alone.' I nod and start to head back downstairs when Ivy calls from behind, 'Amber?'

I turn back to face her.

'I'm glad she wasn't alone, at least,' Ivy says. 'It had to have been really scary. Thanks for bringing her home.'

I nod again, even though I don't feel at all helpful. What did I really do? Watch while a girl lost a part of her soul? Great work.

On my way to the train, I immediately start texting Charlie but pause before hitting SEND. I reread what I've typed several times, looking for any possible pitfalls. I've never second-guessed reaching out to him before, but after my jealous rant the other day, things have been a little off. His words say he's fine, but his body language illustrates otherwise. I don't blame him; I would be acting different if my boyfriend accused me of cheating too. I so desperately want things to go back to normal, I feel like I have to be extra-awesome Amber, steering clear of any weirdness. Hence my hesitation. I scrap the message and text Amani instead, spewing out all the details of the night. Yet even minutes after crafting a horrifying tale that can't be ignored, she still hasn't written back. Hello, if a story about soul-sucking witches doesn't deserve a response, what does?

An entire hour later, I finally hear back. I kind of thought she would call to get the full scoop, but all I get is an *OMG*.

**Where have you been?** I type back.

Sorry! Water Tower. Bad reception, I guess.

**You've been with Kim this whole time?**

Argh! So what, when she isn't suddenly joining clubs with my boyfriend, Kim's now monopolizing my best friend?! GREAT.

Yeah! We got dinner together. She told me the funniest story. . . .

I turn my phone on mute, ignoring her following messages. It's crappy, but I don't want to hear about Amani-Kim Fun Times right now. My evening was scary as hell, and it would be nice to talk to my best friend about it without side stories about shopping. It's great, I guess, that they are becoming better pals. They have a lot in common, and putting my personal problems with her aside, Kim seems like a cool person. It's just weird how your best friend can bond with someone you don't mesh with at all. Isn't there some sort of friendship law of relativity, proving that people within the same social circle should have a tangible thread? Their pairing seems miles apart from what Amani and I share, and it's all so . . . whatever. They both have their free will intact and can do what they want.

I can't seem to stop anything.

# Fifteen

'AMBER, CAN YOU GRAB MY GRIMOIRE WITH THE PURPLE spine?' Mom calls from the kitchen. Ever since Iris's incident, she hasn't left the kitchen, pouring herself into a new spell that's filling the apartment with a metallic smell. It's pretty unpleasant, so if something in that book will make it stop, I'm happy to oblige.

'Yeah,' I call back, pausing *The Great British Bake Off* and popping off the couch. Mom's office is positively bursting with grimoires, so finding the 'purple one' would be daunting if I didn't know where she keeps her personal volumes. Still, it's always fun to take them all in; I've always hoped to stumble across one labeled 'Fun Times at Salem,' but no such luck. Right next to Mom's supply armoire, on a trunk filled with stones, sit three leather-bound books: one deep red, one marigold, one purple. The purple was her second installment, mostly from her teenage and college years, right about when her magic was hitting full swing and life was getting juicy. I flip through the parchment pages (What is it with parchment and witches?), seeing notes in my mother's careful hand about the proper use of agarwood and cautions regarding deer musk. I start heading to the kitchen when a page near the back catches my attention: it's neither notes, nor a list of ingredients, but a long-form, diary-like entry. And because I have no self-control, I start reading:

*Today I met an interesting man. I was meditating near the lake, trying to clear away the negative energy from the night before, when he politely interrupted me. I couldn't believe anyone would be so audacious as to disturb a reflective state, but when I opened my eyes, I was already forgiving him. Not because he was handsome (he was), but because his aura was unlike any I've encountered. No supernatural element, and yet, there was great power emanating from his person; I was instantly drawn in. He asked me for directions back to his hotel (he's from Milwaukee), and I agreed to take him there myself, which was probably a bit forward, but I had to figure out where this energy was coming from. We talked for blocks, and all the while, his spirit grew stronger. It was addictive; I'd only just met him, and*

*yet I didn't want to say good-bye. I've never felt so drawn to a*
*mere human, and I still can't understand why. Even now as I*
*write this, my aura is all lit up, magic swirling inside me.*
*Rather than go out with Victoria tonight, I want to channel this*
*energy into that virility spell that's been giving me trouble. And*
*I owe it all to Tom.*

Tom?! Victoria?!

'Amber! Hello! I need your help here!' Mom yells, breaking me from her prose.

'Sorry! Um, found it!' I scoot into the kitchen, propping the tome on her bookstand. Her hair is all frazzled from the yellowish steam coming from the stockpot, and there are a million sunflower seed shells scattered across the floor. Her face is very stern, and I can tell whatever she's trying to accomplish is not going well. 'What can I do?' I add.

She throws more seeds into the pot, a giant yellow puff hitting her right in the face. 'Can you find the page concerning protection spells? I'm trying to do a variation,' she says through gritted teeth.

'OK.' But I cannot focus on witchcraft when all I want to do is jump to the back of the suddenly very important book. Going out with Victoria, meeting Tom: this is the story of my mom befriending the worst witch of all time AND meeting my dad! Ahhh! I have to know more!

'Did you find it?'

'Huh?'

Mom whips a wild gaze my way. 'THE SPELL.'

'Oh, sorry, I . . .'

She grunts. 'Let me do it.' She impatiently drops her ladle, which hovers in midair, and holds her hand over the grimoire; it automatically flips to the correct page.

'I've always thought that was a pretty cool trick,' I say, trying to ease some tension. 'I wish I could activate stuff with my fingertips.' The angry eyes continue, and I get it; I get frustrated when my recipes go awry too. I also know the only way to deal is to plow through the problem, so I sneak back to my room, head spinning with Mom's written words. I have to know more. I HAVE TO.

I try to sleep, but who can surrender to the dream world when real-life stories are filling my head? Mom never talks about Dad – never – and my clearest memory of him is when he left. Since then, Mom hasn't dated, unless she somehow has a secret second family holed up somewhere, and if so, bravo for keeping such an elaborate cover. I don't have a yearning to learn more about Dad (he left, so BYE, GOOD RIDDANCE), but the idea of Mom being in love is so intoxicating. . . . What was she like? Was she soft and cuddly?

Did she walk around humming Top 40 love songs (ugh, hope not)? Divorce may have pushed the needle toward the mostly solemn creature I know and love, but what other emotions lie under that steely surface? And what in the world is Victoria doing in conjunction with that story? I'm surprised the parchment didn't burst into flames from having her name scribbled on it.

I slip on thick wool socks and proceed to slide to the kitchen. (Old wood floors are notorious narcs: make one misstep and they shout your schemes to the world. Sliding is where it's at.) Mom must've really lost it with that spell; she didn't even clean up, leaving seeds and spoons all over the place. (In witchcraft, even the tools you use can affect the outcome of a spell, so a wooden spoon could wield different results than silver.) The grimoire is open on the same page, so technically I'm not prying. (Ah, the lies we tell ourselves.) I step over a pot filled with charred goo and carefully try to find the section I want; every precise page turn sounds like a sledgehammer slam against the quiet of night. I'm sure Mom's inhuman hearing will catch me any minute, but I finally find the passage I want without being caught. I consider grabbing a cookie and mug of milk to accompany this bedtime story, but decide better to satisfy my curiosity than sweet tooth at this point.

After the initial Dad entry, there are a few doodles and drawings for different spell ideas, but shortly thereafter, she picks up the narrative again. Looks like dear ol' Dad didn't waste any time asking her out.

*Every part of me is tingling, every nerve ending electric. Being around Tom is an experience unto itself. I thought spending more time with him would reveal his magic, but no; our encounters have made me even more curious. The past few days have left me in a state of complete confusion, and yet, I've never been happier trying to solve a puzzle. To have that kind of magnetic charisma, one would have to have at the very least a recessed siren gene, but if he does, he's using an extraordinary cloaking device, which I'd also want to discover.*

*There's something about him I can't understand . . . the way his eyes squint when he laughs, the way he talks faster and faster when he's excited: these things shouldn't undo me, but when he adds four sugars to his coffee or bites the corner of his mouth after I tell him a joke, it's almost too much for me to bear. When he touches me . . .*

Gah! I skip forward to more PG copy . . .

*I want to be near him, constantly, because when I am, I'm simultaneously two feet off the ground yet completely settled, shooting for the moon yet right where I need to be. I've questioned the Fates for their decisions in the past, cursing their*

*seemingly random choices, but now I know: every bend in the*
*road, every closed door has led me here, to this man.*

Wow. Holy sappy. I cannot picture these words ever coming out of Mom's mouth, but here they are, in her handwriting. And Dad . . . he really did bring out something new in her, because the next dozen pages are filled corner to corner with fresh spells, talisman sketches, even notes for opening a magic shop. Some of her most successful spells were perfected during this time: Makeover in a Bottle, Instant Serenity, Miracle Grow (not to be confused with the fertilizer, though this does add a half inch to human height). She was inspired, overflowing with creativity; I can almost feel her excitement from her hurried penmanship, like she couldn't get her ideas down fast enough. She's always so careful and measured, evaluating every detail before she moves ahead, but from the sounds of it, Dad jolted her to her core.

There are several more passages illustrating her growing love, interspersed with magical writings, but the details soon become more and more intimate, and my gag reflex can only take so much. Just because I'm interested in their courtship doesn't mean I want to know the details of my dad's kissing game. BLECH.

For a second, I think I hear footsteps, and I consider hiding in the oven for safety. But after a panicked minute without breath or movement, I decide it must have been the downstairs neighbors getting a 2:00 A.M. snack. Not wanting to test the Fates much longer, I skip ahead, trying to see if Victoria pops up again, and I catch her name on the second-to-last page. A short paragraph, back in Mom's precise writing:

> *It's disappointing, after everything we've been through, that Victoria won't come to the wedding. She's never approved of Tom, but I thought she'd put aside her frustration over my changing course for one day. Just because I'm no longer delving into the darker arts does not mean I've given up on magic; in fact, I've never felt so fulfilled in my pursuit of holistic spells. I guess our friendship really is over after all.*

Whaaaaaaa – now I really do hear something, so I toss the grimoire back on the counter and dive for the fridge, pretending to be in deep consideration over treat options just as Mom wanders in.

'What are you doing up so late?' she asks, pulling her robe tighter.

'Couldn't sleep. Need sugar. You?'

'I thought sleep might bring some perspective on my problem' – she eyes her earlier mess – 'but I don't think I've logged enough hours.'

'You'll figure it out, Mom. You always do.'

She nods, head heavy with a need for more zzz's, and starts a halfhearted attempt at cleaning up. I bend down to help, watching her sleepy face, and think of all the secrets locked behind it. Epic loves. Friendship fallouts. Dabbling in the dark arts?

Oh, you can be sure I'm gonna Veronica Mars the crap out of this.

# Sixteen

MANCHESTER PREP IS ONE OF MY LEAST FAVORITE PLACES in the world, but within these ancient corridors of torture, there are a few sacred spots that can be used to alleviate pain. About a month ago, Charlie and I discovered a bend near the band room that seems to go untouched by both foot traffic and brooms, with the cobwebs to prove it. Still, it's a snuggly little space for a quick afternoon pick-me-up, conveniently located near both of our fifth-period classes.

We took a couple days off, but the lure of our secret spot was too much for both of us, and finally the metaphorical dust has settled. Thank the Gods. I'm blessedly pressed up against Charlie, my hands wrapped behind his neck, when out of nowhere, the visual of my mom and dad making out pops into my brain.

'Gah!' I pull back, shaking my head furiously in hopes the image will leak out my ears.

'You OK?' Charlie asks, slightly breathless. 'I didn't just, like, bite you or something, did I?'

'No.' I laugh. 'I, uh . . . Last night I kinda sorta accidentally read some of my mom's grimoire, and there were some highly illustrative details on her past.'

'I thought grimoires were just like witch shopping lists.'

'So did I, but as it turns out, they are part recipe book, part diary. She had a bunch of stuff in there about meeting my dad and . . . kissing my dad.'

Charlie frowns like he just smelled something gross. 'That's . . . something.'

'Yeah, I mean, I'm not really interested in the intimate details of her love life, and I've definitely already read things I can't unsee, but there's so much about my mom's past I know nothing about. She's not exactly big on sharing, but evidence suggests she was a wild one back in the day. Even her own grimoire has holes, but I want to fill in the blanks, do a little investigating.' I walk my fingers up his tie. 'You in?'

He considers, green eyes gleaming behind his glasses. 'OK. But only if we can wear trench coats and call each other Holmes and Watson.'

'Obviously. And if we could get pipes that blow bubbles, that'd be ideal.'

He snorts. 'You know, Holmes, the best place to start would be my dad, since those two have been tied at the hip since high school.'

'Excellent, Watson!' I give him a squeeze. 'But do you think your dad will be cool spilling my mom's secrets?'

'Well, there's only one way to find out,' he says, checking his watch before he pulls me back close. 'But we only have one more minute before the bell, so we'd better make that count.'

So I lay one on him.

Immediately after the final bell rings, I text Charlie to finalize our meet-up plans but get no response. There's no way he's already off school grounds, so I circle past his locker and a few other places I can think of, but he's nowhere to be found. We don't always see each other after school, since most of the time I'm running off to one of my three jobs, but on my Windy City days, I have some more flexibility and try to grab a hug and kiss when I can. After stomping around the campus perimeter twice, I decide to give up, when I hear laughter coming from the gym (which, to be clear, is not a place I associate with happiness of any kind).

The gym doors are open ever so slightly, so I take a peek through the opening to see an explosion of art supplies: jars of paint, glitter, brushes, and long rolls of white craft paper criss-cross the basketball courts. There are a few painters already in action, meticulously guiding careful brushes across the banners, while Alison Bleeker dashes around the room, giving instructions to the rest of her worker bees. Ah, this must be winter carnival indentured labor, so Charlie has to be here. I scan the room until I see a rolled-up sleeve revealing a forearm of tattooed scales and flames; he's sitting on the floor, smiling, paintbrush perched and ready to go. I adore this boy, but he's not really the best artist, so I can't imagine how his final product will turn out.

I'm about to walk in and deliver a surprise smooch when I notice his attention is already accounted for. He's laughing, and not in a polite, Gods-I-can't-wait-until-this-is-over kind of way. There are too many people blocking my view, so I can't see who is making him so happy, until the crowd clears and my worst fear is revealed: Kim. She's sitting across from him, only twelve inches of paper separating them. I can't tell what she's saying, but Charlie sure does think it's hilarious. She too seems equally delighted by his company, and I start to feel queasy. I watch as she dips her brush into a jar of blue paint, which accidentally (?) splatters onto Charlie's side of the banner.

He mocks offense and sends a spatter of red her way. This only encourages her, and soon the two of them are flinging a rainbow of splotches back and forth, only pausing when Alison's watchful eye passes by. Their banner is completely ruined, but clearly that's the last thing on their minds. My boyfriend's face is covered in a spectrum of colors, but the one that concerns me is the blushing pink behind the paint.

Flirting. This is flirting. There's nothing else it could be, right? My heartbeat is on stereo, blaring through my eardrums and pounding against my rib cage. He told me nothing was going on; he told me to believe him. Should I ignore what's right before me, put my trust in something that feels so wrong? I stand there for a few more seconds before I decide I can't take it anymore and run outside to catch a bus.

I sulk all through my Windy City shift, making a point not to check my phone for possible texts from Charlie. I don't even know if I can believe anything he says, so why bother? A few hopefuls approach my matchmaking table, but I stare at them with such venom, they back away like hikers trying to avoid a bear attack. I even make Bob tumble backward into our display of cauldrons after he asks me about how things are going with Charlie.

After, instead of going home, I take a cab over to the Black Phoenix to talk to Vincent. I wanted to get some insight into my mom's past tonight, and I'm not going to let my detour into emotional ruin deter me.

'Hey, what are you doing here?' Vincent asks as I walk up to the bar. The restaurant is pretty empty, since it's close to closing, but there are still a few creatures nursing cocktails. I slump onto a stool, seeing my grumpy expression reflected in the golden bar top. 'Everything OK?'

'Yeah . . . I mean, no. I'm not sure.'

Vincent grabs a clean martini glass. 'You want to talk about it?'

'Not really. I'm still . . . processing.'

He nods. 'Can I pour you a drink?' I give him a sour face. 'Virgin, of course,' he adds. I shrug, and he mixes together something that tastes delightful, whatever it is.

Vincent makes his way down the bar, attending to his clientele with his usual charm while I slurp down the rest of my kiddie cocktail. When he gets back to me, I say, 'Actually, there is something you can help me with.'

'Anything for you, Miss Sand,' he says with his hand across his heart. Diamond cuff links shine back at me, along with his dazzling vampire smile.

'Did you know my mom when she was friends with Victoria?'

His grin instantly fades; I can tell he's regretting his offer to help. He grabs a rag and starts wiping down the bar.

'Why do you ask?' he says dryly.

'Well, because I'm curious about what she was like back then, and she won't tell me.'

Vincent leans in and stares me down. I try to ignore the smell of blood on his breath. 'Don't you think there's a reason for that?'

'Probably? But I desperately want to know that reason.' He shakes his head, closing out the tab of the fairy sitting next to me. 'Please?! For your favorite employee?'

His eyes are rolling, but his lips are smiling. 'Who says you're my favorite?'

I start to lean back in bravado, when I remember I'm sitting on a barstool. 'C'mon, I know you love me.'

He sighs. 'The truth is, I don't have a lot to tell. I did know your mom back then, but mostly through rumors. You know as well as I do that supernaturals love to gossip.' I nod, thinking about the gabfests most of our shop vendors engage in every time they drop off a shipment. He continues. 'Let's just say, whatever broke up their friendship was for the best because Lucille is now a leader in our community. There's no way she would've gone on to start Windy City Magic if she'd stayed close with Victoria, especially after some of the worst things I heard.'

My skin prickles. 'What were the worst things?' I ask, clutching the edge of the bar top.

He shakes his head. 'Nothing worth repeating. Especially if they aren't true.'

ARGH! 'You are only stoking my curiosity – you know that, right?'

'Sorry, Miss Matchmaker.'

Frustrated, I spin around to see Marcus, all bundled up and ready to head out the door. Upon seeing me, he briefly stops in his tracks before composing himself to come over. 'Hey,' he says, so quiet I almost miss it. I've noticed his shyness skyrockets around Vincent, and I wonder if it's because historically, vampires and werewolves have never exactly been BFFs.

'Nice to see you,' Marcus says, puppy-dog eyes gleaming. And I have to admit, it's nice to see him too, especially since the last few hours have been full of things I'd rather unsee. I don't know how he acts around most people, but he always seems genuinely pleased to share my company, and since I'm feeling very unwanted at the moment, I'm drawn to him more than usual.

'Did I miss anything exciting tonight?' I ask, hopping off the barstool.

'Nah, it was kind of dead . . . No pun intended.' I snicker, and he blushes, his cheeks filling up with a smile. 'So, um, I was just going to head back to my dorm,' he says. He grips the ends of his scarf nervously, rocking back on his heels. He takes a deep breath and adds, 'Do you . . . want to come? Maybe see what campus life is like?'

I feel my phone buzzing in my pocket. Several missed texts with a similar 'where are you?' theme light up my screen. I dismiss the messages with such intensity it's a shock I don't crack the glass. Thinking of Charlie all polka-dotted and happy next to an equally colorful Kim propels me to say, 'Sure.'

# Seventeen

'THIS . . . IS A DORM?'

Marcus is fumbling for his keys outside of a brick four-story building that looks nothing like a typical college residence. When I did my campus tour of the Culinary Institute last year, our guide had mentioned how there's not much student housing on campus, and most tend to get apartments nearby. *Forget about the sprawling college dormitories you've seen on TV and movies,* she said, *because Chicago schools just don't have that kind of real estate.* But I didn't expect this: it looks like a converted warehouse, all open and industrial and cool as hell.

'It's new; they just acquired the building last semester,' Marcus says, guiding me up the stairs. 'I guess they're trying to offer more living space so not as many students will have to commute in for classes, but probably they're just trying to make extra money.'

I'm only half listening, though, because he is living my DREAM and I don't want to hear anything even remotely negative about it.

His actual room is quite small, sparsely decorated, though I haven't spent enough time in random boys' rooms to know if interior design ranks on male living concerns. The space is pretty claustrophobic, with four manila walls closing in, compounded by the fact that half the room is occupied by another human. When we walk in, his roommate doesn't even look up, mesmerized by his laptop. Marcus makes no attempt to get his attention either, and since the two of them are comfortable with mutual avoidance, I do the same, having mastered that skill after four years of high school. Looks like I'm more prepared for college than I thought!

Marcus has several stacks of poetry books around his bed – his BED.

There's nowhere to sit except his bed.

We both seem to realize this simultaneously, eyeing the mattress with uncertainty. He runs his fingers through his closely clipped hair, and I swear I see a bead of sweat drip down his forehead. This was his idea, but Marcus isn't handling having a girl in his room very well. I'm not even a romantic prospect, but he's all jittery, like his inner shyness has clawed its way out to a physical manifestation. And I don't blame him; I mean, something about a bed implies . . . activities. Since I certainly didn't come here for that, and he looks closer to vomiting than putting the moves on me, the whole thing is much more awkward than I'd anticipated. Not that I'd put much thought into this outing in the first place. Hooray for impulsiveness!

We sit, knees practically touching, the muffled sounds of an undeterminable band coming from his roommate's headphones. I can't stand this painful discomfort, so I just start rambling.

'So this is the Culinary Institute.'

He nods, giving me nothing.

'And you like it here, right?'

More nodding. More nothing.

'Right, how could you not? You get to cook all day – for class! That's amazing. I would love to be baking instead of balancing equations and memorizing leaders from ancient civil wars. Your classes must be so awesome; hey, can we go see a classroom?'

This gives him pause. 'It's ten o'clock at night.'

'So?' I say, desperate for a change in scenery.

'So . . . they probably aren't open.'

'But you don't know for sure.'

'I mean, I've never had the urge to make crème brûlée in the middle of the night . . .'

'You haven't?!' I exclaim.

He laughs, breaking the tension, and I can feel his wave of relief as we head back out into the night, yet I almost detect a twinge of regret. That can't be it, though, because he seems much more relaxed and back to his usual amount of Marcus angst once we're outside one of the school's main buildings. We try a few locked doors before finally finding an open one; thank you, incompetent nameless janitor.

Even though it's late and we're technically trespassing, Marcus perks up, a proud pup showing off. We slip into a large room that's easily one of the most beautiful spaces I've ever seen: rows of gleaming metal tables, with hanging pot racks displaying every size of copper pot and saucepan known to man. Drawer after drawer of cutlery, wall after wall of hanging aprons; I almost cry after noticing the Bakers Pride convection oven. It's like the biggest, most well-stocked Williams-Sonoma ever, without the exorbitant price tags to deter you from diving in. I want to touch everything, to fire up the stovetop and cover myself in stacks of recipe books, and I almost do, until I see – the FOOD. A built-in refrigerator that takes up an entire wall, with glass doors proudly displaying all the climate-controlled deliciousness within.

I actually shed a tear.

'Do you just love every single day of your life?' I whisper.

Marcus stands tall, chest out, his surroundings filling him with confidence. For as long as I've known him, his presence has always been partially crumpled, like it's too presumptuous for him to declare a physical space. But here he is poised, self-assured: a complete 180 from earlier. 'I can't complain,' he says with a grin.

'I mean, the Black Phoenix is not too shabby as far as kitchens go, but this . . . this!' I spin around, overcome with joy.

'It's cool, no doubt, but being in an environment like this . . . it's more cutthroat than you think,' he says with an eyebrow perched.

'More cutthroat than having a hell demon as a sous-chef?'

He nods. 'You'll see.'

'You think?'

'I know,' he says, taking a step toward me. 'I've seen you in action; you've got the chops. No one can caramelize a calf's brain like you.'

'Aww, I bet you say that to all the girls.' I take a deep breath, letting his admittedly absurd compliment fill my heart with hope. 'I can't wait. Thank you for bringing me here tonight. I needed this.'

'Happy to help.' Marcus inches forward again. 'I like you being here with me,' he adds quietly.

Somehow we're now in very close proximity, even more so than when we were sitting on his bed. I'm suddenly aware of his woodsy scent, which is usually masked by spices and oils, and how his dark brown eyes are two shades lighter than his skin – again, features I've never paid particularly close attention to. But it's impossible not to notice now, with his eyes tracing the curves of my face, his mouth turned up in a hopeful smile.

*This is not good,* I say to myself. *You shouldn't be here.* It's clear to me now that an innocent campus tour has presented an opportunity for a werewolf to share feelings I didn't realize existed. We've never been alone together, always surrounded by a collection of monsters and kitchen fumes masking any romantic inklings he's been experiencing. Damn it! How did I not see this? Am I the worst matchmaker or what? I have to find an escape without hurting him.

He presses his lips together, leaning forward ever so slightly, and my eyes dance around the room, searching for an excuse. When I land on the clock, I call out, 'Oh my Gods!'

Marcus reels, eyes wide in shock. 'What's wrong?'

'It's eleven thirty!' I cry. 'I'm going to be in so much trouble!'

He snaps into action, free of whatever love bubble was encasing him. 'Let's get you a cab.'

We don't say anything as we stand by the curb, trying to flag down a cabbie. I give him a little wave once I'm inside the car, and he barely manages to wave back, biting his lip like he's just made a huge mistake.

I don't have much time to process, though, because once I exit the cab, I find Charlie sitting on my front steps.

'What are you doing here?' I ask.

Charlie stands, peacoat unable to contain the chip on his shoulder. 'Uh, I thought we had plans? To talk to my dad?'

'Well I didn't know for sure, since you pretty much disappeared after school,' I say, matching his bitter tone.

'I had an MA meeting. I thought you knew that.'

*Oh, I know everything,* I say to myself, brain flashing back to the paint-splattered flirtfest.

'So where have you been? You didn't answer my texts. I stopped by because I was worried about you,' he presses on.

I cross my arms in stupid defiance. 'Out.'

'Obviously. Where? With who?'

I picture Marcus leaning in to kiss me, and my stomach turns. 'Marcus. From work.'

'OK . . .' He waits for more details, but I can't bring myself to share. I stand in the cold, trying to remind myself of the feelings that fueled me to go off with Marcus in the first place, but now everything is cycloning together, like a horrible tornado of guilt, anger, and regret. What am I even doing anymore?

'This isn't like you,' Charlie says. 'I don't understand why you won't just talk to me.'

He's right, I know he's right, but for some reason I can't give him that satisfaction. I feel like I'm on a crumbling ledge, and even the slightest movement will cause a cave-in. I want to reach out, I do, but will he be there if I fall? Do I even deserve to be caught?

When I don't answer, he waves his arms in frustration. 'OK, well, it's late and I'm tired.' He starts walking to his car, before turning back to me. 'Are you gonna go to the carnival with me tomorrow?' he asks, eyes more sad than hopeful.

'Yeah,' I say, the most enthusiastic response of all time. *If you still want me to,* I say to myself.

'Great.' His voice is flat.

Can't wait.

# Eighteen

'I THINK OUR CHOICES ARE NACHOS OR A HOT DOG ON A STICK.'
Charlie reads from a cartoonish food truck menu. Everything
is printed in neon bubble letters, making it impossible to
decipher what kind of overpriced 'food' the vendor is
pushing. 'Although, maybe this says corned beef, instead of
corn dog? That wouldn't be a thing, right?'

I barely look up, choosing to pick at a loose thread on my
coat. 'Corned beef doesn't really scream winter carnival,' I
say through a frown. 'Shouldn't you know what's on the
menu? You spent so much time planning this.'

His face points to the sky, like he's looking toward the
Gods to give him strength. He inhales deeply through his
nose, a string of comebacks surely circling his skull. But

because he's the son of a politician and a natural peacemaker, he simply replies with, 'I wasn't on food.'

I make a noncommittal grumbling sound, and Charlie orders us some cheese fries. You'd think my culinary aspirations would turn me off artificial foods, but I do love me some processed nacho cheese: a point Charlie knows all too well.

'Try to enjoy this, OK?' he says, handing me a loaded fry. 'If not for yourself, then for me. Despite my longtime disengagement from this school, I did try to make this carnival semi-enjoyable, and someday, we'll look back on our senior year winter carnival with rose-tinted nostalgia, right before we yell at meddlesome kids to get off our lawn.'

I bite the inside of my cheek, keeping me from saying something truly horrible. 'Ugh, fine. But only because I'll get to scold children someday.'

'That's the spirit.' He kisses me through my wool beanie, and I try to let his warmth run through. *At least he's trying,* I think. But my heart is struggling to thaw, and it's not from the cold.

The senior class is crammed into Manchester's comically small parking lot, where a series of carnival games, rides, and food trucks are parked for a night of winter enchantment. I'm not one for crowds, or classmates, or rides that were only assembled hours before; all of this is making me scream to go home. But because things between Charlie and me are chilly at best, I agreed to plaster on a smile for exactly one hour, during which we'd meet up with Amani and drink hot chocolate. My soggy marshmallows are almost gone, and we still haven't found her. It seems like every single Manchester senior is here, in pursuit of games with oversize teddy bear prizes and dark corners to make out in. Maybe it's my constant presence at Navy Pier's nonstop carnival, but the whole thing seems ridiculous, except for the part where Charlie's arm is wrapped around me. Even though I hate this, I'd rather he be here, next to me, instead of in one of those dark corners.

Finally, we find Amani, who in turn has found Kim. Fantastic. They're both trying their luck at a game where you have to squirt water at a target to make metal ponies run. The fact that the water isn't frozen is maybe the most magical thing here.

'Five bucks on number nine!' I yell, throwing my support behind Amani's horse in an attempt to get into the spirit of things. The race comes to its photo finish, and Amani and Kim spin around, total losers at the game but winners in effort.

'I was robbed,' Amani says. 'My horse had a bad knee.'

'Yeah, and I think mine had gait problems,' Kim adds.

'Both of which, I'm sure, are undoubtedly true,' I say. Kim sends a bright smile my way, and it takes every ounce of self-control not to shoot back daggers. I quickly lock eyes with her to get her match reel over with, only there's no way to prepare myself for the scene before me. At first, I think I'm having double vision; I see strands of white twinkle lights, just like the ones that hang above us now, and the swirl of a Tilt-A-Whirl, copied directly from the one to my right. Under flashing fluorescents, Kim and Charlie close in for a kiss, slow and sweet, while he holds a pink cotton candy puff and she holds on to him. There's tinny carousel music playing, but is it in my head or in my ears? This scene could be right here, right now; it's practically pulled from the present. I stumble back, breaking our eye contact, and frantically start looking for the corner where the couple in my vision were tucked away for an embrace. I don't see it, but I sense it; the details are blurry, but the feelings are real. Was this a warning, a flash to the immediate future? Are Kim and Charlie about to have their first kiss?

'Are you OK?' Charlie clutches my forearm, his eyebrows knitted in concern. 'You look like you just saw a ghost.'

Normally I take comfort in his touch, but now I'm completely numb. 'I . . . I'm fine. Just dizzy from all this merriment,' I lie. I look up at him for a clue, but having already been treated to a separate scene of his togetherness with Kim earlier, all I see now is worry in his dark green eyes.

Amani signs, *What just happened?* But I shake my head. Our group wanders off to find the next cheap thrill, and I drift to the back, engulfed in angst. The carnival sights and sounds all fade into a single neon hum, matching the pulse of paranoia in my veins. What is happening and what is meant to be melt together into one solid lump where my heart resides. I've seen them together before, of course, but something about the immediacy of this vision gives it an urgency I can't ignore. It replays on an infinite loop, pulverizing my senses and grinding me down to dust.

I'm going to lose him. I can't stop it from happening. And the constant threat of his departure is something I can no longer bear.

I come back into focus just as Charlie and Kim are high-fiving over Skee-Ball, laughing and having fun, and something inside me snaps.

'ENOUGH!' I yell, turning three shocked pairs of eyes my way. Everyone's quiet, like I just let the air out of the fun balloon.

Charlie, still holding a ball, whips around, trying to find the cause of my outburst. 'Amber, what?' he says after coming up empty.

'You! The two of you!' I wave an accusatory finger at the future pair. 'I can't take it anymore!'

'Are you serious?' he spits back. Horrified at being perceived in a negative light, Kim holds her hands up by her shoulders, palms out, displaying her innocence.

'I don't understand. What did I do?' she asks.

Amani tiptoes to my side, like she's approaching a beehive ready to burst. 'Hey, maybe you want to take it down a notch, before it's too late?' she says in my ear.

'No,' I lash back. 'No, I do not. I have literally reached my max.' The vision that should have faded away by now keeps running on its circuit, adding fire to my flames.

Charlie grabs me by my waist, escorting me from the group. I try to squirm away, but he has quite a hold on me. As we hurry off, I hear Kim ask Amani, 'What's going on?'

He guides me to a spot far from the sounds of prize bells and ticket takers, by a relatively quiet cotton candy machine. Pink and blue puffs of fluff dangle from a pole – just like in my vision – while my relationship hangs in the balance.

'I have had enough of this.' He scowls, arms crossed firm. He's mad – beyond mad. I've only seen him like this once, after his dad vanished in goblin cross fire. I didn't know how to reassure him then, and I certainly don't know what to say now. 'Are you having some sort of psychotic break?'

I kick a discarded pop can. 'Maybe.'

'Why? Do you have Skee-Ball-related PTSD you want to fill me in on?'

'No. Don't be ridiculous.'

'Oh, *I'm* being ridiculous?' He gestures to himself overdramatically. 'I didn't just have a fit in front of everyone.'

'Can you blame me?' I take a subconscious step forward, ready to launch into this territory in which there's no turning back. 'It's Kim – OK? I can't stand seeing the two of you together!'

Charlie blinks rapidly, shaking his head in a double take. 'This again? God, Amber, when are you going to let this go? There's nothing happening between me and Kim!'

'Oh, yeah? Then what did I see in the gym yesterday?'

He stares like a game show contestant straining his brain for the final answer. 'I don't know . . . an unflattering display of terry-cloth shorts?'

'Stop it, Charlie! This isn't funny.'

'Why don't you just tell me, then, since you're obviously dying to.'

I don't really want to, but something has taken over me, a monster racing toward the finish. 'You and Kim, painting banners, and each other.'

His jaw drops in a silent laugh. 'So let me get this straight. You're out all night alone with Marcus and that's totally fine, but I was working on a project with a friend, surrounded by a group of people, and you're twisting it into, what, cheating on you?'

I've made it this far; the words are bubbling in my throat, ready to break free. 'She's not your friend; she's your MATCH! Your destiny, your fate.' My arms swing wildly in accordance with the reveal, my thoughts and limbs loose and free. I thought I'd be flooded with terror after sharing the truth, but I've been holding on to it for so long, in this moment it's a relief to finally let it go. 'I've known it since the day you walked up to me for help. I've watched you fall for each other, over and over, every single day, and it makes me sick – physically ill – to watch it unfold in real life.'

Charlie is frozen, his mind working overtime to catch up. I've never seen such a non-reaction after divulging a match; people usually either break into a song of joy or despair. Deep reflection tends not to be a menu option, but then again, I've never delivered a match to my own boyfriend. His face is a blank page waiting to be written, and I can't tell where the story will veer from here. Did I just inspire him to make a break for it? Did I just cast Kim in an all-new light? I've never been one to enjoy suspense, and every second he keeps quiet kills me more.

'Why . . . Why didn't you tell me?' he finally asks.

Now I'm the one in shock. 'Are you serious? Why do you think? Because I didn't want to lose you, and because I love you, you idiot!' I regret it as soon as the phrase crosses my lips. The first time I say 'I love you' to him – to anyone – and it's all wrong. Out of anger, out of the wrong kind of passion. His eyes widen at the sentiment, mouth leaving a frown where a smile should be. All other sound and movement has faded away, with only our aching hearts filling the void.

'But I don't want her.'

I shake my head. 'It doesn't matter.'

'How can it not matter?' He looks like his insides are melting, starting with his eyes. Tears begin to pool in the corners, and I feel my own building.

'Because it's not up to you . . . or me. It's not up to either of us.'

'I don't believe that,' he says, clenching his jaw. 'It doesn't change how I feel.'

'It changes everything, Charlie! You're telling me that knowing this won't affect the way you think of her? You won't be curious about how happy you could be? You can't honestly tell me the thought won't cross your mind.'

He's pacing now, weaving back and forth under the string lights. 'I can't win here! No matter what I say, you'll twist it in your head. Am I curious? It's interesting, at best, but I'm not suddenly dying to be with Kim. And no matter how many times I tell you, you don't seem to hear how much I'm dying to be with you.'

We're at a standstill, neither of us willing to accept the reality on the other's side. Because he's right: no matter what he says, it can't overpower the visions swimming in my head. And there's no way to express how impossible it is for me to push them away.

'Charlie, I can't do this anymore. I can't keep living this lie.'

This stops him in his tracks. 'Is it a lie how we feel about each other? Is it a lie that you love me?'

*Love*. The word makes my throat catch. 'No, but even as we're talking now, all I can see is you and Kim.' A tear betrays me, my voice starting to crack.

Charlie echoes my rupture. 'And we look happy together? Kim and I?'

'Mind-numbingly so,' I croak.

He swallows back tears. 'I can't picture it. I refuse.'

'Well, I have no choice.' I bury my wet face in my fingers, unable to keep my shoulders from shaking. He lightly rests his hands on me, making me convulse harder. I can't accept his affection, not at a time like this.

'Amber, you have to stop this,' he whispers.

'I can't just stop being a matchmaker!' I shout in return.

'No.' He keeps his voice soft, despite my outburst. 'I mean, stop letting these visions overpower reality. That stuff in your head is just that. My words, my feelings: those are real. Focus on what we have. I'm crazy about you! Being with you makes me happier than I thought I could be. Please,' he begs. 'Please hear me.'

He's very close now, resting his forehead against mine, breath warm on my skin. 'Please.' He sighs. I close my eyes and imagine his words as brave knights, swords drawn, ready to tackle the beast that is my visions. They charge into my psyche, pushing past the thorny twists and turns of brain matter, preparing themselves for battle. I want them to win, to slay the dragon, so to speak, but it's too strong, extinguishing them with its flames. Because while Charlie's reassurances are appreciated, even he can't know what the future will bring. He can't guarantee his heart won't go off course, that the things he feels today will be there tomorrow. He can't promise forever, and I can't let myself continue to fall for someone who will eventually slip away.

'I'm sorry,' I choke out, crying with abandon. 'It's too hard. I . . . I love you too much.' I push myself away: away from his warmth, away from the security of his embrace. I fumble into the cold, empty and alone. Charlie stands, gutted, mouth curled in a twist of pain. He looks as horrible as I feel. But the damage is done. I've scorched the earth, and there's no turning back.

Later, buried under layers of blankets and used Kleenex, I feel someone crawl into my bed next to me. Amani doesn't say a word but wraps me in a hug so fierce, she inadvertently squeezes out more tears. With the sound of sobs filling the room, she holds me tight without comment or judgment, supporting me with her silent strength.

# Nineteen

The next morning, Amani's still snuggled next to me. Sunshine streams through my mini blinds, hitting her face just so, and even without the perfect lighting, she looks like an angel. I've yet to meet an actual holy creature, but I can't imagine how anyone could stack up against my best friend. Her halo is visible through the power of friendship.

Her long lashes start to flutter, and I close my eyes so as not to look like some creepo watching her sleep. She stirs, stretching her legs over the end of my twin bed.

'You awake?' she whispers.

I nod.

'You OK?'

I shake my head.

'I'll get you some coffee.' She heads to the kitchen, where I hear her and Mom talk in soft tones. I wonder if she knows. Mom wasn't home when I came barreling into my room last night, but she must've let Amani in. If she does know, I hope she hasn't called John, Charlie's dad and her best pal, to get more details. That's all I'd need right now: the mayor of Chicago and a supreme witch gossiping about my love life.

Amani brings back two steaming mugs, and when I sit up to take one, I feel like I've been hit by a truck. I'm physically sore from crying. Is that even possible? To throw your back out from excessive sobbing? There must be extra gravitational pull in my room at the moment, because small movements feel like climbing Everest. Well, bed, I guess I live here now.

I must look wretched, because Amani is already rummaging through her makeup bag for remedies. Unless she has a power buffer in there, I doubt there's much she can do. She grabs a vial of something and starts sliding a roller ball of liquid under my eyes.

'You knew I'd look awful,' I mutter, steering into the skid.

'I knew you'd be crying,' she counters. 'This helps with puffiness. It has caffeine or something . . . Supposed to have rejuvenating powers.' She takes another bottle of lotion to the rest of my face before sitting back to enjoy her coffee. 'Let that stuff absorb.' We both take a few silent sips.

'So,' she starts.

'So.'

'Do you want to talk about it?'

I sigh. 'What's left to say?'

She twists up one side of her mouth. 'I mean, I feel like there are a *few* things to say.'

'Such as . . . ?'

'Like, aren't you slightly curious what happened after you detonated the bomb?'

'Curious' is not the right word. I've done everything I can to not think about the aftermath of my meltdown; I have had so many stomach-turning thoughts of Charlie and Kim together that if there is even the slightest chance my revealing them as a match actually brought them together, I would sooner permanently plug my ears with an occlusion spell than hear about it.

Amani decides I need to know anyway. 'Charlie was a mess. I tried to catch up with him, but he was a walking shell; he looked at me like he didn't even know who I was.' She pauses, but if notice of a zombie Charlie is supposed to bring me comfort, it doesn't. 'And Kim, well, she was totally confused.'

Just hearing her name sends a dagger through my chest. 'You didn't tell her, did you? About the match stuff?'

Amani looks insulted. 'Of course not. But we need to decide how to talk to her about this because she was pretty upset.'

I don't want to think about her at all, much less figure out how to interact with her. I never had time to relay my I Spy flirtation episode to my best friend, and it seems pointless now. The damage is done. But I guess in my explosion of feelings, I didn't consider that even though I can break up with Charlie, I can't make Kim exit from my life as easily. Why can't people who cause you problems just disappear after you've been inconvenienced? Not die or anything, just stop existing: poof, gone. Now that's a magic trick I'd pay big bucks for.

She takes a long gulp of coffee. 'So? What do we do about Kim?'

'Do we have to talk about this now?' I whine.

'Better now than at school. It's not like we won't be seeing her.'

'Uuuuugggghhhh.' I flop back on my pillow. This is where I want to stay. Forever. No prying eyes, no social awkwardness. Just downy softness. 'I don't know. Can't I just wait to see how I feel when we see her?'

'I mean, I guess.' Her head tilts in disapproval, brown hair cascading down her pink pony jammies. 'But it's probably better to be prepared, don't you think?'

I throw a pillow at her. 'Stop being so wise. You're a precog, not a priest.'

She presses her palms together and raises them to her forehead, bending forward in a yoga bow. 'Wisdom comes in many forms,' she says in an over-the-top Zen voice.

She's right, of course. Because before I know it, we're walking the halls of Manchester Prep, hopped up on expensive beauty products meant to help me not look like a complete basket case. The news of my breakup has already made the rounds — it did take place at a school function, after all — and seeing as how Charlie has always been a highly desirable specimen, girls are already twittering over their second chance at snagging him. Not that I'd expect anything less of my fellow female classmates, but c'mon, the body's not even cold.

Every time I step outside a classroom, my heart floods with panic, knowing that with each footstep I could run into Charlie. I spend the last twenty minutes of each class in intense hyperfocus, planning out alternate passing-period routes based on everywhere he should and should not be at those exact moments in time. I completely avoid our usual meeting spots and take the most asinine paths possible, going up and down staircases I've rarely traveled. I'm starting to consider a career in covert ops, when I see him, down the end of a hallway he has no business occupying. But then again, neither do I, so I guess heartbroken minds think alike.

Everything stops, and if I didn't know for sure that there are currently no practicing witches in this school, I'd suspect a hindrance charm was in play. I'm completely frozen, unable to move or speak or acknowledge his presence, and he seems stuck in the same paralysis. We just stare at each other, unmoving anchors in a sea of students, stubbornly staying put. From across the hall, I watch his face pinch tight, holding back whatever emotions he doesn't want to reveal in public, until he finally turns away and disappears into the crowd. As painful as it is to see him, it's even worse when he leaves, like a vacuum sucking out all the remaining joy in the world. I can hear the bell ringing, but I'm left with such an absolute emptiness that getting to class or even breathing feels completely pointless.

'Is the day over?' I ask Amani later as we make our way to lunch. 'The day's over, right?'

'Hang in there, champ.' She gives me a pat on the back.

The cafeteria is buzzing with its usual hum, but there's only one plaid-clad student who begs concern; I instantly zoom in on Kim, sitting at a table by herself. Sadness frames her face as she slowly pulls the crust off her PB&J. Gods. I don't want to deal with her, now or ever. How am I supposed to explain that her hypothetical stealing of my boyfriend is putting a strain on our friendship without being sent to a psych ward? This is exactly why I don't like people; they expect you to adhere to social norms, when all I want to do is hide under a blanket and mainline sugar. Kim sees us from across the room and stiffens like a deer in headlights. She doesn't wave or smile but has too much nervous energy, so she awkwardly rearranges her food on the table.

'Hey, guys,' Kim says softly when we approach. She can barely look up, and the eye-contact avoidance is mutual. I absolutely CANNOT deal with a Kim-Charlie love mash-up right now. Amani remains standing, waiting for my cue, but I'm so torn between what I want to do (hide) and what I should do (explain), I'm just teetering in place. I need to pick a side and stay there. Kim jumps in. 'Um, I don't know exactly what happened, but, Amber, I want you to know I'd never do anything to jeopardize our friendship. You and Amani have been so welcoming to me since I transferred, and I'd never intentionally mess that up.'

We're still standing, literally looking down on her. The tension is just too much, so I sit down. Amani follows suit.

'We know,' Amani offers. I can tell she thinks I've made a huge mistake but is blindly supporting me anyway. While I don't want her to lose Kim as a friend, my life would be infinity times easier if Kim wasn't around.

'It's kind of hard to explain . . . Um . . .' I say to the table. Of course, it's really not that hard, now, is it? I could just tell her her match and it'd all be clear. But I can't because every single time (last night excluded) I've revealed a match, that person has run straight toward their destiny, and I cannot survive Charlie and Kim being the next It Couple right now. It's physically painful to talk to her, so I hide behind my hair as much as possible. Side-swept bangs are the new shields. I continue. 'I don't know what to say.'

Kim sighs, releasing her shoulders from her ears into a more natural stance. She pinches her lips together, waiting. But while it's morally decent to give her some insight, that doesn't mean I need to bare my soul. She's still difficult to be around; I will need to forever avoid her eyes so as not to be haunted by Charlie. There's a fine line between being noble and sentencing oneself to torture.

I happen to see Ivy scurry by, head down and hair in her face, and for the first time in the history of ever, I leap at the chance to go talk to her. She's alone, giving me the perfect opportunity to escape this mealtime nightmare. From one awkward exchange to the next!

'Uh, sorry. I gotta go,' I say. Kim's eyes widen in confusion, and Amani furrows her brows. If she were a witch, she'd be hexing me right now for sure. But still I call out, 'Ivy!' and leave my best friend to smooth everything else out. OK, so maybe I didn't handle that the best, but what else could I have done?

Ivy doesn't stop or look back; she dumps her trash and sashays toward the door. I manage to meet her side, but she doesn't even give me a sideways glance.

'What?' she snaps, looking straight ahead.

'How are things?'

She makes a low, guttural sound.

'That good?'

'Like you should talk. I heard you just dumped the love of your life.' She takes my silence as confirmation, and adds, 'Moron,' with a championship eye roll.

She stops at her locker, and taped inside are not pictures of the latest Hollywood dreamboat or designer handbag, but shots of her and Iris: There's one where they are very young, sharing a massive lollipop; another more recent, on a ski trip. Riding on a camel past pyramids, smiling on the Great Wall of China – these sisters have traveled the globe together, a string of adventures bound to end once Iris hits the sea permanently. Despite my own personal drama, Iris keeps sneaking into my thoughts. Seeing her transform from a strong, independent defender of the people to a small, defenseless shell of a girl is not resting well in my psyche.

Ivy catches me eyeing her collection and slams the door shut, closing my window to her world. 'What do you want?' she snarls, her nails primed. She turns to me for the first time, and I notice the makeup circling her left eye is much heavier than usual. There's a blackish tint peeking out from layers of concealer that has me instantly concerned. 'We're not meeting until the full moon, right?' she barks. 'What, do you need snuggle time or something?'

'Gods, no.' I recoil. 'That'd be like cuddling an ice cube.'

'Then what?'

Unsure of myself, I venture, 'Um, Ivy? What's wrong with your eye?'

She gently touches the corner of her face, being careful not to press too hard. Her normal scowl is restricted by some swelling. 'None of your business.'

'OK, well, I thought I'd see how you're doing . . . how Iris is doing.' My voice cracks under my discomfort. Clearly, something is going on with her, but I know I'm not her first pick for a shoulder to cry on.

Her nose shrivels up like a stink bomb went off. 'Ew. Well, stop. We're not friends, Amber. I don't see how I could've given you that impression. I don't want you braiding my hair or signing my yearbook. I just want you to help my sister.'

'What is your problem?' I ask. 'I'm not trying to be your friend, but I am trying to help you. That does involve basic levels of human interaction.'

'You want to talk basic levels of humanity?' she snaps. 'How about trying to get a girl with no free will to eat? Hmm? Iris does nothing but lie in a disgusting heap, unwilling to bathe, chew, or get up to use the bathroom. I'm essentially the caregiver of a twenty-year-old baby, but at least babies have the urge to consume foods; I have to force pureed cheeseburgers down Iris's throat to make sure she doesn't die of starvation. My parents are on a cruise, so they aren't home to see this, but that also means I'm all on my own with no one to lean on.'

'Ivy, I—'

'Then, last night, when I'm bringing Iris her nightly milk shake, a freaking black bird bursts through her window and beaks me in the face.'

'Beaked you?'

'Yes! Stabs me right in the eye with its pointy little black mouth.'

'What was a bird doing in your sister's room?' I ask.

'How should I know?' She touches the sore spot near her eye, gritting her teeth. 'And on top of that, now that I'm no longer sirening idiots to do my homework for me, I also have to squeeze in study time, which is not something I'm equipped for. I'm stressed out, I'm alone, and there's nothing I can do about it.' Her eyes are glazed, but she stares at the ceiling until the tears subside. 'You want to know how I'm doing? I'm exhausted. Completely exhausted.'

'I promise you my mom and I are doing everything we can to be ready for the full moon,' I say. 'You'll have your sister back.'

'Will I? Really? Because I'm pretty sure that even if she gets her free will, she'll just be splashing off into the sea, and I'll be left a hot mess. I don't see any winning scenario.'

I can relate to that feeling. Knowing I am not Charlie's endgame was strangling my heart, and now here's Ivy, slaving over a sister who will probably still jump ship once she gets the chance. It feels hopeless, draining, and for a brief moment, we're connected by our losses and magical mismanagements, carrying the burden of sacrifice in the name of love. But before it gets too mushy, she spins on her heel and catwalks off, a picture of perfection crumbling at the edges.

# Twenty

I'M STIRRING A POT OF GODS KNOW WHAT FOR GODS KNOW who at Gods know what time.

'Amber, it's time to – what are you doing?' Marcus asks, examining my efforts with total confusion. His voice breaks me out of the faraway place my brain has traveled to, and I realize I'm tending to the aftermath of tonight's mystery porridge with a spatula.

'Oh, um, sorry,' I say, not remembering wandering over here. The stove is not my realm in the Black Phoenix kitchen, and I don't even want to know the steps involved in making this stew. It looks like a plundered village.

'Are you OK? You've been really off all night.' His face is rumpled in concern, with puppy-dog eyes begging to help.

'This isn't even your day to be here.' He's kept his distance most of the night, but even the awkwardness of our last encounter can't stomp out his protective, wolf-pack mentality.

'Yeah, I just . . . couldn't stand to be at the shop tonight.' Which is putting it lightly. In truth, I avoided my Windy City shift like the plague. Love might as well be leprosy for me right now, except that instead of losing a limb, I've lost my heart. I thought coming here would help; being in a kitchen usually gives me a sense of purpose. But clearly, I'm just as lost here as anywhere else. If only I could roll up the world's biggest pile of dough, climb inside, and sink down, away from everything.

'Oh.' He fidgets. I can almost picture a tail between his legs. 'How come?'

I tilt my head in a weary 'I don't feel like talking about this' slant and add, 'I'm just not up for being a love conduit right now.'

'Gotcha,' he says knowingly. He doesn't press and instead drags the porridge pot over to the sink, filling it with water and soap. Most of the crew has already left; through the window in the kitchen door I see the waitstaff still tidying up. When it's not filled with weird smells and even weirder patrons, the Black Phoenix is actually quite a cool-looking spot, with its gleaming gold tabletops and massive chandelier made out of champagne flutes. There's a lot of glitz and

181

glamour, considering it's an underground hangout for 0.01 percent of the population. I walk aimlessly through the dining room, weaving through the tables.

Usually Vincent is leading the cleanup charge, taking no issue with rolling up his cuff-linked sleeves and wiping tables. But tonight he's at the door, talking animatedly to a lingering customer. I can't see her, but it's clear this individual is getting his best material. I overhear beats of his classic Dracula story, which he only reveals to those deemed worthy, and it shouldn't come as a surprise to see Amani is on the receiving end. What is surprising is there appears to be a smile on her face, and not a fake, 'please make this stop' kind of smile.

Vincent's just hitting the punch line as I approach. 'And then I said, "*Count* me out, Drac!"' They both laugh, Vincent slapping his thigh at his own hilarity, and Amani not actively recoiling as she usually does. Her genuine participation in this type of exchange is a first.

'What are you doing here?' I ask.

Amani's still grinning as she turns to me and says, 'Looking for you. I had a feeling you'd be here.'

'We were just having a wonderful chat.' Vincent beams. He's absolutely glowing in Amani's presence, and I swear he's practically levitating.

'Did my mom send you?' I add, ignoring the sparkling vampire.

'Yeah, she's pissed. Mostly worried, but definitely pissed. Haven't you guys talked about—'

'No, not yet.' I don't want to talk about my love life in front of Vincent, especially when he's off in the stratosphere.

A man of the world, he picks up my deflecting vibe. 'Well, I can see the two of you need your friend time, so I'll let you be.' He gently takes Amani's hand, which she does not automatically pull away. 'A pleasure, as always.' He kisses the top lightly, and it isn't new makeup that's making her blush. My matchmaker senses tingling, I grab my best friend, and we pile into the Sharma station wagon parked out front.

Once buckled, I blurt out, 'What the hell was that?'

'What?'

'That!' I gesture back to the restaurant. 'With Vincent! And the smiling! And not barfing!'

Amani shakes her head, turning the ignition. 'I don't know what you're talking about.'

'Ohhhhhh, yes you do. You were all twirly.'

'I was just being polite.'

'Nuh-uh. I know your polite face: it's a strained combination of societal niceties. This was something else.' I scoot as close to her as the seat belt allows, doing my best to pressure a confession.

She palms my face, pushing me back. 'OK, fine!' She

sighs. 'He said something actually funny and not creepy for once. Sue me.'

'Ha! Consider yourself served.' I take a brief moment of self-congratulation before slipping back into the malaise that coated me all day. Funny how familiar it is, like a Snuggie of pain.

The Sharma family vehicle is a straight-up disaster. Ripped to shreds by her five younger brothers, the interior looks like a holding cell for a feral jungle cat. The front seat is duct-taped together, and the whole thing smells like stale pizza. Which is to say, it's a wonder to behold.

'So,' Amani says, keeping her eyes on the road, 'I think I worked things out with Kim.'

'Oh?' I say, feigning interest. Somehow my brain has managed to push away Kim for the last several hours, and I'm less than thrilled to have her return. 'How'd that go?'

'Do you even care?' she asks with surprising venom. Her demeanor change is shocking, catching me completely off guard.

'What?'

'You just left me there at lunch, Amber, to clean up your mess. I didn't even know what I could or couldn't say to her!'

I clutch the door handle, suddenly feeling very uncertain. 'I had to go talk to Ivy about her sister.'

'Right. Right then? It couldn't wait?'

Streetlights fly by outside, repeatedly highlighting my guilty face. 'I mean, I guess I just figured you and Kim were closer, so . . .'

'Yeah, we are closer, but only because you've kept her at arm's length the entire time.' I try to butt in, but she cuts me off. 'And I get it, I do. The whole Charlie thing makes it a nightmare. But you know what? You let her into our world, even knowing what you knew. You should have just let her go to find a different circle to swim in. But it's too late for that now.'

'Amani . . .'

She clasps the steering wheel tight, not letting go of her grip or stance. 'Kim is a cool person. She's funny and smart and free from most of the garbage most Manchester people carry around. We have fun together. She's my friend, even if she's not yours.'

I swallow hard. 'I never said you shouldn't be friends.'

'You don't have to say it. I feel it. You turn into a damn turtle every time she's around. And I'm not saying it's not justified. But you've put me in a really difficult situation. If it comes down to a decision between her and my best friend, I'm obviously going to choose you, but I don't want to even be in that position.' She turns to me for the first time, a swirl of agony and anger in her eyes. She's never looked at me this way, and my insides collapse. I feel like a monster. The supernatural side of me has taken over, destroying everything

I hold dear: first Charlie, now Amani. A creature that can't be stopped, I've let down the one person who has always defended and cared for me when others left me to rot. What is wrong with me?

And yet, my words start tumbling out on a different tangent. 'And what about me, huh? What kind of position do you think your friendship puts me in?'

'I just said, I know this is hard for you—'

'No, but you don't really know. You don't know what it feels like to see someone bring joy to everyone around you, while in the meantime, your insides are dying. I have to fake a smile when she's around, and avoid eye contact as much as possible. I want her to just disappear, but then she's so nice and sweet, I feel like a demon for even sending any negative thoughts her way. Because what has she done to me? Nothing, technically nothing, except, OH WAIT, she's openly flirting with Charlie.'

She gives me a quick side-eye. 'What are you talking about? I've never seen her do anything out of bounds.'

'Well, then you must have missed the grand showing of their body-paint performance art.' I rub my hand down my jawline like a paintbrush, fluttering my eyelashes like it's the most wonderful feeling in the world.

Amani's shaking her head like she's talking to a three-year-old with an overactive imagination. 'Amber, did that *really* happen, or did you just envision it?'

'Seriously? Of course it happened! Kim's on track to steal my boyfriend, and – based on how quick you are to defend her – probably now my best friend too!'

Pulling onto my street, Amani parks outside my apartment, leaving the car running. The air is so heavy, I can hardly breathe. I'm ready to just stop, drop, and roll onto the sidewalk, but I can tell she has more to say.

She leans back in her seat, laying her hands on her lap. It'd be so much easier if she'd straight-out attack me, release her rage in a flurry of claws and teeth. But she won't, partially because that's not her way, but mostly because she's hurting, which makes it ten times worse. Black-and-white anger is much easier to take than the grays of suffering. 'I understand why you broke up with Charlie. I support you. But now I need you to support me. Kim is my friend, but she's not stealing me from you. She doesn't even know she's meant to be with Charlie. Stop being so self-centered all the time.'

With a final blow like that, I can't help but snap, 'Well, since I'm such a self-centered pain, I'm sure you won't miss me when I'm gone.'

I get out of the car, slamming the door behind me. With the weight of her words on my shoulders, I can barely climb the two flights to my apartment, my body heavy with regret. I don't know what possessed me to escalate the fight like that, even if I do have resentment toward her friendship with

Kim. What kind of person have I become, pushing everyone away? I collapse on the couch, instantly curling into a fetal position. I hear Mom's storming footsteps enter the room, the start of a rant on her lips over my missing work, but she pauses at the sound of my sobs. The words come spilling out faster than I can think them. I tell her about Charlie, Kim, my fight with Amani – everything. Squeezing it all out until I'm nothing but a shell.

Mom sits down beside me, guiding my head onto her lap, stroking my hair like she did when I was little, letting her fingers run gently through the strands. We seldom snuggle like this anymore, and her distant yet familiar touch is intoxicating. I nuzzle into her side, just as she launches into a memory.

'When your father left, it was the worst pain I'd ever known. It was physical, devastating, like my heart had literally broken, and without it, my body seemed incapable of survival.' I look up, and her gaze is elsewhere, reliving the horrible sensation. Sadness clouds her, and though the room is already dark, there's a perceptible change to her coloring. 'I felt like the fire within was extinguished, that I wouldn't have the strength to go on. It sounds foolish, and weak, but . . . that is where I was.'

'It doesn't sound foolish,' I whisper, understanding all too well. I don't really remember my parents being together. Only a few random snapshots of mundane life come to mind.

Dad building my first bike; the two of them talking in hushed tones in the kitchen. And then, of course, the fateful Uncle Seymour wedding, where my matchmaking skills decided to make their grand entrance. I certainly don't remember my mom struggling under the pain she's describing, or even the love she originally felt to get her there. Her grimoire entries about falling in love captured a time so foreign to me, a period of her life I still desperately want to understand. To me, my mom has always been a certified badass who took care of me, her coven, and – through Windy City Magic – the entire Chicago supernatural community. I can't even conjure an image of her being anything less than a pillar of absolute strength. The idea of my mom crumpled, crying, and lifeless does not compute. 'What changed?' I ask her.

Color starts returning to her face, like the early moments of dawn. 'One morning, I couldn't get out of bed. You came in my room and must've seen how sad I looked, and promptly walked back out. When you returned, you placed a giant plate of cookies next to me and said, "These always make me feel better."' She laughs to herself. 'In that moment, I knew I could survive because I wasn't alone. I had you.'

It's almost too much: the honesty in her feelings, the confession of her struggle. How I played a part in her rehabilitation. I want to play it off, make a corny joke to lessen the importance of my role, but though the space is unfamiliar, I actually feel quite comfortable, so I let it lie.

'Things will get better,' she says softly. 'You're a Sand; you have the power to rise again.'

# Twenty-one

MOM FORBIDS ME FROM MATCHMAKING IN MY FRAGILE STATE, saying she doesn't want to scare away customers with my temperamental attitude toward love, so I suddenly have a lot more time on my hands. I take some extra shifts at both MarshmElla's and the Black Phoenix because I need to keep busy; it's the only way I'll get through the soul-crushing agony of simultaneously losing a boyfriend and fighting with my best friend. Every few seconds I reach for my phone, wanting to text either Charlie or Amani something – anything – to prove I'm not a pathetic loser with no social connections. But what would I say? No combination of letters conveys the right feelings, and there's not a sad enough emoji in the world to illustrate my empty heart. Without that release, my thoughts ping around my cranium like loose fireworks, noisy and crackling but ultimately fading away until the next one flares.

School is excruciating. If I thought roaming the Manchester halls was hard before, it's infinity times worse when I'm braving them alone. Weirdly, Charlie has disappeared off the face of the earth, which I guess is a blessing in disguise, except that I miss seeing his cute face and impeccable styling so much, I almost cry when I spot some random sophomore sporting a tie clip. Even though seeing him post-breakup felt like the ultimate torture, *not* seeing him is even worse, and I wonder if Mom has any memory-erasing spells to help wipe the constant thought of him clean.

I do see Amani and Kim walking together at one point, but since I don't know whether to wave or throw a fit, I choose the next best option: hiding. In fact, the second-floor girls' restroom has become my new favorite spot, serving as both a functional space and emotional fort.

I try to channel my energy into learning more about my mom's past, spending a stalker-level amount of time googling her name, the shop, anything I can think of. But since she grew up in the Stone Age (i.e., before social media), the Internet doesn't serve me much past very recent history. I scribble down a list of possible informants, including several of Windy City's vendors and a few coven members, but my brain is not firing on all cylinders, and I can't think of sneaky ways to get any of these people to abandon their loyalties and reveal Mom's secrets.

And even though he'd be the best source, I don't have the emotional strength to contact Charlie's dad.

Two days pass, and I'm on the verge of a nervous breakdown. At MarshmElla's, I've hit rock bottom, funneling pastry bags of buttercream frosting directly into my mouth. In just a few hours, I have consumed my body weight in sugar, meaning I'll probably have a heart attack and be found facedown in this wedding cake I've been tasked with decorating. I suppose there are worse ways to go.

Ella peeks her head in the back room, catching me sucking pink goo from the icing tip. She grits her teeth like she just walked in on someone doing something very naughty, and averts her eyes upward. 'Hey, um, you all right back here?' she asks.

Visibly shaking from the vast amount of sugar coursing through my veins, I must look like a drug addict. I hide the empty bags as if they were previously filled with heroin. 'Yeah, sorry.'

'You have a visitor at the counter,' Ella says, still not meeting my eye. 'But you may want to wipe your mouth first. And, uh, please throw out that tip.' She disappears, and I drag the corner of my apron across my lips; a sizeable streak of blush-colored buttercream gets left behind. As if I weren't jacked up enough, anxiety spikes as I wonder who has come to see me. Amani, wanting to make amends? Charlie, desperate to see me and get back together? Either would be wonderful, though I wish I weren't convulsing like a meth head for this reunion.

Only when I walk into MarshmElla's storefront, I find my mystery guest is neither; it's Marcus, standing awkwardly with his hands jammed in his jean pockets. He shifts his weight back and forth, looking completely out of place surrounded by rainbow-colored confections. He brightens when he sees me, but I can't imagine what possessed him to come here.

'Uh, hey, Marcus.' I clasp my hands behind my back in an effort to get a grip. 'What's up?'

An innocent smile warms his face, and I swear he looks like a puppy hoping for a treat. 'I knew you'd be here today, so I thought I'd stop by and say hi.'

'OK.' I didn't realize he was so conscious of my schedule. 'Can I get you something? We just pulled some snickerdoodles from the oven.'

'Oh, um, I don't really care for sweets,' he says.

'Good thing you're in a bakery, then,' I quip. Ella nonchalantly refills an empty pie tin with a fresh one, pretending not to listen but clearly devouring every word.

'Do you have a break, or something?' Marcus asks. The question seems to pain him, like it's taking great effort to be so forward. He's clearly nervous, which is not helping my already addled state.

'Uh, Ella, can I take my break?' I ask.

She raises an eyebrow. 'I'd say you're due.' I don't normally take breaks here, so I know my asking will require details of this encounter as payment.

'Give me one sec,' I say to Marcus, and I duck into the restroom to assess my damage. After splashing water on my face, I stare myself down in the mirror and barely recognize the creature before me. Careful scrutiny of my own appearance has never been of much interest to me. Beyond the bare minimum of grooming, I know full well no amount of mirror time will drastically change my skin/hair/body/fill-in-the-typical-problem-area-here. I'd also rather spend my money on food or baking supplies than give it to a cosmetics company trying to make me feel bad about myself. Yet this is one of those occasions when I wish I had a basic understanding of makeup. The skin around my eyes looks like it's been through the trenches, sallow and sad. My peacock hair color has lost its luster; it's in desperate need of a refresh. If I had to pick one adjective to describe myself all over, it would be 'gray.' Which is accurate, because that's exactly how I feel. I don't know Marcus well enough to let this all hang out, but I don't know if I have the energy to hide it.

I hang up my apron and slide into the booth where Marcus waits. Ella brought him a coffee that's gone untouched, and while I'd like to take a sip, I think even a drop of caffeine at this point would launch me straight to the moon.

'This is a cute place,' he says, anxiously pawing at his mug. 'I've never been here before.'

'Well, why would you, if you're not a sweets guy?'

He nods, exhaling loudly through his nose, then says nothing. I can feel myself fidgeting, vibrating the booth. This is embarrassing.

I shoot a pleading look at Ella behind the counter, who shrugs sympathetically. The shop is slow right now, so the only sounds are her plating cookies.

'So, um,' Marcus thankfully starts, 'I heard you and your boyfriend broke up.'

Wow. That is not where I thought this was going. 'You did?'

He tenses, like he's walked into a trap. 'Yeah. Vincent mentioned it.' Then he quickly adds, 'But we weren't, like, talking about you or anything.'

What the hell? How would Vincent even know? I don't exactly keep my vampire employer in the loop on my love life. Is there some sort of supernatural social-standing wiki I don't know about?

I must look on the verge of a murderous rage because Marcus observes, 'I've upset you.'

He looks like he'll be sick if this is true. Every part of him tightens, waiting for me to relieve him of guilt.

'No, I mean, yes, I am upset but not because of you.' A considerable weight leaves the booth.

'I brought you something.' He rifles through his coat pocket and produces a tiny square of folded notebook paper. On the top crease is my name, written in that scrawly kind of boy handwriting that makes you wonder how they ever made it through grade school.

'What's this?' I ask, unable to remember the last time someone passed me a note.

'Just . . . read it,' he says, and he bows his head, preparing himself for whatever my reaction to the contents may be.

I flatten the page against the table, taking a second to compose myself. It doesn't take a history of matchmaking or even a general understanding of the written word to see this is a poem. Marcus has written me a poem, and not one observing the frailty of life or beauty of nature: this is a love poem.

Oh Gods, no.

I'm shaking, and he gently places a hand on top of mine to calm me. My instinct is to pull away, but he feels nice . . . warm. I've been so starved for affection. When you become accustomed to a constant stream of cuddles and kisses, their absence leaves a hole unfillable by anything else. Kind words can never take the place of caring hugs.

I try to process his poetry, but my vision blurs, meaning I'm about to either bawl or barf. Marcus must be reading my reaction in a positive light because he takes my other hand. I feel heat coming from his skin, and the room begins to spin.

'Do you like it?' he asks, hopeful.

'I, um, don't know a lot about poetry,' I say truthfully. I want to pull away, but I don't trust myself to make any major movements at this point.

'You don't have to know anything about it; it's just how the words make you feel.' Help. If it wasn't clear before when he almost kissed me at the Culinary Institute, it is now 3,000 percent a go on Marcus having feelings for me. There's no turning back now, and I don't know what to do. Marcus is a great guy – there's no denying that; he's taught me so much about working in a kitchen, and I've genuinely enjoyed the time we've spent together.

But I can't help but think, what is the point of this? Here I am, with another boy who's destined for some random girl. Yet he's sitting here, opening his heart to me. Why? Why go through this charade? Marcus won't end up with me, regardless of what he's feeling now; I can see it in his eyes. Happiness awaits in his future, and I won't be a starring player. So why even go through this dance? It's exhausting, infuriating; I grip the table so as not to let out a scream. Love was always something I thought I understood, but now I'm as confused as ever.

Marcus leans forward and plants a gentle kiss on my lips. It's a bold move for such a shy guy, and I let him linger just to see if anything comes of it. But there's nothing: none of the heat I felt kissing Charlie, that insatiable need to keep his body close to mine. Marcus's embrace inspires nothing, other than an immediate need to let him down gently.

I place a hand on his chest, signaling him to stop. He looks happy, which pains me further.

'Marcus,' I start, having never been in this position before, 'thank you for the poem. You are beyond sweet.'

He smiles, dark skin hiding his blush. 'It was my pleasure.'

I pull my hands away so we're no longer touching. I don't want to hurt him – he's my only friend left – but I can't walk down this path again. 'I'm just not ready for anything else. The stuff with Charlie is still really fresh and . . . I'm still sorting out how I feel.'

'About him?'

'About love, in general,' I admit.

He sits back, disappointed. 'I thought, as a matchmaker, you'd have that figured out by now.'

I laugh to myself. 'You'd think, huh?' We sit for a minute, letting the finality of my rejection settle. I don't know what else to say. Things like 'I hope we can still be friends' or 'it's not you, it's me' seem too cliché to verbalize. So instead, I ask, 'Cupcake for the road?'

'Why not?' He shrugs, getting up from the booth. We walk over to the display case, where he chooses a savory maple bacon like the carnivore he is deep down. 'I've heard desserts help with heartache.'

'I can attest to that,' I say, handing him the pastry. His eyes are so sad, I wish I could help him feel better. 'I really liked your poem,' I add.

'I really like you.'

Another suitor, cast away.

I miss Charlie so much it hurts.

# Twenty-two

I'M SITTING AT HOME, STARING AT MY CALCULUS HOMEWORK like it's written in a foreign language, when my phone rings twice from a number I don't recognize. It scares me at first; I'd all but abandoned hope it would ever chime again, after the exodus of Amani and Charlie communications. I let it go to voice mail, waiting for my mystery caller to leave a message.

*Hello, this is Alexander Pru from the Culinary Institute. I'm calling today to schedule an interview for our undergraduate program . . .*

I drop the phone, causing the case to crack. The voice continues to talk at my feet while my heart skips several beats.

*Please call me back at your earliest convenience. I look forward to meeting you.*

Oh my Gods. It's happening. The admissions people read my application and didn't hate it. They weren't immediately turned off by me like so many others tend to be. They want to meet me, possibly welcome me into their sugar-covered arms. Oh my Gods!

Before I even process what I'm doing, my fingers quickly shoot the news off to Charlie, accompanied by a stream of dessert and star emojis. My insides melt as soon as the 'sent' tone plays.

No!

What did I just do?! It was an instinct, a gut reaction my brain didn't have time to suppress. I received happy news and wanted to share it with someone who makes me happy: simple as that. But what will *he* think it means? I don't even know what he's thinking these days. It's like he's been scrubbed from the earth, leaving no physical or digital trace. It's not that I don't understand it. I personally haven't made any effort to contact him, even though he's constantly circling in my brain like a hamster wheel. And I'm sure a majority of the population would celebrate the idea of their ex ceasing to exist post-breakup. But I guess I thought he would've reached out at some point. Going from being in someone's life 24/7 to no contact whatsoever is the coldest of cold turkey. Maybe he hates me. Maybe I magically mutated all his affection toward me into loathing the moment I said good-bye. If so, this stupid text I just sent will make things even better, since imposing my glee on someone I've caused pain is like kicking someone in the gut and then forcing them to check out your new shoes.

But I can't take it back. There's no 'digital message retrieval' function, though really, there ought to be. I can't be the only person to mistakenly shoot off a text and then regret it a millisecond later. Isn't that what drunk dialing is all about?

I stare at my screen, both terrified and excited at the possibility of a reply. I haven't seen or spoken to Charlie in over a week now, and the lump where my heart used to be aches for him. Part of me wants him to text back, even if it's words of anger, just so I'll know he's OK. But after ten straight minutes of willing my phone to light up, I throw it on the bed, cursing my stupidity.

I'm trapped in a calculus equation I barely understand when I hear the blessed text-notification chime. I spin around in my chair so fast I actually fall over, grasping at my quilt to act like a parachute. I scramble to find my phone within the tangled blanket, breathless from my tumble. I jam the home button to find Good job, Amber staring back at me.

*Good job, Amber* . . . hmm. At first glance, this is a nice message, but it's impossible to sense his tone. This could go either way, like a heartfelt *That's amazing!* Or a sarcastic *Wow, great* dripping with disdain. While I don't think Charlie is the particularly vengeful sort (like I would be), he'd also be totally justified if he wrote me off. Still, I type back a hopeful Thank you.

Minutes go by without a response, and I feel like an explanation is necessary.

**It just felt wrong not to tell you,** I send his way.

His reply comes almost immediately:

I understand.

I think about how my news would have been received had we still been together. I know without a doubt Charlie would have done something to make me feel special, like bring me a bouquet of daisies (my favorite) or a chef's hat embroidered with my name. There would have been fanfare, kisses, and complete celebration. Not the hollowness of a polite response.

Selfishly, I want him to say more, to elaborate on whatever he's feeling, but my screen fades to black.

Knowing full well I'll never be able to concentrate on homework now, I decide to go for a walk and clear my headspace. After a few blocks, I loosen my scarf, taking advantage of an unexpected Chicago heat wave. (You know it's been a rough winter when forty degrees feels warm.) I try to let the cool air purify my thoughts, but after wandering past dozens of local storefronts and apartment buildings, it's obvious no amount of climate change is going to reset my worries. I need to focus on another topic completely, to give my brain another challenge to work through. And since *The Mystery of Lucille Sand* is my most interesting prospect right now, I settle on that.

I make my way to the home of Wendy Pumple, a longtime Sand-family friend and Dawning Day member. I haven't talked to Wendy much since the whole coven-deciding-Amber-is-unworthy incident, but since I'm not one to hold a grudge (ha!), I'm hoping she'll feed me stories of my mom's youth. Wendy was friends with my grandmother, Edith, so maybe she would've been around for the undetermined happenings of way back when.

She lives on the first floor of a vintage Lincoln Park apartment building, and hers is the only name on the list of residents to include a proper prefix: *Ms Wendy Pumple*. I press the buzzer.

'Amber, dear, is that you?' answers her sweet little voice through the building intercom. She buzzes me in and meets me at the door. Almost instantly, I have a cup of cocoa and a cookie in my hands. Her hostess game is on point.

Sitting on a well-worn pink couch that could've only come into existence during a different century, I take my time addressing the subject of Mom. Clearly, Wendy's loyalties lie with all things Wiccan, but the way her dainty wrinkled hand is clutching my knee has me hopeful she'll help me too.

After some general chitchat, I start testing the waters. 'So, Ms Pumple, sorry to drop in here unannounced, but I was wondering if you could help me with a project I'm working on.'

'Oh, of course, dear.' She smiles, blue eyes twinkling. 'What kind of project?'

'Uh, for school.' I hesitate, trying to dream up what ridiculous teacher would ask us to dig through our parents' secret pasts. 'We're doing a unit on . . . biographies, and we're supposed to write an outline on someone we personally know, hitting all the major life points. I'm doing mine on my mom.'

Wendy clasps her hands together and holds them against her heart, letting out a joyful sigh. 'Oh, that's lovely! What a wonderful project! That would make such a nice gift for Lucille.'

'Right! That's what I was thinking. Only, I don't want her to know about it until I'm done. It's, like, a surprise.' Wendy looks so happy, I congratulate myself on this fabulous story I've pulled out of nowhere. This is going to work!

'Well, I would be honored to help,' she says. 'This is just what she needs right now. Poor thing has been so stressed lately.'

This gives me pause, because while *I* know Mom has been pushing herself to the limits in trying to help Iris, my mother isn't exactly a sharer when it comes to personal problems. If the coven has picked up on her emotional state, it must be worse than I thought.

I nod, taking another sip of cocoa. It's so rich and chocolatey, it almost has to be witchcraft. I make a mental note to get her recipe later.

'So what do you need to know?' Wendy asks. 'I can tell you all about how she opened Windy City Magic. She was so happy during that time. And courageous! Opening a shop like that for the public? Such a risk but such a big reward.'

I tap a finger against my cheek, making it look like I'm really wondering what I need from her. 'Well, actually, I think I have that time period covered. I'm most interested in learning about when she was younger, like, say, when she was a teenager, or early twenties?'

My informant sits back, suddenly less interested in this game. 'Oh, well, honey, I'm afraid I don't have much to offer there.'

'Why not?' I ask innocently. 'I mean, I'm sure you and my grandma talked about her.'

Wendy wrings her hands. 'It's not that; it's just . . . that was when your mom was going through her "difficult" phase.'

I cock my head to one side. 'Difficult how?'

'It's not uncommon, really. Almost every witch goes through an experimental time, learning the boundaries of her powers. Some push the limits further than others, of course . . .' She trails off, and I do my best to bring her back.

'Were her boundaries bad?'

'Amber, witches don't like to use labels like "good" and "bad" when it comes to learning magic. Mistakes are made. That's how you learn.'

I'm getting frustrated by yet another dead end. I know the Wicca community is tight, but this is some next-level conspiracy theory happening here. Everything she's saying is so vague. What, does every witch get a He-Who-Must-Not-Be-Named-esque time period that all other witches must keep quiet?

'So you didn't know what she was doing?' I press. 'That she was friends with Victoria?'

Wendy flinches at the sound of that name. 'Of course not!' she says, her voice getting loud. 'Had I known Victoria was previously involved in your mother's journey, I would've personally pulverized her.'

I've never heard Wendy's voice anything above a gentle melody, which causes me to say, 'Wow, so it must've been really bad.'

She takes a deep breath, resetting herself. From the kitchen, she floats the cocoa pot over, and even though I'm always around magic, it surprises me at first because Mom rarely uses her powers to do mundane tasks such as getting refills. She calls it lazy, but I'm guessing Wendy is trying to calm her chi by focusing on something else. She refills my mug without lifting a finger and then sets her attention back on me.

'I know I'm not a witch, but I am her daughter,' I say. 'I just want to know.'

'The truth is,' Wendy starts, her volume returning to normal, 'I really can't say for sure. I know your grandma, my dear Edie, was worried about your mom back then. And Edie herself was a wild one, so for her to be worried was a concern. It was something she didn't like to talk about, though. As her best friend, I could only sense that something was awry.' She places a hand on my shoulder. 'I'm sorry.'

I slump back in my seat. Another dead end. 'But what about my dad? Did you know him?'

'A little. I went to their wedding. They were both enamored of each other.' She gives a sad smile. 'But it was pretty clear from the start they wouldn't be a match. Too bad you weren't around then to tell them so,' she says with a wink.

I thank Wendy for her time and exit as quickly as possible. It feels like I will never learn what my mom was up to when she was younger. My imagination starts dreaming up horrible nightmare scenarios, including puppy sacrifices and cities in flames, but my hellish landscape visions are interrupted by an equally chilling sound coming from the real world.

A shrill cry from high above stops me in my tracks. I look up, but a streetlamp blinds my vision. The piercing call continues, soaring above, so I walk half a block away from the light and search the sky again, finding nothing. The sound circles around me, and it's so sharp, I instinctively cover my ears to keep them from splitting. I look around frantically to find the culprit, but the pitch is so jarring, it's setting my nerves on end.

Instinct taking over, I start running, until a small dark bird lands before me on the sidewalk. A raven, menacing, stares at me with its beady black eyes, chest puffed out, almost daring me to take another step. I've held countless handfuls of raven feathers in my lifetime but never been in the presence of the bird itself. And why would I want to, seeing as how it's a symbol of death? I slowly walk backward, wondering how one bird could be so intimidating. When it decides I've backed far enough off its turf, the bird lets out one final croak before taking off for the sky, and I watch as it soars over the neighborhood, until it's circling one area in particular. I slowly walk under the raven's tight flight pattern and realize where I am.

This is Iris and Ivy's street. This raven is claiming its turf.

This is exceedingly not good.

# Twenty-three

I CAN'T GET THE RAVEN'S SHRIEK OUT OF MY HEAD. IT HAS permanently speared my senses, leaving me on edge. Why was it looming over the Chamberlains' street? Was that the bird that beaked Ivy? It's not like ravens are native to Chicago, and an omen of death is not something to take lightly. I want to call Amani, to see if she can conjure up any visions of impending doom, but I don't think she's in the mood to come to my aid right now. I can't let that keep me from checking in on Ivy and Iris, though. And since Ivy probably won't accept my help, I should probably bring backup.

I'm working on a strawberry glaze to drizzle over animal body parts I can't even name during a particularly slow night at the Black Phoenix. Standing next to me in silence is

Marcus, who is deveining shrimp with extreme care. I don't want to disrupt his concentration, but we've been working here for hours with so few orders and even fewer words. I can't take it anymore.

'Hey, Marcus?' I venture. 'Can I ask you a favor?'

He turns to me with a look that reads 'how dare you?' but then melts into an unresisting 'sure.'

'I have a friend who could benefit from your expertise.'

'Which is?' he asks, all downtrodden.

'Cooking, obviously.'

This elicits a tiny smile. 'OK, I suppose.'

'Specifically, I need some recipes that require little to no chewing.'

He raises an eyebrow.

'It'll make sense when we get there.'

Once the kitchen closes, we snag a few leftover ingredients Marcus needs. He describes a pumpkin squash soup so rich and creamy, I plan to snag a slurp for myself.

The cab ride over is slightly awkward; crammed in the backseat with a heaping bag of supplies, I can feel Marcus sneaking quick glances my way, and I need to be conscious of his crush. I don't want to do anything that could be construed as flirtatious or cute, although I didn't think I was doing those things before, and he developed feelings for me anyway. I try to think of neutral, non-heart-swelling topics.

'How 'bout them Bulls?' I randomly blurt.

'Um, I don't really watch basketball,' Marcus says, staring at the back of the driver's seat.

'Yeah, me neither.' I rearrange my scarf to give myself something to do. The cabbie's incoherent talk radio fills the space.

'Amber,' Marcus says softly. 'I don't want you to feel weird around me.'

'Oh, I don't feel weird—'

'You do, I can tell.' Damn werewolves and their body-language-reading abilities.

'No, Marcus, it's just that . . . I don't have a lot of friends, to be honest, and after what happened at the bakery, I don't want to lose you from my life.'

'I don't either,' he replies. 'The poem; it was too much.' I start to reply, but he adds, 'Please don't let it mess everything up.'

'I won't if you won't.'

'Deal.' He leans back in relief.

'So what we're about to walk into . . . it's gonna be a little strange,' I say.

'Oh?'

I give him some background just as we pull up to the Chamberlains' brownstone. I eye the sky for the raven, but the menacing bird is nowhere to be seen. Ivy answers the door after several rings.

'What are you doing here?' she asks in her usual disapproving tone.

'Special delivery!' I singsong.

'You brought me . . . a man?' she asks. Marcus shifts uncomfortably, looking for an escape route. 'Is this some sort of new matchmaker service?'

'Huh? No! *He's* not for you; it's what he can do,' I say. 'Can you let us in and show us where the kitchen is? It's freezing out here.'

'I guess,' Ivy says. She closes the door behind us and leads the way into one of the most gleaming, most modern kitchens I've ever seen. I start unloading our foodstuffs on the counter. Marcus, back in his element, starts searching through the cabinets for the kitchenware he needs.

'What are you guys doing?' Ivy asks. Having fallen from her previous siren standards, she looks like a complete disaster: barely brushed hair, faded T-shirt, sweatpants. Not to mention the bird bruise. It's more than obvious that being a caretaker is taking a toll. Of course, by Amber standards, she looks like a Tuesday.

'We're making dinner for you and Iris. I figured you could use a break,' I say, whisking some whole milk to prep for a banana pudding dessert.

At full strength, I'm sure Ivy would brush off our offer, making some sarcastic remark about not eating food prepared by peasant hands, but she's so emotionally spent she just sinks into the closest chair and rests her head on folded arms. Her shoulders shake with silent sobs, and Marcus and I share a quick look of panic. Do I go over and comfort her? Or is prepping the food comfort enough?

Before I need to decide, she picks her head back up, wiping away the evidence. 'God, Amber,' she starts, 'how can you be like this?'

'Like what?' I ask, slicing bananas.

'This!' She gestures toward our efforts. 'I have been nothing but horrible to you. How can you even be here right now? Is this, like, a witch thing? Putting positive energy into the world so that similar energy comes back to you?'

I shrug, trying to focus on the task at hand. 'Nah, I mean, yes, that is a witch thing, but I wasn't thinking that. I'm not a witch, remember? And I don't know. You are definitely the worst, but you're also going through the worst time ever. And anything is better with pudding.' Marcus smiles as he stirs the beginnings of his soup, and Ivy accepts my answer without reply.

Once everything's ready, we take a tray up to Iris, who is in almost the exact same spot where I left her days ago. She makes no acknowledgement of our presence and barely blinks as we set up next to her. Marcus approaches her carefully, like a dog sniffing out a stranger. Even though I explained the situation beforehand, it's much different seeing a human compost pile than hearing it described.

'So this is what a person looks like without free will?' he asks, watching her closely. He gets the same stern look on his face I've seen on him when he's trying to figure out a new recipe: lips pinched, brow furrowed. He's clearly horrified but doing his best to keep his expression in check.

'I guess so,' I say. I brush a strand of her blond hair back, to no reaction. He brings a spoonful of soup to her lips, and Ivy was not joking: Iris doesn't move to slurp it down, even with how delicious it smells. We have to physically open her mouth and guide it down, letting her throat muscles take over from there.

Marcus is so gentle with her, taking his time with a painstakingly slow process, and I am filled with gratitude. 'Thank you for doing this,' I say.

'I'm happy to help you,' Marcus admits. 'I've seen a lot of things, working at the Phoenix, but nothing like this.'

'What's the craziest thing you've ever seen? Before this, obviously.'

He scoops another bite. 'Hmm, probably the time a random vampire got staked. It was nuts. Vincent lost his mind.'

'Yikes.'

'But even that was not as intense as this. That vamp had it coming. This girl doesn't seem like she would deserve this.'

'She doesn't,' I say, but have to wonder: Do any of us deserve our battle scars from love? How often are the innocent damaged just because they opened their hearts? Even Marcus, fresh off a rejection, must be still licking his wounds, and yet he's here, working beside me. Why do we do these things to ourselves?

The two of us wander back downstairs and start cleaning up the kitchen. Ivy is collapsed on the table beside us, her soup bowl licked clean. There's a trail of drool coming from her mouth, and while the past me would've taken a picture for future blackmail, the current Amber lets it slide. She seems to be in the world's most uncomfortable position, and yet she's sleeping soundly, so we let her lie. Until, that is, we hear the front door click open and shut.

'What was that?' I ask Marcus, my skin instantly prickled in goose bumps.

He too is on sudden high alert. 'I don't know,' he says, barely moving, like a guard dog trying to detect danger.

I tiptoe out of the kitchen, peeking around the corner. Did Ivy's parents come home early? Or maybe the butler is dropping off groceries? 'Hello?' I call out into the darkness.

After no reply, Marcus picks up a rolling pin, and the two of us venture farther into the house. He walks ahead of me, reaching back every so often to make sure I'm there. Room after room is filled with silence. The less we find, the more imaginary spiders crawl up and down my spine.

'We didn't imagine it, did we? That sound?' I ask, voice shaking. 'Someone came in the house, right?'

He nods, keeping the rolling pin raised liked a sword. 'Or left it,' he adds. We lock eyes for a split second and then bolt up the stairs to Iris's room.

'Iris!' I call out, flinging open the door. But she's not there. Minutes ago, she couldn't even feed herself, and now she's disappeared. 'Iris!'

What just happened? How could she suddenly get up and walk away? Victoria told her not to leave until the full moon. Did the magic wear off? Did her free will come back? What is going on?!

We run back downstairs, and I shake Ivy awake. 'Ivy! Get up! Iris is gone!'

She snaps up, bewildered, practically falling off her chair. 'Huh? What? What do you mean she's gone?'

I don't have words – I don't know what's happening. But Ivy must see the fear in our eyes, because she jumps up, and the three of us grab our coats and boots and tumble out the door.

We run around the block, trying to pick up Iris's trail. It's getting late, and it's pretty cold, so it's not like there are tons of people crowding up the sidewalks.

'She couldn't have gotten far,' I say, more to convince myself than anything else. 'I mean, right? She hasn't been mobile in days.' We look ahead a few blocks in every direction until we spot her, headed west on Webster Avenue. She glides like a ghost, her white coat and blond hair shining beacons in the dark, and we sprint toward her.

But just when we're getting close, a familiar shrill fills the air, and the raven dive-bombs us from seemingly nowhere. Like a scene from the Hitchcock film, the bird attacks me, digging its claws into my shoulder. I scream in pain, and Marcus whacks it away, but within seconds, the raven circles back for more, pecking my ears and neck with its beak. It feels like the tip of a cheese knife: not sharp enough to break my skin but pointed enough to do some damage. I swing my arm blindly and connect. The bird squawks and moves on to Marcus and Ivy – relentless. Ivy screams in fury as the bird tangles in her hair, nearly scraping her cheek with its talons.

Then, out of nowhere, the raven backs off, soaring up into the sky in Iris's direction. We pause to catch our breath, but even before we're fully restored, Ivy charges off again toward her sister, and the bird suddenly swoops in for an extra round.

'Wait a minute,' I say to the sound of Ivy's shrieks. 'Ivy! Just hold still for a second.'

'What?' she screams, blond hair flying among black wings. 'STOP MOVING TOWARD IRIS!'

'Why?' she cries, but does as she's told. The second she stops, the raven detaches from her and flies off after Iris again.

'I think . . . the raven is protecting her, or something,' I say, watching it hover above Iris like an evil bodyguard.

'How could it possibly be protecting her?' Ivy snarls.

'I mean, it's watching over her. It seems like it's trying to make sure she gets to wherever she's going without interference. Every time we try to get close to her, the bird circles back, giving a warning swoop.'

Marcus, who's been relatively quiet, looks at me and adds, 'I think you're right. That raven is on a mission.'

Ivy shakes her battered and bruised head. 'So, what, we just let her disappear into the night with this bird babysitter?'

'Maybe we can get Iris to come to us instead,' Marcus suggests.

Keeping a safe distance, we each take turns yelling Iris's name, but she never looks back, never stops walking forward. Although we can't get close, we keep her in our sights, while trying to stay out of sight from the cracked-out bird.

While we continue ducking around corners and crouching behind parked cars, Ivy starts to cry, a mix of exhaustion and terror taking over her. Marcus wraps an arm around her, assuming the role of pack leader. 'I don't understand,' he says as calmly as possible. 'How can she choose where to go without free will?'

'Well, there's no way she's *choosing* this,' I say, glaring up at the black devil in the distance. 'No rational person starts heading off in the night into the middle of nowhere with a kamikaze avian accomplice.' I turn to Ivy. 'Was that the bird that attacked you?'

She wipes her nose, huffing. 'Yes. That vile piece of feathered garbage! What is it doing to her?' She gestures ahead toward her sister. 'How is she just following it blindly?'

This has Victoria written all over it, and even though I don't want any more harm coming Iris's way, trailing her may help us learn more about what that crazy witch is up to. Having a siren as a puppet is a scary weapon indeed; when you manipulate the ones who can manipulate others, is there any greater power than that?

# Twenty-four

WE FOLLOW IRIS TO A DIRTY TUNNEL UNDER THE EXPRESSWAY. The dark entrance swallows her white outline whole, while the villainous raven swoops in behind. I'm surprised, really, that the evil thing doesn't set up shop outside like a surly bouncer, making sure no one follows in. But I guess it is a birdbrain, after all. Once Iris disappears, Marcus, Ivy, and I slump down next to a trash can that looks like it hasn't been emptied in years. Our tired faces are covered in shadows.

'Now what?' Ivy asks, resting her forehead on her knees.

Rationally, I know none of us should follow Iris in there; Gods only know what's waiting on the other side. A vampire den? A demon nest? Calling for backup or heading for the hills would be the smartest choice, but there's no time for either, because if we can gather even a crumb of information that will help us later, jumping into the unknown will be worth it. 'We keep following,' I respond with dread.

Ivy looks up, eyes so heavy they could easily just retreat to the back of her skull. Her lip is on the verge of quivering as she says, 'I don't think I can.'

I honestly don't know if I can either. It's not a place I'd want to be anyway, since after spending an hour being the world's most inexperienced secret agents, we're exhausted, sore, and all out of adrenaline to keep us moving. But we've gone this far, and Iris could be in serious danger.

'I'll just go, get the deets,' I say, standing to brush some dirty snow off my pants. 'You guys stay here till I come back.'

'No way,' Marcus says, getting to his feet. 'You can't go in there alone.'

'Well, Ivy can't sit out here alone, and I don't think it'd be good for her general well-being to see her sister put through a potential second round of magical torture.'

Ivy doesn't even flinch at my suggestion of suffering. She's definitely hit a wall of her own. We are not exactly in the best part of the city, and having her sit here like a tasty treat for unscrupulous souls is the worst idea yet.

'Fine,' Marcus says, following my wavelength. 'But be safe. Stay out of sight. Please.' He squeezes my shoulder as his face pinches in synchronized concern.

'I will be careful. Extra careful. All the careful.'

And with that, I head into the unknown, resuming the tiptoe walk of the night. As soon as I step inside the tunnel, the city backdrop disappears, and I can only assume this passage is enchanted with portal-like qualities. Great. In an effort to remain unseen, I press myself against the walls, which feel like they're covered in slime. The crisp night air has been replaced by a foul *eau de death*. I can barely see my hand in front of my face, so I rely on the goo walls to guide me, inching ever inward.

There's a light at the end of the tunnel – literally – and my eyes start to adjust. I hold my breath as I get closer, partially because of the smell but mostly because I don't want the raven to detect my arrival. I hear a murmur of voices and strain to pick out the words. Finally, I'm close enough to see two figures – Iris and an old man – so I pick a spot in the shadows to crouch down in a ball, making myself as small as possible as I eavesdrop on the conversation already under way.

'I was told you could help me,' Iris is saying, in a voice that echoes her own, yet is completely detached and emotionless. After spending forever staring at her back, I finally have a view of her face, not that there's much to see: her eyes are glassed over, her jaw slack, no life in her body or voice. Without her free will, this is definitely not the passionate speaker I've come to know. She may as well be a reanimated corpse.

'Perhaps,' says the man, a toothless grin peeking through a long, unruly, navel-length beard. It's the most magnificent yet bizarre tangle of facial hair I've ever seen; it may be the dim lighting, but it almost appears like there are streaks of moldy green woven throughout the gray. I squint to make out more of his details. He's sitting in a massive pile of trash, wrinkled skin grabbing on to his makeshift garbage throne. His feet are submerged in a puddle of very murky water, and the whole scene has me craving a scalding hot shower.

'We are one and the same, after all,' robot Iris says. The old man strokes his mildewed beard in approval. *One and the same?* What does that mean? How could Iris be the same as this trash dweller?

'Tell me more about this witch you want to punish,' says the man, with a weird amount of excitement.

'She's your typical two-faced, goody-goody Wicca,' Iris starts, her words biting but her face neutral. 'She puts on this Mother Earth facade, but it's all for show. I'm tired of her thinking she's better than everyone else.' I wish she were talking about the actual witch who has caused her harm, but it's clear she's describing my mom, like a recording of Victoria that's been run through a distortion filter.

The man sends a creepy chuckle echoing down the tunnel. 'Yes, witches are a terrible breed. Completely worthless. They have to use silly words and potions to get the job done. They don't have any real magic inside them, not like us.'

I'm racking my brain, trying to understand how this jerk pile has the balls to associate himself with Iris, when it hits me: he's a nix. Of course! Hello, Amber! Basically the male equivalent of sirens, nixes are water sprites that also have the ability to mind-warp unsuspecting creatures to bend to their will. Only problem is, a nix loses his powers way faster than a siren, usually burning through his allotted magic before he's barely figured out what to do with it. This leads to an almost universal hatred of any supernatural who can sustain her ability for more than half a second, with witches being enemy number one. You don't come across many a nix, since most of them become so intolerable post-magic burnout that they find it hard to trick someone into reproducing. They sure do love sirens, though, since they share the whole from-the-sea, limited-time specialness.

'Agreed,' Iris monotones. 'So you will help me?'

He plunges a hand into his garbage heap, rummaging around. I can't imagine what he will pull out of there, but it can't be good. He digs down deeper, at one point tossing his lengthy beard out of the way; I realize now the green strands are traces of seaweed. From out of the wreckage he eventually pulls some sort of black orb, about the size of Windy City's average-size crystal balls. With a dirty sleeve, he attempts to polish it up, only adding to its smudge.

'This pearl . . . in the hands of a witch, this could do real damage,' he says, eyeing his treasure, 'which is why I'd only

226

ever share it with someone like me and not one of *them*.' With two hands he gives it to Iris, like the passing of a precious family heirloom.

So this is the real reason Victoria took Iris's free will. She needed a body to get here and do what she could not. Nixy here is clearly some prejudiced buttwipe that would never give a witch this magical item, and Victoria needed a siren – someone a nix would trust – to run her errand. That murderous raven must have sent some wacko decoded message to Iris to get her here. I don't know what that black pearl does, but it can't be good.

My legs start to fall asleep in my balled-up pose, and I tumble back, bottom landing in more of the tunnel's putrid water. The raven, which has been chilling on one of the nix's trash piles, darts its attention toward the darkness, feathers ruffled, and I hold my breath in panic. After a few seconds of silence, the bird relaxes, but my heartbeat continues at a furious pace. I need to get out of here. If this water sprite was going to hurt Iris, he would have done so already, and it looks like she got what she came for.

Or, I should say, what Victoria came for.

# Twenty-five

'MOM, HAVE YOU EVER HAD USE FOR A BLACK PEARL?' WE'RE in our kitchen the next morning, getting ready. It's a big day, for sure, because I have my Culinary Institute interview in a few hours. Too bad my head is now filled with nightmares of the nix's seaweed beard strangling the life out of me while Zombie Iris and her pet raven watch. Mom's sipping coffee while I stir waffle batter in an attempt to calm myself. I know I need to tell Mom about what happened, but I'm scared she will strangle me after learning about my involvement in last night's events.

'Black pearl? No,' she says, not looking up from her grimoire.

'Are they, like, scary or something?'

'They are incredibly rare. I wouldn't say the object itself is scary, but I've heard the spells one can unlock with them are rather dangerous.' With this, her suspicion grows, and she sets down her mug. 'Why?'

I take a beat, ladling brown sugar blueberry mix into the waffle maker. 'Um, because I have it on good authority that a certain witch may have acquired a certain rare item.'

Mom's face grows stern. 'How good of an authority?'

The sizzling batter behind me matches my crackling nerves. 'Uh, a personal account?' I tell her everything, every super-weird detail, but though I expect her to eviscerate me on the spot, she remains still, her face changing from initial anger to fear. Real, tangible fear fills the room, and I know she's lost hold of her usual Wicca serenity. When I'm done, silence sits between us, with only the timer from the waffle maker beeping.

'This . . . is much worse than I expected,' Mom finally says, gripping the table for stability. 'Victoria is using this poor girl as a weapon, to get back at me.'

'Get back at you for what, though? Kicking her out of your coven? She had no right to be there in the first place. You were staying cool to keep everyone safe.'

Mom shakes her head. 'It's not about just that.'

'Then what?'

She stands abruptly and walks out of the room.

'Mom!' I call after her. She doesn't stop, so I grab her arm. 'Why won't you just tell me?'

'Because!' she yells, the sudden volume change startling. 'Because there are some things you don't want your teenage daughter to know, all right?!' She shakes her arm free and storms off to her room, slamming the door. The waffle iron beeps again, and I walk over to pull the plug, my appetite lost.

So much is happening, and I have no one to talk to. My best friend thinks I'm horrible; my own mom won't even have a real conversation with me. And Charlie ... He's practically disappeared off the face of the earth. I miss sharing my experiences with him, the way he'd always listen even though my world is so much different from his. He never judged or made me feel crazy; he took the supernatural struggles in stride. I'm thinking of him when the words I need to see you ignite my phone.

Charlie.

He misses me. He wants me. He has not given up on me.

Elation. Pure elation. How five little words can set off fireworks in my veins is a mystery I don't need explained. I start flitting around the room like I imagine fairies do when they can finally unfurl their wings after a long day of assimilating in human society. Maybe I was wrong all along. Maybe Charlie and I have a connection that defies the basic patterns of love and courtship. Somehow, someway, our pairing is stronger than signals pointing us elsewhere. Screw destiny, screw the Fates. I told Charlie his match yet he still wants ME. That has to be saying something.

I'm flying so high, I'm about to mix myself one of Mom's sedative elixirs to calm myself down, until I realize the text didn't come from Charlie after all: it's from Ivy. I got so caught up in the message, I didn't bother to check the sender. My manic twirling stops, mood slashed and gutted.

What's wrong? I text back, my fingers groaning with every letter.

**Just meet me at Diversey Harbor in 30 minutes.**

I kind of have an important appointment today, I text back.

**AMBER.**

Fine!

It will take me that long to get over to that part of the city, but at least I'll have something to do other than wallow.

As I step off the bus, icy wind lashes my face, and I think, *I could have been with Charlie right now.* Reunited, wrapped up warm in his arms, instead of braving frigid lake effects. Except that I couldn't, since he doesn't need to see me and everything is just as it was.

Diversey Harbor is a bend in the lakefront where the members of Chicago's upper crust park their booze-cruise boats during the warmer months. The docks are empty now, their tenants holed up somewhere much cozier for winter, mass vacancy casting an eerie feel. Ice-cold water gently laps at the shore, and I pull my coat tighter as I look for Ivy.

I spot her sitting in silence, sunlight illuminating her blond curls. She rocks herself gently, blowing hot breath into her mittened hands. She's practically blue: not at all at home with the ice I tend to associate her with.

'What's wrong?' I call out as I approach, scaring her to the point of nearly knocking her off the bench. Clearly, the aftermath of last night is sticking with her too. 'Did something else happen with Iris?'

This would be the part where Ivy delivers her requisite glare, but she doesn't, looking at me instead with tired eyes. 'C'mon,' she croaks, and starts plodding off farther down the dock, forcing me to follow.

'For reals, what is going on?' I repeat, once I catch her side.

She blinks furiously, eyelashes crusted with snow crystals. I myself have blurred vision from the freezing wind.

'Iris's phone has been buzzing like crazy,' she begins. 'I wasn't going to do anything about it, but the sound she has set for text messages is like a chirpy bird that won't stop squawking. Since she doesn't have the free will to check it' – she gives me a piercing side-eye – 'I needed to make it stop. I thought about smashing the damn thing, but decided setting it to silent would be nicer. Once I picked it up, I saw all the texts were from Brooke.'

I stop walking. 'I'm sorry, but how does a mermaid have a cell phone? If my phone touches water for a millisecond, I have to submerge it in rice before it short-circuits.'

'Amber, keep up!' Ivy turns back to me. 'I don't want to be out here all day; it's freezing!' I hear her cursing under her breath, even from several feet away. 'And it's not like Brooke's carrying an iPhone in her seashells. Iris got her a burner she keeps on the shore so they could stay in communication during this transition phase.'

This is blowing my mind. 'But how does she even text? Aren't her fingers all pruney? Can she even work the screen?'

'STOP IT. You are focusing on the wrong crap, OK? She has a phone; they text each other. The end!'

'OK, OK, sheesh.' But I still have more questions. 'Brooke is living in Lake Michigan, though? That sounds really murky. Not to mention cold as hell. Aren't mermaids supposed to be best friends with dolphins?'

Ivy rolls her eyes. 'You know, for someone who takes such offense at witch stereotypes, you sure do like to pull out ridiculous tropes for others.' Zing. 'And besides, she's not living there permanently. She's just waiting for my sister, and then they'll swim off toward the Gulf, where it's warm and tropical and fitting of your perceived visual.'

We've stopped now, pausing on the edge of slip number nineteen. It's just an empty rectangle of water, but Ivy is peering down like there's treasure at the bottom.

'When I picked up her phone, Brooke's messages were getting progressively more panicked. *Where are you? . . . I'm worried . . . I love you, please respond . . .* Blah, blah. She's been freaking out, so I texted back that I'd come meet her.'

'Aww, that's so sweet of you,' I say, more condescending than I mean. 'But I thought you don't want them together? Why even bother? Why not just let Brooke drift aimlessly out to sea?'

'I *don't* want them together,' she says. 'But that doesn't matter now, does it? And besides, I've spent a lot of time feeling completely clueless over how to reach my sister, so I know it's not a good place to be.'

I'm about to congratulate Ivy on her growth as a human being, when something pokes out of the water. Tentative at first, like a submarine scope surveying the shore, Brooke's aqua eyes hover on the water's surface, ensuring she is safe. She's so still, barely causing a ripple, as if she is actually part of the water itself. If I hadn't come here specifically to meet a mermaid, I wouldn't even notice her careful emergence.

She recognizes Ivy, eyebrows knitting in confusion. After glancing around for Iris, her head fully pops out of the lake, revealing long strawberry-blond strands that curl around her shoulders like a shawl. I can't even imagine how cold the water must be. She surely must need any type of cover she can get.

'Ivy, what are you doing here?' Brooke asks, grabbing on to the side of the dock. 'Where is Iris?'

'She . . . can't come,' Ivy says, genuine regret lacing her words.

'Why not? Is she OK?'

Ivy bites her lip, a shiver running through her. She's so timid, reserved. I don't know if I'll ever get used to her being something other than a commanding Ice Queen. She seems paralyzed by the events of last night, so whether I'm supposed to or not, I step in. 'There's been a development. With Iris's spell.'

Brooke splashes over to me, suddenly aware of my existence. 'What do you mean? What happened?' I can't tell if her lip is quivering from the cold or fear of what I'll say next.

I give a high-level recap of Iris's free-will extraction, leaving out the frightening visuals that will haunt me for a lifetime. Ivy, for one, doesn't seem like she could handle it right now, and I'm not familiar with Brooke's constitution.

The mermaid sinks back into the water once I'm done, like the *Titanic* surrendering to the sea. For a moment only the sound of our frozen breath fills the air.

'Do you think she's OK?' I ask Ivy.

'How could she be? *I'm* not OK.'

I nod, searching for scales beneath the surface. There's a faint green glimmer hovering below, and we wait to let her process.

Brooke peeks back up, eyes cloudy, and I wonder what it feels like to cry underwater. 'I didn't mean for this to happen,' she says. 'I didn't realize it would be so hard.'

This hits Ivy the wrong way. 'You mean, you didn't think it would be so hard to switch species? Hello! She's getting a tail *for you*. All of this is because of you!' She looks like she's about to stomp on Brooke's fingers clinging to the dock, so I gently pull Ivy back to a safer distance.

'It wasn't my idea! Iris wanted to do this,' Brooke says. 'When we met, I didn't even allow myself the thought of us being together, because how would it even work? But Iris reassured me it could. She said it wasn't a big deal for a siren to return to the sea.'

'Not a big deal?!' Ivy yelps.

'In that sirens had done it before, I guess,' Brooke clarifies. 'She made it seem like it was almost expected. If I had known this would happen . . .'

'What? You would've told her not to?'

'Of course!' Brooke cries, splashing in frustration. 'Do you think I want anything bad to happen to her? I love her!'

With tensions rising, I step in. 'No one wants anything bad for Iris,' I reply. 'We all have her best intentions at heart, even if we want different things.' Realizing an opportunity, I press on. 'Brooke, I have to ask: What will Iris's life be like once she's a mermaid?'

Brooke tilts her head to one side. 'What do you mean?'

'Like, what do you do all day, beside swim with the fishes?'

She looks confused, like she's unsure what I'm asking. 'Well, I do a lot. I wake up, I go to work—'

'You have a job?' I interrupt.

'Of course I do,' she says, slightly offended. 'Merpeople are the ones who keep the oceanic community running. I mean, you can't rely on sharks to be law keepers.'

'So you're, like, in the government?'

'Yes. Iris has told me my job is the equivalent of what a mayor does on land. I hold weekly reef meetings, alert the community to current changes, send out public service announcements on the dangers of fishermen's bait. Once Iris joins me, she wants to get involved as well. Or . . . *if* she joins me . . .'

'Wow.' I guess life as a mermaid isn't a 24/7 tropical vacation after all. Maybe my worries are unfounded? 'Don't worry, Brooke, we won't let Victoria win. My mom is a witch, and she's doing everything she can to overturn this trick.'

237

This reassurance does little to calm Brooke, and why would it? She doesn't know me or Mom. She only knows her girlfriend is in trouble. I kneel down, laying my frosty hand on top of hers. Our eyes meet, and I'm given another view into the mermaids' romantic future. Brooke and Iris, swimming together, hand in hand, in water so clear, I can see all the way down to the ocean floor. They're surrounded by tropical fish and hot-pink coral, and their smiles are so bright, they're like sunlight kissing the waves. I squeeze her freezing fingers, wishing I could transfer this vision to give her hope.

'You'll be together,' I whisper. 'It's meant to be.'

Her expression brightens slightly. Perhaps Iris shared her matchmaking experience with Brooke. Still, our news has clearly exhausted her, and she seems eager to be alone.

'Thank you,' she replies. 'Please, try to keep me updated with any changes. I'll be there on the full moon, waiting.' She starts sinking back, but not before adding, 'And tell Iris I love her. Hopefully . . . that will help.' Brooke swims away, her shiny tail lapping the water a few times before she disappears completely.

Back home, I can't seem to get warm, no matter how many blankets I pile on. The events of the morning have left me drowning, submerged in cold from my head to my heart. Thinking of Brooke, and the guilt she must be feeling over setting her love on a difficult path, I can't say it's something I'm unfamiliar with. The choices we make while under love's spell sometimes have unexpected consequences.

# Twenty-six

I'M FIDGETING TOO MUCH. PROBLEM IS, I KNOW I'M FIDGETING too much, and the acknowledgement of my fidgeting is making me fidget more. Everything is uncomfortable: this plastic waiting-room chair, this too-tight-across-the-shoulders blazer Mom insisted conveys professionalism and maturity, this scent of slightly burning pie crust wafting from down the hall. This is the Culinary Institute, for Gods' sakes! Shouldn't someone be telling that inexperienced noob to take out the way-too-golden dough already?! The smell of that alone is enough to give me hives.

Multiply all of that by the fact that any minute now, Mr Pru will be ushering me in for my interview. I can't even imagine what he will ask me, and the thought of having to answer questions about myself in real time is pushing me over the edge. It took months to finish my application essay questions, and those were only a few basic queries. Everything I wrote always sounded either too corny or too insincere; finally, I managed to put together something balancing my severe need to be accepted without verging into desperation. But now the questions will surely be harder, and I won't be able to edit my responses. If only there were autocorrect for speech.

It doesn't help, either, that I'm still exhausted from last night's adventure and this morning's mermaid rendezvous. Why all of this had to happen right before the biggest conversation of my life is an unfair mystery. I let out a huge yawn just as Mr Pru emerges from his office. Tall and lanky, with a neatly piled man bun, he's not exactly who I pictured meeting with. Though I envisioned a French pastry chef with a curlicue mustache, now I realize that was probably unrealistic for someone who works in admissions.

'Amber Sand, I presume?' he asks, outstretching his right palm. I shake it heartily (a firm handshake equals success!) as I hop up to my feet. Even though I'm business-casual on top, my trusty Chuck Taylors keep me grounded. I brush back a few wayward peacock strands and do my best to stand tall and confident, even though I'm so nervous, my bones feel liquefied.

'Nice to meet you,' I manage, flashing an unnaturally wide smile. I know they say you should be yourself at these kinds of things, but my instincts are on the verge of tears, which would probably not be the best impression.

'Please, right this way.' His office is filled with expertly photographed pictures of food – extreme close-ups of dripping chocolate and moist cake crumbs. I don't know how he'd get any work done in here, with so many visuals always stimulating his palate.

'So, Amber, the admissions board was quite intrigued by your application,' he says, taking a seat across from me. 'You submitted some of the most unique essays we've read in a while.'

'Oh?' 'Unique' is one of those special words with a large spectrum of definitions, ranging anywhere from 'amazing' to 'what in the world is happening here?' 'I'm not really a writer, you know. It's just that baking is my passion, and I wanted to put that out there.'

He smiles, and my blood pressure goes down a few levels. 'Well, you succeeded on that front. I've never had anyone go into so much detail regarding her feelings toward butter.'

I squeak out a nervous laugh, shifting in my seat. 'Butter is a building block of baking, after all.'

'Indeed.' He beams. 'When did you first start?'

'Um, I've always spent a lot of time in the kitchen with my mom. She' – I try to create a visual that doesn't involve frog legs or bubbling cauldrons – 'taught me the fundamentals.'

'Wonderful. And I see you have some real-world kitchen experience, working at MarshmElla's, is it? Tell me about that.'

'Of course!' And we begin a real dialogue, exchanging kitchen catastrophes and successes, touching on some of our favorite recipes and techniques. It all spills out so effortlessly; for a good while, I forget he's evaluating my responses. The next time I look at the clock, thirty minutes have passed by, and I realize I've stopped sweating profusely.

'Well, Amber, the reason I brought you in today is that here at the Culinary Institute, we work very closely as a team, especially once you choose your specialty,' Mr Pru says. 'Since you're learning a trade, you won't get the experience you require from a textbook, which is why everyone needs to merge together toward a common goal. I like to meet potential candidates to see what kind of vibe the freshman class is gathering, and if students will mesh well together.' He leans forward. 'A true chef, as you know, is difficult to capture on paper. It's essential to understand the beating heart that moves the hands.'

I nod, hoping my heart has proven true. Everything he's saying, everything surrounding me, has 100 percent convinced me that this is where I'm meant to be. I hope he can sense that too.

'I'm conducting these sit-downs throughout the week, and it won't be long thereafter that we make our final decisions.' He stands, walking over to the door. 'In the meantime, it was a pleasure speaking to you, Amber; I thoroughly enjoyed our conversation.'

'Me too, thank you,' I say, shaking his hand again. 'I look forward to hearing from you.'

I leave with a swirl of pride and confidence: two feelings I haven't encountered in quite some time. I'm practically skipping down the street when I hear a familiar voice call out to me. 'Someone's full of sunshine.'

At first, I'm convinced I've imagined it, that my happiness must be manifesting into something truly epic (and delusional). Cautiously, I turn around, just in case the voice's owner is actually there and not singing in my head.

'Charlie?' He's here, in the flesh, not a figment of my imagination. And I've been imagining him a lot, especially since he's been MIA at school and in my life as a whole. I'm left stunned on the sidewalk, because he looks . . . so damn good, as always: the same smushable face and ridiculously warm glow. His peacoat is unbuttoned, revealing a pink button-down with navy-blue woven tie. And a coordinating tie clip, of course. It's all working toward one emotionally paralyzed Amber. 'What are you doing here?'

'I knew you'd be here. Thought I'd see how your interview went.' Putting aside the fact that he came here – FOR ME SPECIFICALLY – I can't help but notice how he's hanging back, not allowing any less than five feet between us. Maybe that's the requisite distance needed while interacting with an ex, or maybe he doesn't trust what either of us would do if we came even closer. If it's the latter, I can't say I fault his logic; seeing him after such a long absence has me ready to smother him on sight. Better to test the waters slowly.

'That's very sweet of you,' I say, keeping myself within the allotted boundary. 'It went really well, I think.'

'Good, good. I'm happy for you.' We're both looking around like it's raining squirrels. Every time I steal a glance his way he's staring elsewhere, and I wonder if he's sneaking peeks at me too. He has to be, right? Or why else would he have come?

'Where have you been?' I ask. 'I haven't seen you at school.'

'Oh, well, my dad had a trip to Shanghai – it's one of Chicago's sister cities. He thought it would be educational for me to come along.'

'China. Wow.'

'Yeah. He goes on trips like that a lot, but I don't always go. The timing for this one . . . happened to work out.'

Good Gods, I didn't realize I had driven him out of the country. That has to be some sort of all-time matchmaker low. 'Was it cool?'

'Honestly?' He lets his gaze finally rest on me. 'It was a nightmare.' I try to fight it, to keep my eyes from meeting his, because the last thing I want is for Kim to interrupt this moment. But there's nowhere else to look; I can feel him staring, begging me to meet his eye. So I do, bracing myself for a scene I haven't had to endure in a while.

Only . . . there's something wrong in the transmission, because when our eyes meet, I'm not flooded with the usual courtship barf-fest I've come to expect. I don't see Kim; I don't even see Charlie: everything blurs to a fuzzy static, like old-timey television stations that didn't have 24/7 programming. I rub my eyes, wondering if I'm having an aneurysm, but the static continues. Charlie, interpreting my reaction as emotional (and not technical) difficulties, asks, 'Are you OK?'

'I'm sorry, I'm just . . . I feel bad you didn't have a good time,' I say, which isn't completely untrue.

'Yeah, well, I was a little distracted,' he admits, turning away, giving me the opportunity to stare without embarrassment. What happened to my visions? Did I short-circuit? I have never, ever looked someone in the eye and been greeted with anything less than total clarity. Am I doing something wrong? Or is it like with Ivy — have I made so many matches that my magic is all used up, leaving me a washed-up matchmaker with nothing left to give?

'I know what you mean,' I say, trying to concentrate on the conversation at hand.

'Do you?' When he looks at me again, his eyes are starting to shine.

'Yes, Charlie, I do. Do you think I wanted to break up with you? That that was fun for me? I lasted as long as I could, but it was eating me alive.'

'And now? How do you feel now?' he asks with accusation, as if the possibility of me feeling better now would be a crime.

'Awful, I feel awful. Everything that's happened has left me totally ripped up inside. I only did what I thought was right; I followed the code I've learned to rely on. I want what's best for us – for you – but I don't know what that is.'

He shakes his head, unsatisfied with my answer. But it's the truth. My heart wants me to leap into his arms, to kiss him like no one is watching, but my head knows I'll only end up in the same place, tortured by his future with another girl. No matter how hard it is for either of us, staying apart seems like the only option.

'Yeah, well, your visions were wrong,' Charlie says.

'You can't know that.'

He kicks a dirty clump of ice. 'Actually, I can.'

Without warning, my heart takes off, thumping so hard it's hard to breathe. 'What do you mean?'

Keeping his focus glued to the sidewalk, he says in the quietest voice possible, 'I kissed Kim.'

Everything around me starts to spin like a Tilt-A-Whirl. 'You . . . what?'

He swallows hard, shaking his head. 'I kissed Kim. I was so mad at you for believing in something other than us that I just had to do it. To prove you wrong.'

247

I laugh in disbelief. 'Let me get this straight. To prove me wrong you went and did the exact thing I predicted?'

'Yes, which I know sounds dumb, but when I kissed her—'

'Stop! I don't want to hear it.'

'When I kissed her,' he repeats forcefully, 'I felt nothing. Like, even less than nothing, if that's possible.'

'Sure, I bet,' I sneer, tears building. 'And I'm guessing she hated it too because kissing you is such torture.'

'She acted like she did. She pushed me off her, saying she could never betray you like that.'

'Well, that makes one of you,' I say.

He frowns, a single tear rolling down his cheek. 'That's not fair.'

Every single vision I've ever had of the two of them starts to play in my head at once, fueling my anger. 'No, you're right. None of this is fair!' I yell. 'It's not fair that I fell for someone destined for someone else, and it's not fair that I'm always right.'

'But you're not! That's what I'm trying to tell you!'

'Whatever. I can't . . . deal with this right now.' He takes a step toward me, but I brush him off.

'Amber, please. I'm telling you this because I love you.'

It takes a second to fully let his words sink in. I'm frozen, the bomb shrapnel paralyzing my heart. Charlie loves me, Charlie loves me . . . but Charlie kissed Kim. What am I supposed to do? I don't know what this means, or how I should feel. Pissed that he kissed another girl, or satisfied that my visions were true? My visions . . . which have suddenly gone offline, feeding me a new layer of supernatural torture. Though I guess if my magic is truly maxed out, I won't have to witness any more visions of Charlie and Kim's love life. Maybe it's a blessing in disguise.

Finally I regain blood flow to my limbs, and I run off, ignoring his calls behind me. I don't want to talk to him again until I process, and until I figure out what this fuzziness in his eyes means.

# Twenty-seven

'BOB, PLEASE STAND STILL. YOU HAVE TO WAIT FOR OUR SIGNAL.' For probably one of the first times in his life, Bob is a bouncing ball of energy, practically hopping from foot to foot. Of course when I need him to stop blocking the dry herb supply closet in the storage room, he's a four-hundred-pound glacier, but when asked to be part of a spell, he's all over the place. Mom's put a lot of effort into his rehabilitation, slowly building his access to magical situations, but since he's twittering like a toddler on Christmas morning, I'd say he still has a way to go.

'Bob! Seriously!' I scold, taking hold of his massive shoulders in an attempt to glue him to the floor.

'I'm sorry, Amber, I just . . . I'm so excited,' he says. He takes a deep breath, inhaling for five long seconds before letting it go. Awareness of breath is a very Zen thing, beloved by Buddhists, Wiccans, and recovering magic addicts everywhere. Bob repeats this several times and finally manages to hit his mark.

'OK, are you ready?' I ask, taking cover behind my matchmaking table. I'm not really a fan of magical side effects; one wrong ingredient and you can find yourself with an extra appendage in the morning (which I know is ridiculous, because obviously it takes more than twelve hours to grow an arm, but still).

Bob exhales his final breath and nods. Mom takes her stance at the opposite end of the shop and pulls a handful of what looks like black sand out of a pail. She gives me the signal, and I yell, 'Charge!'

With surprising speed, Bob barrels toward Mom, fists balled tight and jaw clenched. Mom tosses the sand in Bob's direction and calls out, *'Prohibere!'* in hopes that she will freeze his attack. For a moment, he does stop, both legs dangling midair like giant sausages. It's quite a sight, seeing a man his size suspended in space like he's caught in Jell-O, but his will is too strong, and he breaks free, instantly crashing into Mom and the two display tables flanking her. Feathers and vials go flying as Bob lies lifelessly in a body-crushing heap.

'Mom!' I leap out from my hiding spot and grab hold of Bob's shirttail, trying to roll him off my poor mother. He slumps over, unconscious, into a puddle of hair-removal tonic that broke open. Yikes, that won't end well for him. 'Mom, are you OK?'

Other than a few stray feathers sticking out of her hair, she seems unscathed. 'It's still not right,' Mom grunts, pushing herself up on her elbows. She doesn't seem to care that she was knocked to the ground and almost suffocated to death, or that the shop looks like a rabid donkey ran through it. 'It's not strong enough.'

'But he did pause, at least,' I offer, helping her off the ground. 'That's progress, right?'

She takes no pleasure in small victories, dusting the wreckage from her ankle-length skirt in angry swipes. Ever since Victoria turned Iris into a mindless slave, Mom has been extra hard on herself, spending every moment of free time working on offensive combat spells. Her plan is to have all angles covered on the night of the full moon, making it impossible for Victoria to walk away the victor. But since Mom's usually more of an earth-mother, white-light kind of gal, the darker stuff is taking much more effort. I think about Victoria's words, about Mom abandoning her 'dark' practices, and how that's hurting us now. Not that I want my only parental unit to subscribe to the dark arts, but given the circumstances, I do wonder what the previous Lucille could have whipped out of her arsenal.

Bob comes to, shaking his head like a dog stuck in mud. His shoes crunch glass, and he looks at me with guilt. 'I guess it didn't work?' he asks.

'It's not your fault.' I shrug as Mom storms back into her office. The way she whips the curtain behind her is the clearest 'do not disturb' sign I've ever seen. Bob cringes like he's been given a lashing. 'Don't worry about her,' I add. 'The spell messed up, not you.'

He lumbers to the back room, returning with a broom and trash can. Carefully, we start piecing the store back together, being mindful not to touch any of the liquids with bare skin. 'I just want to help her,' he says, the words laced with sadness.

'Well, Mom's done a lot for you, so that makes sense.'

He shakes his head. 'Not your mom. I mean, yeah, I want to help her too, but I was talking about the girl.'

I stop midsweep. 'You mean Iris?'

'Yeah.' He scoops up an entire display case of tiger's eye stones in one meaty paw.

'You don't even know her.'

'Doesn't matter.' The stones drop back in their wooden bowl, plinking as they pile on. 'I know Victoria.'

I almost drop the broom. 'You do?'

He looks up at me, surprised. 'Yeah,' he confirms, like this isn't a big reveal. 'How did you think your mom and I met?'

I run my fingers through my hair, literally scratching through a decade of memories and references to Mom and Bob's relationship. Did I know how they met? I remember when she first brought him around. I wasn't even working at Windy City yet, but I spent enough time here to be well aware of the minutiae. At that time, we had another employee, Carol, who was obsessed with charm bracelets. I never understood how a witch could allow herself to wear such loud accessories. Didn't she ever need to sneak up on people? Of course, I was obsessed with sneaking up on *her* and stealing the charms one by one, so that's where my seven-year-old head was at.

The first time I saw Bob, he was a snarling, writhing, and frankly frightening version of himself. Today, he can still scare small children just by giving a polite wave, but back then, his presence would have melted their skin. There were times when he'd completely freak out, trying so hard to fight a craving, he'd actually roar with yearning. Hair standing on end, eyes perpetually bloodshot: whatever coursed through his veins was wicked, and the withdrawal process was brutal. Mom didn't let me around him much during his junkie detox stage, saying she'd found him running with a 'bad crowd' and felt he needed a positive environment. I guess I never really pressed for details on what that meant.

'Were you . . . friends with her?' I ask, trying to conceal my burning desire for details. This whole time I had a treasure trove of information right in front of me, stroking a damn rabbit's foot.

'Yeah, we both were: your mom and me.' He frowns. 'Though I don't know how friendly that time was.' His eyes start to glaze over, so I need to be careful not to lose him.

'Tell me how Mom found you.'

He sniffs, rubbing his nose against his bare forearm. 'I don't remember how, exactly. I'd been hanging around Victoria for a while, though, doing . . . bad things.'

'You don't have to tell me about your, um, extracurricular activities,' I say (although I'm desperate to know). 'But I'm confused; I thought my mom had stopped talking to Victoria, like, before I was born.' Based on Mom's grimoire timeline, it seemed like the two parted ways around my parents' wedding.

Bob shrugs. 'Not sure. But Victoria talked about your mom all the time, telling me I could be one of the greats, like how Lucille Sand could've been.'

'Excuse me, *could have*?'

He throws his hands up as if under interrogation. 'Not my words! It's just something she said a lot.'

I shouldn't be surprised – Victoria has made her feelings known about Mom's 'squandered potential' multiple times – but I figured those were insults reserved for in-person assaults. I didn't realize she was slandering Mom's name across the supernatural community.

'And how was she "guiding" you to be better than Mom? Forcing you to sacrifice kittens and drink the blood of the innocent?'

Bob grimaces.

'Oh Gods! I was kidding!' I exclaim.

'But your mom saved me from all that. She is a good witch, and a good person.' He scratches the back of his neck, forehead creased in worry. 'And I bet Iris is a good person too. I don't want her falling into what I did . . . into what Victoria can do.'

I sit back at my matchmaking table, letting everything absorb. The more I learn about Victoria, the more it's hard to picture her being a part of my mom's life. 'I can't believe Mom was friends with someone like that,' I find myself saying aloud.

'They weren't just friends,' Bob says, heading toward the back with a garbage bag slung over his shoulder. 'They were best friends.'

No. No, that's too much. BEST friends? Best friends take companionship to a whole new level. Best friends create an understanding found nowhere else. They rely on each other, offering support and backup without being asked – no need for justification. They crave each other's company, knowing that when they're together, it will always be fun even if they're not doing anything at all. They see the world from the same filter, even if the individual perspectives differ.

Amani and I are best friends. We share everything. There's no way Mom and Victoria could've had a friendship like that.

Amani. I need to talk to my best friend.

# Twenty-eight

'WELCOME TO THE MADNESS! PLEASE WATCH YOUR STEP,' Mrs Sharma says, ushering me inside her home. She has two paper airplanes lodged firmly in her loose waves, and behind her, a primal shriek, the kind only a small boy is capable of, wails through the house. She grips the door as if it could help propel her into the night, far away from the catastrophe building in the background, yet she smiles with acceptance of her fate.

Several more airplanes fly overhead, and I spot the boys crouching behind the couch. They have a small forest of aircraft ready to launch.

'I'm Swiss!' I call out, waving my hands above my head. 'Hold your fire!' The boys giggle as I dash up the stairs. I didn't tell Amani I was stopping by. Hopefully she doesn't kick me out.

I knock on her closed door, admiring her collection of 'Keep Out!' signs. I'm surprised her parents haven't allowed her a lock, in light of the battle zone below.

'Go away!' answers Amani's muffled voice. Maybe this wasn't such a good idea.

'It's Amber,' I reply through the doorjamb.

She hesitates, then says, 'Come in.'

I slip inside, shutting the door behind me. The volume level drops several decibels, and it feels like stepping onto another planet, not just into another part of the house. Amani is curled up on her bed, cocooned in a blanket with her laptop perched on her knees. She could easily be a prisoner of war, rather than a high school student working on English homework.

I stand on the edge of her pink shag rug, not knowing where to place myself. Sitting next to her on the bed would be my normal move, but it seems too forward at the moment. Yet sitting at her desk would be completely unnatural since not even Amani sits there. I stand awkwardly, realizing I should have brought some sort of edible peace offering, so at the very least I'd have something to do with my hands.

Amani, knowing full well I tend to be crap in these kinds of situations, usually takes the lead, but today she sits in silence, fingers on the keyboard but eyes on me. I came over because I needed her, but I need to give her what she needs first.

'How's life?' I ask, feeling stupid as soon as the words leave my lips. *How's life?* Great opening, Amber.

'Life is life,' she says coolly.

'Right. Cool.' I seriously consider throwing myself out the window, but then the words tumble out first. 'Only no, not cool. My life has been crap. It's only been a few days without us talking, and everything feels like garbage. I miss you so much, and it's all my fault. I've been a complete selfish baby when it comes to Kim; of course the two of you are friends. I guess I was so wrapped up in my own head, I didn't realize she had become important to you.'

Amani closes her laptop. 'Amber—'

'No, I'm not finished yet. I feel like I'm broken. Like I can't get anything right. I've been so used to trusting what was happening inside my head, I stopped looking at what's happening before my eyes. Clearly, I need to put less weight on my matchmaking, because who knows if it's even accurate anymore? Iris is matched with Brooke, and now she's sitting like a lump of mashed potatoes because of it. You are matched with Vincent, and yet he makes your skin crawl.'

'Amber—'

'Please let me finish.'

'NO!' she blurts, pounding a fist into her pillow. 'I have to tell you something.'

I stop short, unsure of what this revelation could bring. That I've been replaced, my short absence resulting in Kim being named as the official Best Friend? That I was right all along, and now Kim and Charlie have fallen madly in love? I cringe, as either is definitely an end-of-the-world scenario.

'I . . . went on a date, with Vincent,' she says, choosing her words carefully as if she doesn't quite believe them herself. She winces, mouth curling up in a question, and I can't tell if she's about to burst into tears or song. 'It was an accident, actually.'

I snort unintentionally. 'Um, how do you accidentally go on a date with someone?'

She relaxes, exhaling a small laugh. 'Well, it takes skill. Definitely an advanced move.'

I'm stunned. This is not at all what I was expecting. 'How? How did it happen?'

'I went by the Black Phoenix, hoping to catch you. Vincent met me at the door, and said you weren't there, but we got to talking . . . then somehow, we ended up in a booth, drinking lattes. The place was closed, so it was just us, sitting in the dark with a few tea lights.' A faint smile blossoms. 'With no one else around, he seemed to mellow a bit, you know? Not so flashy-flashy and over the top. He talked to me like a real person.'

I can't believe it. I mean, I should believe it; I've been envisioning it for years. But Amani's first reaction to him was filled with such disgust, I thought she'd never recover. To hear her recall time spent with Vincent in a positive light is shocking.

'That's awesome,' I say, tempering my enthusiasm so it doesn't come off like an 'I told you so.' 'Do you think . . . you'll go out with him again?'

She shakes her head, but the sunshine remains. 'I don't know. I haven't really processed it yet.' Her glance falls downward, long waves concealing her face. 'I didn't have anyone to talk to.'

I approach carefully, choosing my steps as if anyone could set off a land mine. I sit down before her and pick my words with the same precision.

'What about Kim? She seems like she'd be really good at this stuff.'

'Yeah,' Amani says, 'but it's not the same. She doesn't have the backstory, and it's too exhausting to explain it. It's better to talk to someone who just knows and doesn't require footnotes.'

Our eyes lock, and I instantly feel like I'm going to start crying. Not because Amani and Vincent are taking a moonlit stroll through my head (they are), but I'm so relieved she's missed me just as much as I've missed her. I don't deserve it – I've legit been the worst – but I still welcome it, praising the Gods I haven't lost my true soul mate.

'I know exactly what you mean,' I say. My head is so crammed with the events of the past few days, there's barely room for normal brain function. 'If I didn't say it before, I am really sorry.'

'I know.'

'You are my best friend, and I cannot take you for granted.'

She nods and reaches out for me. I lunge forward, practically suffocating her in a ferocious hug. It feels so good to be reunited with this magical girl, I may never let go.

'So,' I start, my arms still squeezing her rib cage. 'Did he kiss you?'

Amani delivers more details of the date (no kiss, but there was a friendly hug) and how Vincent's texted her a few times. She asks me what I've been up to, and I unleash a tidal wave of emotions, going on about Marcus's poem, Iris's tunnel trip, my school interview, and Mom's true relationship with Victoria. It feels like I'm talking for hours, but Amani lets it all sink in, and we slip right back into our usual rhythm. In retelling everything that's happened, it reinforces how lost I've felt without her, and I know I can never survive this life if I don't have Amani.

'Yikes,' she says, leaning back in her pillows. 'So how is Ivy? I'm surprised she hasn't murdered you.'

'She can't.' I shrug. 'She's powerless now. And besides, she needs the Sands more than ever.'

'How many days until the full moon?'

'Seven.'

She looks off at the corner of her room, and I'm hopeful she's having a vision. Any insight into Iris's fate would be a huge advantage right now. But nothing comes to light.

'I should tell you,' she starts, bunching up a wad of blanket in her fist. 'I did tell Kim about Charlie being her match, and that it's why you've been screwy toward her.'

Whoa. 'WHAT?!' I blurt out, but then catch myself, trying to maintain Zen. 'What did she say?'

'I think she was weirded out at first; she didn't know how to handle being responsible for a breakup while being an innocent bystander. But she did understand how hard it must have been for you.'

I don't want this circling back to the 'poor, tortured Amber' mentality that got me here in the first place, so I spin it back around. 'Is everything OK, though? You two are still friends?'

'Oh, it's fine. She asked if she should call you, but I told her to chill. And that it probably wouldn't matter what she said to you anyway: your matchmaking visions are your truth.'

'Yeah, well, you're not wrong.' Although, I really wish she was. A sinking feeling worms its way into my heart, dragging down the elation of the moment. There was a small part of me hoping maybe my matchmaking was cracked, and I shouldn't rely so heavily on what I see. Knowing my match for Amani was way off base gave me a small trickle of promise toward love inconsistencies. Even though it goes against what I've practiced and preached since I was seven years old, I was beginning to think maybe my visions were thoughtful suggestions, a peek into what *could* happen, not what 100 percent *would*. But if Amani is turning a corner toward Vincent, it just reconfirms what I already knew: there is one match, and only one match, for everyone. This means Kim and Charlie probably aren't far behind. I'd be fooling myself to think otherwise.

'Did she, um, happen to mention that Charlie kissed her?' I ask.

'Wait, what?' Amani shoots up. 'When?'

'I'm not sure. I just know that he did. He . . . told me.'

Amani shakes her head in disbelief. 'I don't believe this. C'mon, Charlie! Why would he do that?'

I shrug, though it's a much more casual gesture than the situation requires. 'He said he was trying to prove me wrong.'

She slouches back in her pillow, frowning. 'Boys are so dumb. That makes no sense. This had to have just happened, and, not that I'm trying to lead the Kim parade or anything, but I can't imagine she actively participated in the kiss. I mean, when I told her about Charlie being her match, she genuinely didn't get it. She started rambling off reasons why he'd never be her type: too many tattoos, not athletic enough. She thinks it's funny you picture them together,' she adds, certainly sensing my shift in demeanor. 'She can't see it.'

Right. Until one day she does – just like Amani now sees Vincent, once an object of her disgust, in a whole new way. The day will come when Charlie says or does something so hilarious or adorable, Kim won't believe she's ever let such a precious creature out of her sight. When he turns to her and suddenly he's the only person on the planet.

When she sees him like I do.

# Twenty-nine

At lunch the next day, with Amani joyfully beside me, I decide I need to hear Kim's side of the story on this kiss. If she truly doesn't like him, if it was truly some disgusting plot point in her life, she shouldn't mind telling me, right? And I should just be strong and listen to her actual words, instead of spinning them into the Kim-Charlie fairy tale I've been writing in my head, right?

I get to the cafeteria as early as possible, choosing a table right near the exit, in the event that I suddenly have to bail. I also make sure there's no cutlery within reach, in case I go into a blind rage. Safety first, friends.

I spot Kim walking in, searching the room for a friendly face. When she spots me with Amani, she does a quick double take, which then melts into a genuine smile. She starts bounding over like a puppy excited that her owner's come home, and Amani dangles an oatmeal chocolate-chip cookie in front of me like a sugar-covered carrot (a store-bought cookie, not from this cafeteria, because she loves me) and gives me a thumbs-up of encouragement. 'You got this, champ.'

'Thanks, Coach.'

'Amber!' Kim says excitedly, setting her tray down across from me. 'You're sitting with us today?'

'Yes, ma'am,' I say, looking at her directly, being bold (for once) and not avoiding her eye. I prepare myself to see Charlie, only . . . he's not there. In fact, nothing is. A fuzzy crackle plays before me, showing me nothing of Kim's love life except static. It's just like what I saw (or didn't see) with Charlie the other day, a visual disconnect. I lean in closer, really trying to get in there, but the blur continues, leaving me with nothing.

Am I broken? Is my brain bleeding? I quickly turn and try to make eye contact with some rando in the cafeteria; a freshman girl happens to catch my stare, and I see it: she's frolicking with a cute leading lady, all happiness and happily ever after. OK, so, clearly *I'm* not defective, but some screw is loose in Kim and Charlie's future; something has thrown their love story off track. I have no precedent for this; I've never had a match un-match, if that's even what's happening.

But having this static pop up for both Charlie and Kim after their allegedly unsuccessful kiss has me more interested in the event than I ever thought possible.

'Amber, I have to tell you something,' Kim starts, looking nervous. 'Um, Charlie kissed me.' She waits for the inevitable blowback, but when I don't react, she twists up her face in confusion.

'Oh, yeah, I know already,' I say, working overtime to iron out my nerves.

'Y-you do? And you're still choosing to sit here?' Kim looks at Amani for a lifeline, clearly debating whether she should jump ship.

'Yes. I want you to tell me about it. Every detail,' I say, folding my hands on the table. Amani gives Kim a reassuring nod, but Kim is not convinced. 'No, really, this isn't a trick. Charlie is supposed to be your match, but . . . something weird has happened.'

'What do you mean, weird?'

'Well,' I say, 'usually when I look at either of you, I see scenes of you both together, being all . . . lovey.' I swallow to keep bile from coming up. 'But last time I saw Charlie, those images weren't there. And looking at you now, he's erased.'

'Erased?' Kim asks. 'Is there someone in his place?'

Hmm, how to put this delicately. *Actually, Kim, right now it looks like you're destined to disappear into nothingness. Congrats!* 'I'm not sure yet.'

'Well, that's depressing,' she says, sitting back in her seat.

'I mean, yeah, that doesn't sound great. But honestly, I've never had this happen before, so I don't know what it means,' I say, trying to be comforting although I'm still in need of comfort myself.

Amani speaks up. 'I think what Amber's trying to say is that she needs your help to fill in these blanks.'

'O-kay,' Kim says cautiously. 'Just promise you won't get mad, because it wasn't my fault.'

I make a cross-my-heart motion, even though I really can't keep a promise like that.

Kim starts. 'There's really not so much to tell, I guess. After the winter carnival, we had a follow-up MA meeting, to talk about how the event went, how it could be better next year, blah, blah. I wasn't totally listening, since I'm graduating, so who cares about next year, you know? And Charlie . . . he was there – physically – but mentally, it was pretty clear he was elsewhere. He kept giving me weird looks, like he was mad at me or wanted something from me? It was super uncomfortable. When the meeting was over, he asked if we could talk, and since I knew everything was so hard between the two of you, I wanted to just stay out of it. Then the next thing I knew, we were lip-to-lip.'

Even though I'm dying inside, I maintain eye contact the entire time, waiting to see if any part of this recap will stir up an accompanying visual. But there's nothing, NOTHING AT ALL.

Kim continues. 'I pushed him off me, like, "What the hell are you doing?" And he just buried his face in his hands, saying he was sorry, and that he just "had to know." I had no idea what that meant, not until Amani told me about the match thing.' She pushes around some unidentifiable meat on her tray with her fork, taking a minute to choose her next words. 'This whole thing is crazy, Amber. I wish you would've told me earlier. Then you would've known I don't have any feelings for Charlie.'

'Yeah, but—'

'No, no buts,' she says with more force than I thought she could muster. Kim has always been a gentle unicorn girl, but now she's giving me the horn. 'The kiss . . . it was like nothing, free of any emotion besides maybe sadness. Charlie didn't kiss me out of passion; he kissed me because he was dying inside and was looking for some kind of relief. He kissed me because he wants you.'

It's the weirdest sentence in the history of language, but somehow in this context, it makes sense. Amani squeezes my leg under the table as my heart swells.

I've handled this all wrong. Why *didn't* I just say something about the match? That's what I'm supposed to do, right? A matchmaker isn't supposed to keep information under lock and key, and by doing so, I sent myself on a pain spiral, tormenting myself, Charlie, Amani, and Kim in the process. I was so afraid of the truth destroying me, I didn't even think that maybe it could set me free.

I'm trembling, but for the first time in a while, it's not out of fear. There's a glimmer of hope building inside me, lighting me up in a way that's been dark and dormant. Somehow I feel like this kiss has set off a cosmic string of events, and now it's up to me to connect the dots. Screw the Fates, screw destiny; what was meant to be has gone and passed, and new possibilities await.

'Thank you, Kim. I mean it,' I say. 'This was more helpful than you could ever know.'

As if I'm being filled with helium, I rise from my seat, my feet carrying me out of the cafeteria. I run straight to Charlie's locker and wait for him there, practically exploding with excitement. I want to tell him that I'm sorry, that I was wrong, and that I love him, really love him. I want to declare mutiny against everything I've known about love, and step bravely into the unknown. And I want to do it with him beside me.

But when the bell rings and he hasn't stopped by, I deflate slightly, trudging off to class in defeat. I spend every following passing period looking for him outside his classes, but he's nowhere to be found. Did he stay home today? Damn him! Charlie, how can you not be here when I'm having a revelation?! I send him a can we talk? text, but to no reply.

The second school's over, I'm out the door, hailing a cab for the Gold Coast. I tumble out at Charlie's building, the doorman (with whom I'm well acquainted) gesturing me inside. My heart pounds on the elevator ride up, and by the time I'm knocking at his door, I'm practically on the verge of hysterical tears. Please, Charlie, PLEASE answer the door.

As the door opens, I'm ready to fling myself into his arms, but luckily I refrain, since it's his dad, John, who greets me.

'Amber!' he says, wiping his giant football-player hands on an apron that reads 'Kiss the Cook.' 'This is a surprise.'

'Yeah, um, samesies,' I reply, suddenly feeling self-conscious. What is John doing home at this time? Shouldn't he be overseeing Chicago's well-being? I can't profess my love to Charlie with his dad in the next room!

John smiles. 'I came home early to make a surprise dinner for Charlie. He's been so down lately, but nothing turns a frown upside down like homemade lasagna!'

I'd prefer homemade pie, but I get the gesture. 'Is he here?'

'No, but I expect him any minute now. You can come in and wait,' he says, stepping aside to let me in.

I've never been here without Charlie. Usually, I'm so focused on his cute face, the details of his luxury penthouse don't really register. Everything feels so . . . grand, while my insides are slowly caving in. I have all these emotions and no way to release them! Trapped, I figure I'd better put my mental energy toward something else before my brain short-circuits.

I take a seat on a kitchen barstool, while John resumes stirring the marinara sauce bubbling on the stove. The Blitzman kitchen is something out of a Pinterest fantasy, with beautiful quartz countertops and top-of-the-line appliances; it's light-years away from the tiny galley setup we Sands work with. I can't believe I've never asked Charlie to let me bake here.

'Smells good,' I offer, realizing I haven't really talked to John since the whole Cassandra debacle. He seems good, considering that a leprechaun stole his heart and tried to trick him into marrying her only a few short months ago.

'It's an old Blitzman recipe,' he says, adding a pinch of basil. 'Hopefully it'll do the trick.' He fills a stockpot full of water, then pulls out a box of lasagna noodles from the pantry. 'How's your mom? We've been playing phone tag.'

'Oh, she's . . .' And that's when I remember: John! Mom's best bud! He can surely tell me something about her past! Seeing as how I saved him from marrying a gold-digging leprechaun, I figure he owes me one. 'She's been better. I mean, this whole Victoria thing has her pretty rattled.'

He shakes some pasta in the pot. 'Yeah. I've never been a fan.'

'I can't picture them being friends,' I add, hoping he'll pick up what I'm putting down.

'It's a good thing they're not anymore, because it almost ruined *our* relationship,' John admits.

'Really?'

'Oh yeah. Your mom was not herself, suddenly getting into trouble all the time, and playing around with spells she'd never even thought to touch before.'

'Like what?' I press.

'Don't know for sure; it's not my realm, clearly.' He turns back my way to grate some cheese. 'But I thought I was gonna lose her. It's a miracle she got pulled out when she did.'

'How? What changed?'

The mayor looks up at me. 'She met your dad.'

I knew this, kinda, from reading Mom's grimoire. But John's eyewitness account makes it even more real. He reads my face, trying to determine if he should go on or not, and when I don't show any results of inner turmoil, he continues. 'Even though her involvement with Victoria was alarming, being with your dad was an addiction of a different nature. The obsession was mutual, but most harmful toward Lucy.'

I'm no cheerleader for my absentee father, but I don't understand what he's getting at. 'But why?' I wonder. 'If she turned away from black magic for him, wasn't that good?'

For some reason, John's face turns even darker than when he was talking about Victoria. 'Sure, but she almost gave up magic completely. Tom pretended to be intrigued by her talent, but really, it scared him. The longer they were together, the more he tried to steer her away from witchcraft. He thought it was a hobby, something she did for fun. He never understood that it was part of her, essential to her existence.'

Suppressing a supernatural talent is not healthy. Back when Amani was fighting to reject her precog ways, she would turn all poltergeist when a vision did manage to break through, eyes spinning and limbs shaking. Only recently has she been able to glimpse into the future without going full freak show. Mom repeatedly lectured her about being true to herself, about how much harm Amani was inducing. I thought Mom was just reciting from some Official Supernatural Handbook, not speaking from personal experience.

John shakes his head while slicing tomatoes. 'Because she loved him, she almost gave up a part of herself.'

Now that is a resonant theme. If I were sitting under a lamp right now, it would be lighting the hell up, because a big piece of the puzzle just fell into place. No wonder Mom didn't want to help Iris transform into a mermaid! It wasn't about messing with the Fates or harnessing darker powers – she didn't want the siren giving up a part of herself in the name of love. Having been burned before, she was trying to protect Iris from traveling down a similar path. And Victoria, being the vindictive witch she is, was probably dying to throw this back in Mom's face.

So many complicated feelings about love. I wonder how Mom felt when her only daughter emerged as a matchmaker, destined to spread the emotion that almost destroyed her. It couldn't have been easy. I spent a long time thinking she was disappointed I wasn't born a witch, but maybe instead she was sad I was accessing the emotion that caused her so much pain.

'I'm sorry. I shouldn't be talking like this about your dad,' John says, pausing.

'It's fine.' I brush it off, though his story has taken some of the wind out of my sails. 'It's not like—'

Just then, the front door opens and Charlie walks in. He drops his bag and hangs up his Manchester jacket before taking a deep inhale of the wafting Italian aromas. 'Hey, something smells . . .' He turns and spots me, face morphing into shock. 'Oh. Hey.'

I give a little wave, gritting my teeth in an awkward smile.

'I'm making lasagna!' John declares, slicing the tension with a metaphorical knife.

'My favorite,' Charlie confirms quietly. He's glued to his spot, and the three of us share an uncomfortable silence.

'You know, dang, I got marinara on my sleeve; I'd better go rinse it off before it stains.' John makes a quick exit, leaving us alone to the sound of bubbling sauce.

'Wh-what are you doing here?' Charlie asks.

I bite my lip, unable to proceed with my earlier plan. While I'd like to run across this giant apartment and throw myself into his arms, it just isn't the right time or place.

'I texted you earlier,' I say.

'Oh. Sorry, my phone died during Chem.'

'Oh.'

We're still standing several feet apart, neither knowing whether to advance or stay put. From this distance, I can't lock eyes to see if his static filter is still in place. The awkwardness is killing me, and Charlie looks equally tortured. He nervously rolls up his sleeves, bright flames and scales from his dragon tattoo peeking through. His face is flushed, and even though this is his home, he darts his eyes around like it's unfamiliar territory.

John walks back in and, upon seeing us still stuck in the same spots, almost tries to spin back around to give us more time. But it's too late, and anyway, my earlier plan will have to take a rain check.

'Well, I should let you guys get to your dinner,' I say, crossing the room to grab my coat. Charlie doesn't move, and our arms brush up against each other as I bundle up. Even through the fabric, the close contact gives me goose bumps, and I look up at him expectantly as he shares my intense gaze. I feel his breath on my cheek as I'm flooded with a vision, or anti-vision, since it's just a jumbled discord of nothingness. Still, I let the chaos play out between us, until finally I'm left with his forest-green eyes.

Drenched in pine with golden flecks peeking through, I don't think I've ever fully appreciated how beautiful they are. With no written future, I can finally see.

# Thirty

'MMM, A LITTLE MORE LENGTH. HER HAIR'S IN A BOB, NOT A bowl cut.'

Bob sweeps his pencil around the page, while my hopeful customer looks on. The shop is positively buzzing, and I can't tell if it's because it's Saturday or the full moon is almost upon us. This always seems to happen around celestial events; people get subconsciously wound up, being pulled by forces they can't feel or recognize. Scientists may say the moon has no effect on our moods or motivations, but the magical community knows the truth. Tides change, and people flock to the shop, looking for answers to cloudy questions. It's good for business, anyway.

'Does she have a nice butt?' my customer asks with sincerity. Ugh. I try not to cringe, because I get this question more often than I'd like. I'm supposed to be delivering true love, not true booty. 'I always pictured myself with a girl with a nice butt.'

'You won't be disappointed!' I say in my 'you're paying me by the minute' voice. I'm sure the girl Bob's busy sketching will be into what this superficial beefcake offers, so it'll all work out in the end. 'But my partner here will only be drawing her face.'

'Sure. Awesome.'

It's weird, holding a dude's hands when he's talking about butts, but I hold on, relaying the final details to Bob. Behind this guy, a few more hopeless romantics are queued up, meaning I better hustle if I'm to release all my Cupid's arrows before closing. It's been a while since I sat here, as I haven't really been in the mood for talking romance. After getting major interference from looking into Charlie's and Kim's eyes, I worried my matchmaker signals were broken, but I've had no problems matching all my customers today, seeing everything from beauty marks and hidden fangs to how they fill out their jeans. Since everyone else's romcoms are still playing in high-def 3-D, Charlie's offline visions are raising my hopes like freshly baked cake. Which is to say, deliciously.

Butt Guy finishes up, and I'm on to the next. I match a partial pixie with a farmer, a kindergarten teacher with an insurance salesman, and a vampire with a hematopathologist (go figure). The shop is finally starting to clear out, so once the vamp skips off, I bend down to grab a bite of coffee cake I stashed under my table, since I'm in desperate need of sugar. I end up wolfing down the whole thing in three massive mouthfuls and lay my hands down on the table before I've even finished chewing, just as my next patron sits down. A woman wearing a fur hood clutches my fingers and shakes her coat back to reveal her face. I almost choke when I see it's Victoria.

'Ahhh!' I scream, spitting crumbs everywhere. I yank my hands free and jump back against the wall. 'I touched her cloven hooves! I am unclean!'

Upon seeing Victoria's face, Bob goes stone-cold, eyebrows permanently raised in shock. Mom runs over, immediately placing herself in between the wicked witch and me and Bob. Victoria feigns shock at our alarm, then slowly stands, revealing a black dress with fabric that somehow looks wet. It's an effective scare tactic; between the massive animal carcass on her back and the slimy sheath on her front, she looks like something that just crawled out of a cave (one stocked with overpriced styling and tanning products but a cave nonetheless).

'You are not welcome here,' Mom says, fists clenched at her sides. I hope to Gods she has some sort of talisman or repellent powder hidden in there.

'Goodness! Is that how you treat all your clientele?' Victoria makes a tsk-tsk sound, waving a shaming finger. 'That can't be good for customer satisfaction, Lucille.'

'What do you want?' Mom hisses.

'Oh, I'm just doing a little last-minute shopping. I have a big night tomorrow, you know, and I realized I was out of candles. Silly me! You can't turn a siren into a mermaid without candles; everyone knows that.'

We're all on high alert, waiting for her next move. She could just as easily pull a snake out of her hair as wave good-bye and saunter off. Why she'd show up here the night before the spell is a mystery to me, but she has to have her reasons.

'Now, I can't say for sure,' Victoria says, 'but I have a feeling the three of you must be working together in some sort of effort to stop me.' She gives each of us a quick visual examination, waiting to see if someone will crack. Her eyes settle on our gargantuan friend. 'Bob, I expected more from you.'

To his credit, he stays still. I can't imagine the scenes from their past that must be playing in his head. I wish I could slip him his lucky rabbit's foot for comfort.

'Don't talk to him,' Mom commands, 'and don't pretend to know our plans.'

Victoria laughs, deep and throaty, clutching a strand of pearls vaguely resembling teeth. 'Of course I have no idea what you could be up to, darling, but when Amber here showed up the other day with Iris, well, you can understand my assumption.' She turns to me, and I grip the wall as a reflex. 'How is Iris, anyway?'

'As if you don't know,' I spit with anger. 'Since in addition to leaving her a mindless lump sitting around her house, worrying her sister sick, you have a crazy raven manipulating her like a remote control!'

'Oh, I wouldn't know anything about that,' Victoria says, waving me off. 'Perhaps she's recently taken up an interest in bird-watching.'

'Right, because the perfect time to pick up new hobbies is when you've lost your free will,' I sneer.

'Why are you doing this?' Mom asks. 'She's just a young girl. She didn't do anything to deserve this.'

'Lucille, she came to me. I'm providing her a service. How I complete that service is at my discretion.'

'But taking someone's free will? That's low, even for you.'

Victoria shakes her head with a puffy-lipped smile. 'You're just jealous.'

'Jealous?' Mom scoffs.

'Yes. Jealous. You know in your heart you could never pull off this spell, and you're kicking yourself for abandoning your practice.'

'Look around!' I blurt out. 'She hasn't abandoned anything. This whole shop is filled with Mom's spells!'

'Amber,' Mom warns.

'Darling, I never said she stopped doing magic,' Victoria says. 'But her practice is what disappeared. She let her heart fall in love and out of what mattered.'

Mom glances at me, and Victoria, sensing Mom's discomfort with the subject, continues with pleasure. 'When I met your mother, she was a wild young thing, a force of nature, ready to take on the world.' Victoria takes a deep breath, reveling in the memory. 'She was ready and willing to flex her magical muscles as she saw fit, doing whatever she wanted in pursuit of becoming a better witch. Right, wrong; dark, light; there were no distinctions. Only exploring, discovery.' A wicked grin starts to spread. 'I once watched her debone a live fish in midair, just so she could see how it worked.'

I shoot Mom a stare, but she doesn't flinch. It's not the most disturbing thing I've ever heard – witches use bones and animal body parts all the time in spells – but the visual of a fish exploding out of water is not pleasant. I'm sure the smell alone was very off-putting.

'Well, so what?' I declare, chin held high. 'So she played doctor on some guppy. I dissected a frog in biology; it's just a gross part of life.'

'Is it, now? Well, how about using those same powers on a human?'

I shake my head. 'No. No way.'

Victoria smiles, lips curling viciously. 'Oh yes. She held an innocent bystander in midair and—'

'Stop it right now!' Mom yells.

'—made his heart beat right out of his chest.'

I try to keep my stomach calm because it's definitely wrestling with keeping that coffee cake down. I know the reaction Victoria wants; she's hoping I'll freak, be appalled at Mom's past behavior, and rescind my stronghold. And honestly? It's working because I am more than a little surprised to hear she flexed her mystical prowess through the flesh of an actual person. I know I've been supersleuthing it to learn more about her secret past, but I never in a billion years thought the skeleton in her closet could be torturing someone.

'How dare you?' Mom growls in a violent whisper, close to shooting actual lasers out her eyes. 'What gives you the right to share that with my daughter?'

'Well, as your daughter, don't you think she has a right to know who she's fighting for?' Victoria asks, words dripping with innocence.

Enraged, Mom starts to advance in attack, mumbling some Latin under her breath. But before she lets the spell fly, she catches herself, closing her eyes and burying whatever she was about to unleash.

And there she is – the mother I know and love. She's capable of destruction – I've seen her attack Victoria before. Even if she turned her back on the dark arts, those shadows still live within. But she fights them every day, taking the higher path 99 percent of the time. That's the witch I'll always stand beside; I won't give Victoria the satisfaction of a meltdown.

'I do know who I'm fighting for,' I say, using all my focus to control any shaking in my voice. Mom turns my way, doing her best to remain expressionless, but I can feel her heart breaking.

'Mmm-hmm, sure.' Victoria rolls her eyes. 'But it doesn't matter anyway. Once she met your dad, she walked away, abandoning her true self in pursuit of love. And we all know how that turned out.'

'ENOUGH!' Mom yells, charging toward Victoria again. 'This is my business, my story to tell should I choose. If you came here in an effort to shake my confidence, you've only made it stronger.' For a second, I think she's going to grab a chunk of Victoria's fried blond hair, but she hovers just within the boundaries of personal space. 'I have taken you down before, and I will do it again.'

I look at the two of them – a hair's distance apart and ready to brawl – and think, *They were best friends*. Confidants. Two peas in a twisted pod. But when Mom found Dad, it all fell apart, and their bond transformed into a rivalry. How quickly the lines between love and hatred can blur, that raw emotion easily swayed to live on either side.

'You know, on second thought, I'm sure I have plenty of candles at home,' Victoria says, taking a step back. 'I'll see you all soon, I'm sure.'

And as quickly as she rolled in, Victoria exits, leaving a wake of misery in her path. We take a beat to let our nerves settle back to a natural state, while Bob, who remained frozen during the entire exchange, takes his first breath in several minutes.

'Amber, come with me,' Mom instructs wearily. She leads me to the back room, pulling the red velvet curtain shut. I take a seat on a star-printed floor pillow and stare blankly into the crystal ball before me. *Thanks for nothing, buddy,* I think. *You couldn't have given me a heads-up on all this?* Mom lights some lavender incense and sits down next to me, taking my hand.

'I want you to know,' she starts, avoiding my eye, 'I appreciate you standing up for me, even after hearing what I did.' She squeezes my fingers. 'I'm sorry Victoria shared that with you, but I'm even more sorry you had to hear it from someone other than me.'

'Mom, it's—'

'No. I'm ashamed, for many reasons. I was a different person back then; thinking about that time, I don't even recognize myself. It'd be easy to blame it all on Victoria, but she didn't make me hurt that man. I let myself get to that point.'

'Did he . . . survive?' I ask, metaphorical fingers crossed.

'Yes, thankfully. It happened so quick, we were able to put him back together again.' She's bent over, shaking her head in regret. 'I think the scars stayed with me longer than they did with him. If I didn't have good people in my life, like John and your dad, to help me get back on track, I don't know what I would've become.'

I think about John's words, how Dad tried to put a stop to Mom's magic. 'Dad doesn't really seem like a hero to me.'

Mom looks up, eyes glistening. She never talks about him, so I know she's struggling to find the words now. 'He was, and he wasn't. I was so scared of where I was heading, I threw myself into him, hoping he was the answer. I was willing to sacrifice everything just to ensure I didn't end up a lost cause.' She's so small, all curled in a ball, I squeeze her hand back in support, encouraging her to go on. 'But he didn't understand me either, tried pushing me into a mold that didn't fit, just like Victoria did.'

'People should know by now: Sand women *break* molds,' I say, hoping for a laugh.

Mom smiles weakly, sniffling a bit. 'I should have obliterated Victoria the second she came to town, but I didn't want to submit to those old urges. And I should have helped Iris instead of turning her away. I refused to work with her for my own selfish reasons, and it's caused nothing but trouble.'

With the past finally out in the open, there's a closeness between us I've never felt before. People make mistakes – Gods, I'm certainly not perfect – but owning up to them is half the battle. You can't course-correct until you realize you're on the wrong path in the first place. That's what Mom did, and I hope I can too. 'You're a good witch, Mom, and a good person too.'

She leans in for a hug, and I bury my face in her long hair. The incense stick burns out, and the last of the sweet-smelling smoke curls around us.

# Thirty-one

I FEEL LIKE WE'RE PACKING FOR THE APOCALYPSE, AND MAYBE we are. The night is dark, the moon is full, and Mom is stuffing what seems like the entire contents of her supply cabinet into a satchel. But because she's a witch, she's enchanted the bag to go all Mary Poppins, allowing her to cram as many items as she wants without anything spilling out the top. It's a pretty neat trick.

'Amber, can you pass me that crucifix?' Her hair is tied up in a messy bun, but she's moving so frantically around the room, gray strands keep waterfalling down her face.

'I didn't realize we'd be facing the undead tonight,' I say, passing her the wooden cross.

'I just want to be prepared. We're bringing backup; I don't see why Victoria wouldn't do the same.'

Yes, backup. The moon is full, and the Fates are ready for a supernatural showdown. In the Sand corner, we have a witch, a matchmaker, a precog, an ex-siren, a mermaid, a vampire (thank you, Vincent), and our wild card, a werewolf, in the form of Marcus (well, I guess technically he'll be in the form of a dog). Marcus was sweet enough to offer his services, although I really can't picture how he'll contribute, besides scaring the crap out of everyone, myself included. I've never seen a werewolf in person; something about the whole going-feral-in-the-moonlight thing is not exactly enticing. He reassured me he'd be able to control himself enough to know who's a friend or foe, but I'm packing some wolfsbane just in case.

When we get there, Iris and Ivy are already by the lakeshore. Iris is sprawled out on a large rock, still lacking free will. Brooke is clasping her hand in the frigid water. Our posse hangs back, letting the darkness conceal our location. But even from a distance, I can tell Brooke is comforting her girlfriend, running her fingers through her hair and whispering words of encouragement. Ivy keeps looking over her shoulder, either for us or the wicked witch, but also lets her eyes linger on her sister. Ivy's never been the warm and snuggly type, but she too has a reassuring hand on Iris, stroking her upper arm.

One of the provisions I smuggled in Mom's bag o' magic is a thermos of hot chocolate, which I pass around to the group. Mom and Amani take long pulls, while Vincent passes. I gulp down as much as I can, letting the warmth fill my throat and belly, hoping that if my core temperature rises, my fingers will stop feeling like icicles. The fact that this full moon had to land on one of the coldest nights of the year is a sick joke, one I'm sure the Fates are enjoying at our expense. No sign of Marcus, though; maybe he decided to wolf out in his parents' basement after all.

Just when it feels like all my nose hairs have frozen together in one solid clump, Victoria emerges from the darkness, wearing a long black velvet cape. I've never seen her adorned in anything but some sort of animal print, so the fact that she's chosen to go with a stereotypical witch costume for this event seems highly comical. It's almost like she's expecting supernatural paparazzi to catch her in this epic spell, and she'd better look the part. She takes long, careful strides, like a deranged bride walking down the aisle to hell, chin raised in self-importance. This spell is definitely all about her, not the nearly lifeless girl who's about to switch species. Victoria has crowned herself Queen of the Night, and is relishing every moment.

'Where's her entourage?' Amani asks the question we're all wondering.

We scan the area for possible associates. It's so cold, there's no way any Chicagoan would be outside without a pressing reason. Besides the Chamberlain sisters, I don't even see anyone else, yet there's no way she showed up for this alone. Then, without a word, Mom points to the sky, where countless black birds circle the scene.

Ravens. OF COURSE.

'Nothing like a literal sign of death,' I say under my breath.

'Could be shape-shifters,' Mom suggests. 'Hard to tell.'

'Or just the worst pets ever,' Amani adds. Vincent snickers.

Mom shoots us a glare. 'Quiet, please.' She fumbles through her bottomless bag, pulling out a flat, clear stone used for uncloaking hidden truths. She peers through it, examining the ravens as they hover over their master. Mom squints, turning the stone a few times, then drops it in frustration. 'It's too dark.'

'I'm not sensing any supernatural traits,' Vincent says. 'But that doesn't mean she doesn't have them specially trained for vicious tasks.'

'Oh yeah, she definitely has them targeted to prey on weaklings,' I confirm.

'Good thing we're not weak,' he says with a wink.

Mom stares at us disapprovingly; we're talking too much. From out of the bag, she pulls out what seems like nothing, clutching chunks of air. Except I know better: she enchanted a blanket to make its wearer temporarily invisible, which will hopefully let us get closer to the scene without being detected.

'Now, it is imperative we remain hidden until Iris gets her free will back. We cannot intervene until she's fully restored.' She wads the balled-up see-through blanket and passes it to me. Holding invisible objects is always such a mind bend. I can feel the soft chenille, but all I see are my gloves. Weird. 'Are you ready?' Mom asks me.

I nod, swinging the non-blanket around my shoulders, draping it over my head like a hood. My view stays the same, but Amani's and Vincent's eyes both widen at my disappearance.

The plan is for me to sneak over to Iris and cover her with the blanket as soon as she's re-will-ified. (Willed? Will-full? Hmm.) If Victoria can't see the siren, she can't change her into a mermaid. Because, in addition to Iris's safety, what's most at stake here is this wicked witch gaining access to a power none of us can even begin to comprehend; the consequences of that are . . . Well, let's not think about that. I creep out from our hiding place, being careful not to step in snow and leave proof of my presence. I'm crazy nervous, and my accelerated breathing fills my blanketed space, sounding much louder to my ears than probably anyone else's. I swerve far from Victoria, assuming she can smell blood or some other creepy dark witch trait, and take my place next to Ivy just as

Victoria steps up to her victim. I texted Ivy about this earlier today, but she still jumps when an invisible finger pokes her back.

Ivy rises, placing herself in between the witch and her sister.

'You're lucky I'm not a siren anymore,' Ivy sneers, 'or I'd be having you light yourself on fire like your Salem sisters.'

Victoria smiles. 'How precious.'

Brooke, clearly panicked about pissing off the creature who's going to perform mystical surgery on her girlfriend, tries a different approach. 'Will this hurt her? I don't want her to be in pain.'

'Of course you don't,' Victoria says. 'But surely you must know that love and suffering go hand in hand. Or in your case, hand in fin? I'm not really sure how that works, to be honest.'

Ivy's siren rage funnels down to her fists, and Brooke starts splashing around in fear, until finally, Victoria raises both her arms, letting her cape cascade behind her as a crackling bolt of light passes between her palms. Ivy and Brooke both jump back in surprise, but Iris, still unable to act on her own, continues to lie still. As the crackling continues, though, Iris's body starts to move, beginning with a twitching at her feet. It moves upward, shaking her nervous system, almost as if Victoria is reanimating her. And maybe she is, because slowly, Iris comes to a stand. It's awkward, her muscles undoubtedly struggling after so much lethargy, but she makes it, standing shoulder to shoulder with her sister. Ivy wraps her arms around Iris, who truly observes her surroundings for the first time. She clutches onto Ivy, clearly afraid, but when she sees Victoria, it dawns on her where she is.

Brooke pulls herself up out of the water, splaying her tail on the shore. She reaches for Iris, who instantly notices her girlfriend's out-of-water shivering. Iris unzips her coat and drapes it over Brooke, signaling to everyone one clear truth:

Her free will has returned.

Wasting no time, Mom springs into action, grabbing her bag as she crawls out from our hiding spot. She runs over and takes her place alongside Iris, whose confusion and fear is broadcast across her face. Until, that is, I whip off the blanket and drape it over her, making her disappear from the scene.

'Lu-ci-ille!' Victoria chimes, in a singsong that chills my already-frozen blood. 'And the matchmaker! How adorable,' she says to me, laughing at the thought. 'You think throwing a rag over this poor girl is going to result in a happily-ever-after?'

Ivy flashes her trademarked glare, and for a second, I kind of love her. 'This isn't a fairy tale, though it's pretty clear you're the villain.'

'Happy to play the part,' Victoria says with a bow.

'Don't do this!' Iris cries, probably not even realizing no one can see her. These are the first words she's spoken in weeks; her voice cracks due to lack of use. I can't imagine what it'd be like to wake from what essentially was a supernatural coma only to be the center of attention in a magical showdown. Disorienting, for sure. 'I don't want your help anymore.'

'Are you kidding me?' Victoria laughs. 'Do you realize how much power I'll unlock by altering a member of the human species? There's no way I'm stopping now.'

Mom steps in front of invisible Iris, acting like a human shield. 'Think again,' she says.

Victoria and Mom start to duel in true Wicca fashion. Victoria begins by muttering in Latin and flings what looks like a bath bomb into the air, which explodes at Mom's feet, causing her to stumble back. While on the ground, Mom skids a disk filled with herbs over to Victoria, which causes the witch to sneeze uncontrollably. I can tell Mom is still trying to use lighter magic to disarm her enemy, but if she wants to stay in the game, she's going to have to do more than cause hay fever.

While Mom and Victoria are busy trying to one-up each other, I get back to my task: getting Iris away from the scene. I feel around for her hand, which is much harder than it sounds. 'Iris, we have to get out of here.'

Whether she looks at me or not (I can't tell), she replies, 'No. I won't leave Brooke.'

The mermaid, still trembling inside Iris's coat, shoots a

worried glance my way before turning in the general direction of her girlfriend. 'I'll be fine, love. It's not safe here.'

'NO!' Iris yells out from the void. 'I'm tired of getting yanked around.' She pulls the blanket off her face, leaving an unsettling visual of a floating head.

A finger taps me from behind, and I jump a mile high, spinning around. 'Vincent! Gods!' He and Amani have left the safety of our hiding spot, ready to help.

'Sorry. Should I just throw them over my shoulder and run?' he asks me.

'Unless you can carry all three of them, I think it's useless. Iris is not going to leave Brooke to be potentially tortured in her wake.' Argh. A perfectly good invisible blanket gone to waste.

'Well, I can't just do nothing.' He springs into action with surprising vampire speed, racing off toward the witches before either Amani or I think to stop him. He entraps Victoria, pulling her away from Mom and pressing two warning teeth into her neck.

Amani gasps at seeing Vincent's fangs for the first time. I too am taken aback, having grown so comfortable with his charming, polished facade. It's easy to forget that behind the martini-shaking Casanova is a thirst for blood. I reach for Amani's hand to comfort her, but she doesn't seem afraid; she's positively transfixed by Vincent's strength and power over this wretched wench.

With her opponent caught under the tension of Vincent's teeth, Mom lowers her arms, taking the opportunity to quickly blow some protection powder toward Ivy, Iris, and Brooke. I don't think it'd be enough to guarantee safety against a strong spell, but it may offer a few extra seconds of safety, which is sometimes all it takes.

Just as I think things may be moving toward our favor, Victoria whistles a three-note tune, causing her birds of prey to halt their circling and change direction. The ravens swoop toward me with frightening speed, and before I can run, they've pinched my shoulders in their beaks and raised me high above the ground. I scream out in fear as my legs dangle over the icy waves of Lake Michigan.

'Amber!' Mom yells.

'Release me, or my birds release her,' Victoria cries.

Vincent retracts his fangs but keeps her locked in his arms, waiting for Mom's signal. She nods wearily, never taking her eyes off me. Once Victoria is free, the ravens lower me slightly, but I'm still several feet above, with a terrifying plunge below.

It's the perfect setup, with me as the perfect hostage: Mom can't do anything to the birds without me tumbling into subzero waters. Instant hypothermia awaits.

'Now, you'll let me complete my spell, unless you want an ice cube for a daughter.'

I'm crying, which doesn't help, as the tears leave frozen streaks on my cheek.

Then, as if things couldn't get worse, I see a blur of black barreling toward the scene. From way up high, I can't make out the details, but anything moving with that fierce determination is something not to be messed with. No one on the ground detects the incoming horror, but just as I'm about to let out a warning scream, I realize it's Marcus.

He cuts through the group, snarling past with crazy speed. Everyone jumps back, as the wolf himself makes a fantastic leap straight toward me. His wolf fangs bite into one of the ravens, and they all release me instantly. My arms and legs flail hopelessly in the wind, and I try to prepare for the frigid temperature below. The water is like a million tiny needles simultaneously pricking my skin, even through my winter outerwear. I try to push my way up to the surface, but it's so unbelievably cold, my movements are stilted, as if I truly am turning to ice. It hurts to see; it hurts to breathe. Yet just as I feel I'm being bled dry, arms wrap around my waist, pulling me back toward oxygen. Slippery scales undulate next to me, as Brooke tugs me back to shore. Ivy and Iris grab my blue hands as I cough out the lake from my lungs. Amani rushes to my side, covering me with her coat.

Mom, Vincent, and a very wet wolf have Victoria surrounded. She looks tired but not yet defeated, as if she's saved her best move for last. A wicked grin starts to spread, and Victoria quickly stops her incantation, lowering her arms and emitting the creepiest cackle I've ever heard. I'm shaking on the ground, the wicked witch towering over me, but my best friend is lying beside me. Then her eyes light up with a glimpse of the future.

'Ms Sand!' Amani screams. 'The black pearl!'

Victoria removes the onyx orb from her robe, and it instantly begins to glow from within. Her acrylic nails tap against the incandescent globe, which casts a ghostly phosphorescence on her skin. She went to great lengths to get this mystical item, only she doesn't know we've come prepared.

Mom stops her before she starts, gathering a clump of snow and mixing it with a single blue drop from a stopper. The coloring spreads through the mound like a snow cone, causing it and all the snow in the immediate area to activate, swirling up from the ground. A tornado of ice begins to circle Victoria, curling faster and faster until particles combine into something stronger.

Ice. It rises up like a winter stalagmite, trapping Victoria's feet and literally freezing her in place. Victoria, realizing what is happening, raises the pearl above her head, trying to keep it away from the frozen water. She shrieks a stream of Latin, causing the globe to glow brighter, but it's too late: the snow travels faster, working its way up her body, encasing her within the elements. Finally, the maelstrom overtakes her head, closing off the screams that have been filling our ears until she's frozen. Once it reaches her raised fingers, they lose their grip on the pearl, which turns back to black and bounces down the side of the evil Popsicle. The silence is haunting, and we all stand by, our panicked breath the only sound. In the middle of our circle stands a solid witch statue, Mother Nature wrapped around her tight. But from behind the sheath of ice containing her, Victoria's eyes continue to blink.

Mom walks up to her frozen creation and taps on the ice right above Victoria's distraught gaze. 'Now, chill out, and watch a real witch do some magic,' she whispers to her defeated opponent.

The coolest burn of all time.

# Thirty-two

WITH VICTORIA LOOKING ON FROM HER ICY PRISON, THE GROUP gives a collective sigh of relief. Iris re-covers a dripping-wet Brooke with her coat; Vincent wraps a comforting arm around Amani. Mom and Ivy converse in hushed tones. And I, still pulsating with adrenaline, roll over toward Marcus, who has paused to lick his paws. It looks like one of the ravens clipped him, as he's lying on his belly, tending to a small wound. Marcus is incredibly cuddly in human form, but since I'm still unsure of his wolfish tendencies, I approach with caution.

'Marcus?' I start through chattering teeth. Even though I wasn't in the water for long, the waves definitely penetrated my core, and the midnight wintery wind is not helping. 'Can you . . . understand me?'

He continues nursing his paw, uninterested in my advance. Yet when I crouch down and offer a peaceful palm for him to sniff, he does respond, looking up at me with those same kind eyes. Despite his black fur and frightening fangs, I recognize that serene soul within, and I slowly, cautiously, place my nearly numb hand on his shaggy head. He leans into the gesture like most dogs would, encouraging me to sink my hand over and scratch behind his ear. And while I'm sure canine Marcus would appreciate that gesture, human Amber can't really deal with giving a good nuzzling to the boy who wrote her poetry.

'Thank you,' I offer instead. I don't know if he'll remember this when the moon cycle moves on, but hopefully some of it will stick with him. 'You saved my life.'

He whimpers in acknowledgement, then comes to a stand. We're now eye to eye, and I hold my breath, hoping my werewolf friend will maintain his momentary tranquility while so close. He's massive, like a small bear, and could easily devour me. Instead, he licks my cheek, then turns to run, howling away in the moonlight. That sly dog, sneaking in a kiss. Well, I guess he earned it.

I'm shaking on all fours, unable to stop. Mom comes up beside me and rubs a strong-smelling lotion on my exposed skin, working her way behind my ears and down my neck. It's cold at first, causing obscenities to spill from my lips, but it instantly warms, growing hotter and hotter until it feels like summer sunlight bronzing my skin. I sigh in relief, letting the heat run through me, and I grab her lotion bottle and dump the remains down my shirt. Soon I feel like I just jumped out of a pool on a warm August day, rather than having escaped death in an arctic lake.

'What happens now?' I ask, once my lips return to their natural color. Everyone has huddled close for warmth, congregating alongside the shore. Iris and Brooke are curled up against each other, a shimmering tail entwined with UGG boots. Even in the moonlight, it's clear how content these two are together.

'Well, that is up to Iris,' Mom says. 'If you still want to go through with this, now would be the perfect time.'

'But how?' Iris asks. 'Everything got completely out of hand.'

'That's true,' Mom agrees. 'But the moon is still full, and I have an entire supply cabinet here in my bag. I can help you see this through.' She was so against this spell to start, and now here she is, offering her services.

'But why?' Iris asks, reading my mind. 'Why now?'

Mom takes a long pause. 'For a long time, I thought that choosing love had made me weak. I altered my path to follow my heart, and it led me to sadness and regret. But now' – she looks first at the Victoria statue, and then at the water-bound couple – 'I know I was wrong. I did make a choice, and it did change my life, but not for the worse. Had

I never ventured down that road, I wouldn't be where I am now.' She looks at me and smiles with love that further warms my heart. 'I am not a Fate; only you can choose your life path.'

Iris takes a long look at Brooke, who strokes her jawline. Watching the two of them together, you get the sense that everyone else fades from their peripheral vision, their worldview very small in the best possible way. It's good to see Iris with life in her eyes, and it's clear that life is Brooke.

Ivy stands over them, biting her thumb. To her credit, she offers no opinion, letting the scene play out without her influence. Either she knows fighting is futile, or she finally sees that silent support is the best way to help her sister.

'I'm ready,' Iris says while still looking at her girlfriend. Brooke breaks into a crazy smile, her tail slapping against the rock. Both of them grab on tighter to each other, flashing ecstatic smiles bright enough to light up the night. 'I'm ready.'

'OK.' Mom smiles back. 'Let's begin.'

I didn't realize when Mom was packing her bag, her real intent was to complete the original spell. Stopping Victoria was key, but helping Iris reach her goal safely was Mom's plan all along. One by one, she pulls out the necessary elements for the spell, starting with several white water lilies and floating candles. Mom steps into the water, interspersing the flowers and flames in a buoyant circle, and sprinkles a golden powder around the perimeter, which dissolves into a shimmering glow. Although I know the water is still freezing, the space Mom creates looks warm, welcoming, like a gentle portal to another world. And it is, awaiting not a victim but an active participant, ready to start her life.

'We're all set, Iris,' Mom says quietly, backing away to give Iris some space.

Iris kisses Brooke on the forehead, then stands to face her sister. Ivy, who's been remarkably strong throughout the whole ordeal, immediately starts to crumble. She throws herself at Iris, burying her face in her sister's coat. From the way her shoulders are shaking, it's clear she's crying, though she doesn't let a single tear show. Iris lovingly cradles Ivy's head, laying her cheek in her golden hair.

'This isn't good-bye,' Iris whispers, at which Ivy balls up her fists tighter. 'I could not live if I didn't have you in my life. You are my sister, my champion, always looking out for me; I wouldn't even be here right now if it wasn't for you.' Ivy sniffles. 'Even though we're very different, your love fills the spaces where we split. Just because I'm choosing this does not mean I'm rejecting you. I love you, now and forever.'

Ivy nods, and skillfully wipes her face clean before coming up for air. Her eyes are puffy, yet she's smiling, still holding her sister tight.

'Well, at least now Mom and Dad will be forced to take me to the Caribbean on a regular basis,' Ivy jokes.

'See? Silver linings.' Iris takes Ivy's face in her hands. 'Everything is going to be OK.'

After one more embrace, Iris turns back to Mom, who gestures toward the shore. I stand next to Ivy, occupying the space Iris left, and take her hand. For once, Ivy doesn't resist.

Iris removes her coat and shoes, and tests the icy waters. She shivers but plunges in anyway, with Brooke floating beside her. Iris paddles to the incantation circle and treads water, her form swimming in moonlight. From the shore, Mom begins her spell.

Chanting in Latin, her hands raised toward the Gods, Mom closes her eyes and lets the magic flow through her. A path of light traces from Mom's toes to Iris's body. An invisible force pulls Iris under the waves, and Brooke dives down in tandem. The rest of us are shielded from view, as the light grows stronger and stronger, almost like a supernova engulfing the coast. Iris and Brooke disappear completely, and Ivy squeezes my hand to the point of pain. They stay under the water for longer than any human could hold her breath, and I realize we're all holding ours.

Like a firework fading from the night sky, the light dims, and all we can see are two heads bobbing in the water. Mom lowers her arms and steps back to join the group.

'Did it work?' Ivy asks, rushing to the water's edge and inadvertently dragging me with her. 'Iris?'

Iris turns our way; she's dripping wet, but some of that moisture is from her own tears. Tears of relief, tears of joy, because poking out from the surface is a second tail, a shimmering collection of blue, sapphire, and cerulean scales. Ivy gasps, and Iris swims over her way.

'Are you OK?' Ivy asks, crouching down. 'You look . . . beautiful.'

Iris reaches for Ivy's hand. 'I've never been better.'

'Can I . . . touch it? Your tail?' Ivy asks.

Iris, learning how to navigate her new appendage, awkwardly flops her fin on the rocks. Ivy removes one glove and gently grazes her sister's scales. Iris giggles and immediately falls back into the water.

'That tickles!' She laughs. Ivy smiles despite herself; it's the first time I've seen any positive emotion cross her face in weeks.

Brooke swims up beside her girl, and the two of them fall into what can only be described as an absolute snugglefest, tumbling over each other, trying to find the perfect position that leaves as little space as possible between them. As I watch the couple, so happy and carefree, I realize that this whole time I completely missed the point of Iris's journey. I've been so focused on what she was sacrificing – her family, her home – that I didn't even look at what she's gaining.

Brooke is crazy in love with Iris, and in return, Iris is positively floating, and not because she has a tail. It's true she had to make a leap of faith to get here, but just because she jumped doesn't mean everything else got left behind forever. She still has her sister, she still has that love in her heart, but because she took a chance, she gained even more. Turning away from Brooke would have been the logical choice; the status quo is always easier to swallow. But look at what she would have missed. The real sacrifice would have been to play it safe, to lock herself in a cocoon where nothing ever happens.

The Fates dealt her one hand: a pair of legs restricting her to a land-ridden life. But Iris refused to accept it as her final option. She carved out something new, a different kind of fate, more in tune with her heart's desire. If she'd been paralyzed by what was supposed to happen, she would have ultimately sacrificed the love of her life.

My gut drops, and all the emotions of the night catch up with me. The joy in seeing a true love connection proves to be a massively powerful stomach punch. Now more than ever, I realize how I've let my visions handcuff my future, surrendering without a fight. I've been living life from a laminated road map, while Iris went ahead and just threw the guidebook out the window.

I have to remedy this, if I even can.

I walk over to Amani, who already has her arms outstretched for me. In her wise, future-predicting way, she seems to know what I'm thinking and whispers into my frozen hair, 'You broke his heart, but you can fix it. You're a matchmaker; it's time to make that match.'

# Thirty-three

'AM I REALLY DOING THIS?'

'Yes, you really are.' Amani releases a chunk of my hair from her curling iron, setting it in an unfamiliar, twisted shape. I've never seen my hair be anything but stick straight, and now I have a pouf of shellacked curls framing my face. It feels like a helmet, ready to protect me for battle. Only I hope tonight I won't be a casualty of war.

I'm going to the winter formal to make a Romantic Grand Gesture in hopes of winning Charlie back, and I'm in such uncharted waters that I'm seconds away from drowning.

'How is one supposed to move with such crunchy hair?' I ask, touching a freshly sprayed curl before Amani smacks my hand away.

'Hair does not move during dances. It locks in perfection for a limited time, ensuring picture-perfect memories.'

'Stop it.'

'I'm serious. Do you think Cinderella's hair moved at the ball? No. Those mice locked it down so she could focus on other things.'

'Apparently not her footwear, though.'

Amani playfully slaps me again. 'You are the worst. You need to get in the right mind-set.'

'Which is?'

'Love, dammit. Romance. You can't go sweep someone off his feet when every word is dripping in sarcasm.'

'I guess you're right.'

'I know I'm right. Now, be quiet and hold still while I apply your mascara.'

I do as she says, though it's hard to stay motionless when your heart is racing and someone is poking your eye with a stick. Watching Iris and Brooke collapse into each other's arms, I knew I'd messed up. I put my trust in the hypothetical when I should have listened to my gut. I used to pity those people: the ones who'd openly defy my advice, who'd follow their hearts despite explicit consequence. How could they veer left, when I warned them to go right? Did they have any idea what they were doing?

Maybe not, but they knew something I didn't: You have to try. You have to fight for what you believe in. Even if it's hard, even if there are obstacles in your way. They say that all's fair in love and war, but for that to be true, you need to be part of the crusade.

'OK, it's done!' Kim walks in from the other room, cradling a long black dress. 'I gave it a good steam, and now it's ready to take the dance floor.' True to her word, even considering my horribleness, Kim went out and found me the perfect dress. I don't know how she did it, or even why; I've given her zero reason to be nice to me. But here it is: a simple black sheath, as comfortable as a T-shirt but acceptable for formal occasions. That such a thing exists is pure magic, and that such a person is in my life is a true blessing.

'Kim, I love it,' I say. 'And I don't use "love" when describing clothes.'

She blushes, scrunching up her shoulders toward her ears. (Reason number ninety-two on the list of Kim's positive attributes: doesn't hold grudges.) I give her a hug, crunchy curls hitting her face, and she hugs me back, like really. A tight embrace, like we're both squeezing out any lingering weirdness between us, so that moving forward, everything will be fresh.

'Thank you,' I say.

'Anytime.'

I give her a long, steady look in the eyes, wondering if I'll see anything beyond static today. It's still fuzzy, but right before I look away, new scenes start coming into focus. I see Kim, laughing on a beach, fingers tangled with a deeply tanned hand. Two burly arms wrap around her and pick her up, swinging her around a few times before tossing her in the sea. Her match jumps in afterward, and she shares a long kiss with the guy.

A guy who is her match.

A guy who is not Charlie.

'Is everything OK?' Kim asks, probably seeing the explosions in my brain.

I take a manic breath. 'Everything is GREAT!'

While Amani and Kim go put their dresses on, I grab a final look in the mirror. With my fancy dress and hair, I almost don't recognize myself; I run my fingers through the sticky spirals, pulling them out to be less perfect. I know Amani likes things proper and pretty, but my life's a little messier. And that's OK because I feel a weight has been lifted. It's been such a burden, carrying all my fears and worries with me constantly; they were dragging down my ability to see. When you're always wondering 'what if,' you can't see 'what is.' And it's not like I'll never have doubt in my life again, but right now, I'm taking on the Fates to see how I can bend my destiny. I may completely crash and burn, but at least the mistakes will be mine and not clouded in speculation. I don't know what will happen tonight. It's scary and also somehow liberating.

You'd think a private school would shell out for a fancy venue, but here we are, pretending the gym is a suitable spot for an unforgettable night. An archway of blue, silver, and white balloons beckons, begging me to cross the threshold of a teenage milestone. The winter formal. It's a setting I never pictured myself in. Yet despite the overuse of glitter and willingly sharing oxygen with my peers, this is where I need to be. I don't even care if it's clichéd to chase destiny at the Big School Dance; I may think it's cheesy, but Charlie won't. A black-tie event is when the rest of the world finally rises to his level. He was born for crap like this.

'Flying solo?' asks a redheaded ticket taker wearing a tiara. 'There's a big surprise.'

'I'm sorry, do I know you?' I respond, handing over my ticket.

'Probably not, but everyone knows the idiot who dumped Charlie Blitzman.' She leans in to me. 'I just saw him, and damn, he looks good.'

I blow past without a response, a smatter of snickers in my wake. I don't have time for jerks who think they know me. *I* know me. That's all that matters.

Crossing into the gym, I'm overwhelmed by deafening beats immediately pulsing through my brain. When your life's playlist consists mostly of piped-in pan flute, hip-hop feels like an auditory assault. Not to mention the accompanying scarring visuals, as my classmates gyrate in ways I can't even picture my body moving. Everyone moves to the rhythm, taking breaks to make out or swish quick sips from concealed flasks, and every inch of me is screaming with discomfort. Several sweaty bodies bump up against me, and I squirm through the horde, effectively grossed out.

Normally, it's easy to pick Charlie out of a crowd, since he dresses better than 99 percent of the population, but with all the boys in monkey suits and strobe lights skewering the scene, I can't find him. He's here, though; I know he is. If only I could use a spell to lift him above the mindless masses and bring him to me. I've done a perimeter check and trudged through the dance floor, but he's nowhere to be found. For a moment, discouragement rolls in, cursing my foolish optimism. A football player barrels into me, nearly spilling his date's punch all over my magical dress, but he wobbles away toward the stage, and that's when I see it: the microphone.

Before I can talk myself out of it, I'm hiking up my skirt and climbing onstage, blending into the scene like a shadow. As the DJ fades the end of the song, I snake my hand through his setup, switching on the mic before the next anthem sounds. While still cloaked in darkness, I croak out a quiet 'Hello?'

My timid question bounces through the gym, heads craning to spot the source. The DJ almost knocks me off the stage as he spins around, calling out a 'Hey!' over his stolen equipment. Somehow, a spotlight gets pointed in my direction, and I squint in piercing light.

Unable to see anything, I focus on my mission. 'Um, I'm looking for Charlie Blitzman.' A female from the audience responds with a 'Me too!' causing a ripple of laughter. But I stand my ground. 'Charlie, are you here?' Mercifully, the spotlight swings away, searching the crowd for my lost boy. It circles the gym, and heads sway in tandem, wondering where it will land. Finally, it stops in a back corner, where Charlie stands alone. The light bounces off his plum-velvet blazer, his face illuminated in shock. I can't tell if he's happy or mad that I've singled him out for the whole school, but he hasn't run away, so that has to count for something.

'Charlie,' I continue into the microphone. 'Will you dance with me?'

If he's feeling the pressure of a whole room of eyes, he doesn't show it, focusing only on me. I'm about ready to faint off this stage, when he finally nods in consent. He starts making his way through the crowd, spotlight documenting his trail, and I hand back the mic, hopping down to the dance floor. We meet in the middle, haloed by blinding light, but it's fitting because all I can see is him. His face, his body, his heart: they are all right before me, and even if we only have this moment, I feel like the luckiest girl in the world.

If we were a different couple, one beloved by our peers, maybe our reconciliation would be met with cheers and applause, but since everyone hates me and likely has no interest in us making up, we stand in awkward silence. The spotlight grows bored, and the audience turns back to their business. Luckily, the DJ has the good sense to put on a ballad instead of a banger.

Pianos and violins fill the air, and everyone pairs up, pulling their partners close. A disco ball spreads sparkles around the room, and Charlie's face dances with light. He put his hands on my hips but keeps an arm's-length distance. We're dancing like middle schoolers.

'Amber, what are you doing here?' he asks.

I've been practicing a speech in my head for hours, but I don't know if it will come out right. I wish I could blurt it all at once, so he could know exactly how I feel as soon as possible, but I should probably try and converse at a regular, human rate. 'I knew you wanted to come to this, and I wanted to see you.'

He stares off, clenching his jaw tight. He has such a tentative grip on my waist, I can barely feel him. 'But why?'

'Because . . . I love you.' I hold my breath, hoping someday I can use these words in a less high-pressure situation, and say them out of happiness: not out of anger, not out of sadness, but because I'm so filled with love that I can't possibly say anything else.

Charlie's face continues to tighten. I can't be sure in the dim light, but I think his eyes are glassy. Fingertips press into me slightly, but we still maintain our two-foot distance, swaying like robots.

'But . . . why?' he repeats.

Speech powers, activate. 'Because you laugh at my stupid jokes. Because you never ask me to be something I'm not. You're funny and thoughtful, and I want to kiss you all the time. I think about you when you're not around, and I love our time together. You are the one person who can make me simultaneously calm and excited, and it's a weirdo, hybrid feeling I can't get enough of. You've made me see the world in a different light, and I'm forever in your debt.'

He bows his head, probably overwhelmed by my compliment train. 'Thank you,' he says quietly. 'But what I meant was, why do you still love me? After what I did?'

'We both made mistakes in the past. I want to focus on right now. Together.'

He looks me straight in the eye, and I brace myself for what's on the other side. Here we go: time to see if a new leading love will emerge for him like it did for Kim. Am I really ready for this?

I resolve to stay tough as my sight is filled with static once more. Pixelated gray confusion swirls before me, relaying a whole lot of nothing. I wait, as patiently as possible, to see if anything (or really, any*one*) will emerge, but the fuzz plays on, finally disappearing without revealing anything new. Like a reflex, I quickly evaluate the possible meanings. Either (a) the Fates, still reeling from having been wrong about pairing Charlie with Kim, have not yet chosen a new match for him and are taking their time to find the right person or (b) maybe, just maybe, I'm falling victim to a magical loophole, unable to cast myself in the role I most want to fill.

Charlie, surely knowing by now that looking my way is not an innocent act, asks, 'What is it? What do you see?'

I resist the urge to shake his shoulders. I'm not going to play these games with him anymore. 'It's not about what I see; it's about what I feel.'

'Oh really?' he asks with a small laugh.

'Yup,' I confirm, chin held high. 'I'm a changed woman. I've learned some stuff.'

'What kind of stuff?'

'Well, first of all, I learned you can turn a witch into an ice cube. Second, mermaids have different-colored tails. And third . . . I'm learning how to live in the present. My whole life has been defined by endings, but I've never understood the journey. When you flash-forward to happily-ever-after, you miss all the milestones on the way. And maybe that's obvious to the world, but I never thought about it before: what it takes to get to "the end." Life is kind of messed up, and even though the Fates are pulling some strings, we have control too.' I pause. 'I want to have better control over my future because I want you to be there with me.'

He pulls me a little closer, and I can't help but admire the view. Charlie, so sweet and kind, with a face that reflects his inner beauty. I love this boy; I do. I don't ever want to lose this sight again, but it's not just up to me.

'I think . . . we still have some things to figure out,' he says. 'You coming here tonight, standing in front of everyone, looking so amazing: it means a lot. Like, I actually can't believe you did that.'

I smile and nod. I can't believe I did either.

'But it has been a rough couple of weeks, for us both. Before we get swept up in the grandeur of the evening' – he waves to mass hangings of balloons and crepe paper – 'let's take things slow. Like you said, we don't have to rush to the end. And I'd rather take my time with you.'

Charlie leans in, but not for a kiss; he gently rests his forehead on mine and finally wraps his arms around me. His touch consumes me, and I close my eyes, letting myself be fully in the moment. In a room full of people, we're the only two around, and I can't think of anything more magical.

Happy endings do not always stem from seamless beginnings. Life is not linear; there's not one straight path. Mistakes and misfortunes are part of the game; the Fates certainly see to it. Love is a surrender, giving in to the unknown and hoping for the best. But no matter how much we stumble and fall, we eventually find our way.

I've found mine.

# Acknowledgements

MY MOM USED TO ALWAYS SAY, 'THE ONLY THING CONSTANT in life is change,' and it would make me crazy. Not because she was wrong (she wasn't) but because I am not great with change. I'm good at randomly bursting into song or having ice cream at the ready, but change? No. Even happy, positive shifts seem to throw me for a loop, plaguing me with uncertainty and doubt, and it's usually not until I've made it to the other side that I can finally relax and realize that moving in a new direction is not a sign of the apocalypse.

So I want to thank all the magical unicorns in my life who help me pierce through the clouds and show me silver linings. Thank you to my friends and family who read my lengthy texts, answer my panicked calls, and hear my rambling worries.

You are the heroes of my story, offering sage advice and strong guidance every step of the way. Your encouragement and support mean the world to me; I would be lost without you.

# Discover where it all began for Amber Sand ...

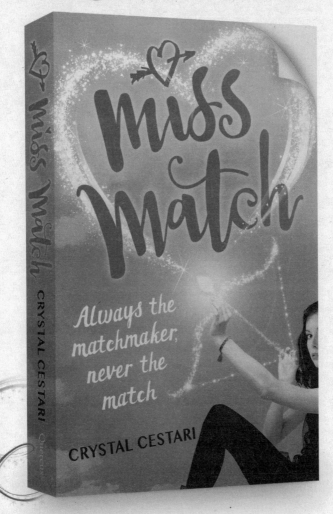

'A wonderful blend of snarky attitude, laugh out loud fun, and some killer magical moments that will have you asking: do you believe in fate?'
*Crossroads Reviews*